A HIGHLANDER OF HER OWN

"Wonderful. . . . Melissa Mayhue captures the complications and delights of both the modern woman and the fascination with the medieval world."

—*Denver Post*

SOUL OF A HIGHLANDER

"Absolutely riveting from start to finish."

—*A Romance Review*

"Mayhue's world is magical and great fun."

—*RT Book Reviews*

HIGHLAND GUARDIAN

"Mayhue not only develops compelling protagonists, but her secondary characters are also rich and intriguing."

—*RT Book Reviews* (4 stars)

"A delightful world of the faerie. . . . Snappy dialogue and passionate temptations . . . are sure to put a smile on your face."

—*Fresh Fiction*

THIRTY NIGHTS WITH A HIGHLAND HUSBAND

"Infused with humor, engaging characters, and a twist or two."

—*RT Book Reviews* (4 stars)

"Melissa Mayhue rocks the Scottish Highlands."

—*A Romance Review*

ALSO BY MELISSA MAYHUE

MELISSA MAYHUE

WARRIOR REBORN

POCKET BOOKS

New York London Toronto Sydney New Delhi

Pocket Books
A Division of Simon & Schuster, Inc.
1230 Avenue of the Americas
New York, NY 10020

This book is a work of fiction. Names, characters, places, and incidents either are products of the author's imagination or are used fictitiously. Any resemblance to actual events or locales or persons, living or dead, is entirely coincidental.

Copyright © 2012 by Melissa Mayhue

All rights reserved, including the right to reproduce this book or portions thereof in any form whatsoever. For information address Pocket Books Subsidiary Rights Department.
1230 ~~Avenue of the Americas, New York, NY 10020~~

First ~~Pocket Books~~ ... November 2012

POC ... trademarks of Simon &
Schu... Inc.

For i ... es,
plea ...
1-86... or business ...

The ...rs
to yo ...
ever ...
1-866-248-3049 or visit our website at www.simonspeakers.com.

Designed by Jacquelynne Hudson

Manufactured in the United States of America

10 9 8 7 6 5 4 3 2 1

ISBN 978-1-4516-4088-5
ISBN 978-1-4516-4091-5 (ebook)

This book is dedicated with love to
Marty and Courtney.
May all your days be blessed with the Magic of True Love.
And may this be only the beginning of your
Happy Ever After!

ACKNOWLEDGMENTS

I send my sincere thanks to a number of people for their help in seeing this book completed.

To Elaine Levine for the constant challenges and soul-replenishing lunch meetings.

To Megan Mayhue for her willingness to read bits and pieces along the way.

To all my readers for their constant encouragement and enthusiasm.

And to my new editor, Micki Nuding, for helping me to look at my writing from a different perspective. Thanks for your patience and all your hard work!

WARRIOR
REBORN

Prologue

NOTHING WAS AS it should be here.

Not this place and certainly not him. Surrounded by all this natural beauty, no one should feel such an overwhelming sense of disappointment.

Chase Noble loosened the shoulder straps of his pack and dropped it to the ground, then settled onto the bench overlooking Fairy Falls. He pulled a long swig from his CamelBak and stared into the cascading water, losing himself to dreams and memories. With nothing but the sounds of water and wind for company, he gave free rein to the dark, lonely place in his heart that drove him to keep searching. Searching for a home and for that special someone to share his life.

If it weren't for his unwavering faith in his father's promise, he could easily believe he'd never find the spot he could call home. The one spot where he truly belonged. The spot where his fate, and his SoulMate, awaited him.

Foolishly, he had allowed himself to have such high hopes this time. Even the name of the place had held promise. Every word his buddy Parker had spoken in describing it had convinced him it would be the place he'd sought his whole life. Maybe it had been because Parker had spoken so lovingly of the place he remembered from his childhood. Maybe it had been the shimmer of heat waves wafting up from the ground, lending a surreal haze to the moment. Or maybe it had been no more than the small dark patch of mud in the Kandahari dust—all that had remained after they hoisted Parker's lifeless body from the ground for their return trip to the outpost.

He'd known at that moment that he had to come here, just as surely as he'd known he wouldn't sign on for another tour of duty.

Though he had no doubt he was intended for the life of a warrior, he hadn't belonged in that faraway land any more than he belonged here.

Chase squinted up toward the sun dappling down through the canopy of trees.

"You could make this easier, you know, Da. You could at least point me in the right direction. One small hint is not so much to ask after all these years."

His father rarely answered, and then only in whispered riddles that wafted to him on the breeze.

Having a full-blood Fae for a father wasn't easy.

Patience.

The word settled around him as the leaves rustled overhead.

"I've been patient, Da. It's not like I've had any other choice. But now I feel as though . . ."

He let the thought linger on his tongue, not at all sure he could find the words to explain even to himself. Lately it felt as though he was running out of time, as if all his options were used up and he stood at the edge of a vast precipice.

The vision was so strong, he could actually see himself taking that first step, soaring off into a blue sky of possibilities.

"Yeah, right," he muttered, leaning over to lift his pack onto the bench beside him.

If his older sister were here, Destiny would be sternly warning him to keep his feet planted firmly on the ground and his eyes focused on the future. It was a lecture his bossy sister had given often, before he'd taken off to find his way in the world.

The thought of her made him smile.

She was correct. No more flights of fancy. He needed to set some priorities and stick to them. First on the list, find a place to crash and get a job. His savings wouldn't last forever. Maybe then he could try to locate Destiny and Leah. It had been much too long since he'd seen his sisters.

Soon.

The wind ruffled through his hair, feeling like his father's fingers as he stood and hoisted his pack onto his back.

"Oh, yeah?" he asked, looking up toward the dark clouds billowing overhead. "*How* soon?"

Four fat raindrops plopped on his face, one after another, as if to tell him the conversation with his father was over.

He turned and headed back down the trail. No point in rushing. The skies had already opened up, pelting down on him through the breaks in the foliage. As his mom used to say, he wasn't made of sugar; he wouldn't melt.

In spite of today's failure, he felt better than he had in months. He had a plan and knew what he would do next. And best of all, though he still didn't know where he belonged, half an hour on that mountain had restored his hope. Hope that he would find his spot in the world.

Soon.

One

JUST BECAUSE SHE could never tell a lie certainly didn't mean Christiana MacDowylt could never deceive. She'd become well practiced in the art of truthful deception. She'd been forced into it. The truth, the whole truth, could get her killed in moments like this.

She kept her eyes fixed on the retreating forms of her brothers and the women they protected as they disappeared into the forest, leaving her behind.

I dinna want to leave without you. Her brother's parting words echoed in her ears.

It wasn't as if she wanted to remain behind. But staying was the only choice she had if they were all to survive. The gift she had inherited from her ancestor, Odin, the dream visions that displayed the future, had shown it to her.

As always, the future had presented itself as multiple paths, the inherent choices of the participants reflected in each. Two had been brighter than the others. On one pathway she accompanied her brothers in their bid for her freedom. That pathway led to a bloody battle, far worse than the one that had ended here within the past hour. The one she foresaw ended in the deaths of all.

On the second pathway, she remained behind.

There was no real choice. Her freedom was a small price to pay for the lives of those she loved.

Besides, a radiant light beckoned her down this pathway. A radiant light she'd been allowed to glimpse before. A radiant light that promised the freedom she sought, and more. A hazy, half-obscured face. *His* face.

If only she knew who he was or when he would come. But the Norns hadn't shared that knowledge with her.

Still, her brothers were on their way, headed toward the shelter of Castle MacGahan. Patrick, Malcolm and his new wife, and the Elf upon whom so much now depended.

When no trace of her brothers' party lingered, neither a hint of them through the trees nor a glimmer of sound from their escape, Christiana released the breath she had been holding for the last several seconds. Their safety was assured.

For now, at least.

With only moments to ready herself before the warriors arrived, she scanned the grove of trees, erecting a series of mental barriers to shield herself from the remains of the massacre where she stood. A deep breath to prepare herself sent the coppery tang of blood stinging up her nostrils.

Her half brother, her captor, Torquil of Katanes, mighty laird of the MacDowylt and descendant of Odin, lay at her feet, lifeless.

Lifeless, but not dead.

A being as powerful as he could hardly be felled by so minor an item as the fork that protruded from his neck. Had the unlikely weapon been made from anything other than the wood of the rowan, he would never have been felled by it.

Even though he was trapped in the middle world between life and death, the evil emanating from his soul permeated the clearing, lashing out with frenzied tendrils to find release. She felt it slither around her ankles as it bathed in the carnage littering the clearing, snaking through the hacked and decapitated bodies of the men who had accompanied Torquil. Swarming along with the flies around the body of her youngest brother, Dermid. Sweet, cherubic, maddened Dermid, who had betrayed them all.

No! She could not allow what had happened in this grove to distract her from what was to come. When Torquil's warriors reached them and revived her tormentor, she would need to be at her most vigilant.

Indeed, it was these moments for which she had been forced to perfect the art of truthful deception.

Returning to the spot where she had lain when

the battle had begun, she dropped to her knees. Tears rolled down her cheeks as she wept for those who suffered, for those who'd lost their lives so needlessly. For the younger brother she had lost, though in truth, he had been lost to her long before the battle here. And she wept for the horror of the life she would return to.

Lying back, she rested her head against a tree and closed her eyes. Her only possible defense in Torquil's view would be her having been lost in the grip of the Visions during the battle. Her escape from Tordenet Castle would certainly compound his anger, but she would walk that fine line when the time came to explain.

For now, she must retreat to the only place of shelter afforded her. Pushing all that had happened from her mind, she silently called upon Skuld to show her what was to come.

As the darkness of another Vision descended, she heard the pounding of hooves nearby, the shouts of men. But they were too late to catch her. Already her mind had escaped to the crossroads that represented the future. Already her soul floated in the eyes of the warrior who would be her savior.

THE HEAVY, MURKY dark strangled him, suffocating him as it coalesced around his naked body. Its thick, sticky tendrils tightened their thorny hold, piercing his tender skin, wrapping around him as if he were some otherworld mummy.

Torquil MacDowylt fought against their over-powering strength, marshaling his will to tear them from his body. His struggles only seemed to intensify their movement. For each piece of the squirming, stinking menace he ripped away, two more replaced it, thicker, tighter, more deadly than before.

Though his strength faded, he would not give up. He could not give up. He fought for his life.

Desperation crowded his mind as the tendrils closed over his face. He screamed, instantly regretting the explosion of air rushing from his chest even as the long, dark fingerlings tightened around him, immobilizing him, preventing his next inhale.

A sudden explosion of sound battered his ears and the tendrils burst apart, tiny pieces of them merging and re-forming above him as his body was flung away from them as if by some invisible giant hand.

His body flew through the dark at impossible speeds, beyond his ability to control. Beyond his ability to understand.

A second explosion slammed his body to a stop, this one a burst of light brighter than any fire he'd ever seen.

"My lord Torquil?"

A voice filled with hesitancy. A voice he recognized. The captain of his personal guard, Ulfr.

"I . . ." His voice cracked as he tried to answer, his throat on fire with pain.

"Our lord, Torquil of Katanes, lives!" Ulfr's triumphant shout reverberated in Torquil's ears. "Lie still, my lord. Fetch his things to me, William!"

Torquil struggled to get his bearings. The last thing he remembered was Malcolm's face. So close to his own . . . and yet, not his.

He remembered now. He'd managed to call the wolf to form. He'd been the beast! His half brother's puny neck had been so close to his muzzle, he could see it snapping within his jaws. Malcolm's strength had begun to weaken. He could all but taste the pleasure of his detested brother's death.

But then . . .

His eyes flickered open and he pushed up to one elbow, his other hand covering a spot on his neck.

His brother's wife had attacked him. Though he couldn't imagine how she'd managed it, the bitch had done something that had ripped the Magic from his body and plummeted him to the mercies of the between worlds.

"Where is she?" he managed at last, his voice raspy. Where were they all?

"She sleeps, Master. We've been unable to awaken her."

"Sleeps?" With Ulfr's arm to assist him, Torquil made his way to his feet.

The last dregs of whatever had possessed him scattered from his mind as he straightened, shivering.

By Odin, he was cold! Little wonder since he was completely naked. Where was Dermid? His brother had carried his clothing after he'd made his physical transformation into the wolf.

"I need . . ." He struggled to form the words. Pain radiated from his neck up through his face, and his jaw shivered from the cold gripping him.

"Allow me, my lord."

With a nod of permission, Torquil raised his arms, allowing Ulfr to drop a tunic down over his head, followed by his plaid and a heavy fur draped over his shoulders.

He could feel his strength returning and with it, his determination.

"Take me to her," he ordered.

The Lady Danielle, wife of his brother Malcolm, would pay for her crime against him now. He would wring the life from her with his bare hands after she disclosed to him how she'd been able to do whatever it was she'd done to him.

"This way, my lord."

As he followed Ulfr across the clearing, he took stock of his surroundings for the first time.

The men who had accompanied him were dead. Yes, he remembered that now. Another crime to lay at Malcolm's feet. To his left lay the crumpled body of his youngest brother, Dermid.

A pity, that. The weak-minded lad had been easily controlled to perform Torquil's bidding. But no matter, there were others who would substitute as well.

As he approached the woman's body propped

against the large tree, his irritation spiked. His sister Christiana laid there, not the woman he sought.

He realized as he scanned the clearing that none of the others were here. The bodies were those of his men only.

"Malcolm? The women?" he demanded of Ulfr. "Where have they gone?"

The captain shook his head. "There were none here when we arrived but those you see now, my lord. Only you and Lady Christiana, and we have not been able to awaken her from her sleep."

Torquil strode to the spot where his half sister lay.

Little wonder they hadn't been able to awaken her; it wasn't sleep that claimed her. Though her body was present, her spirit was gone, flying on the wings of one of her Visions. The red blotches staining her cheeks, the darting of her eyes beneath the delicate sweep of her lashes, the almost imperceptible movement of her full, soft lips were sure signs that Christiana inhabited a vision of the future.

She wouldn't awaken until Skuld released her back into this world.

Her ability to see the future was the one gift she'd inherited from their ancient ancestor, Odin. The one gift he wanted for himself above all others. It was the reason he allowed her to live, and the reason he would never allow her to leave Tordenet Castle.

"Bring her," he ordered, fisting his hand as he turned away, fighting the impure thoughts that plagued him each time he looked upon Christiana.

It was her gift—and *only* her gift!—that he wanted from her. Anything else was unacceptable. "We return to Tordenet."

There was no use in following his brother Malcolm now. He would wait, preparing himself, building his strength. In time, with proper planning, he would have his revenge. Malcolm and all the MacGahan would fall to him, as would everyone else. With his powers and Christiana's Vision to guide him, he would one day return the world to the way it should be. The way it had been when the Ancient Ones walked the land.

And he, Torquil of Katanes, heir of Odin, would take his rightful place as ruler of all.

T WO

"W HY?"

Torquil's voice rang loudly off the high stone ceiling of his solar. Christiana had known this question was coming from the moment she'd made the decision to remain behind in the clearing. She only wished her thoughts weren't so muddled, so she could better reply.

Her body felt as weak as a newborn lamb and her mind was dull, as if it were wrapped in layers of freshly shorn wool.

Her eyes flickered up to meet her brother's angry glare before returning to the floor at her feet. She needed time to gather her wits. Time to find the words that might satisfy Torquil. The words that might save her life.

The stones beneath her feet seemed to shift and roll as she stared at them, and she lifted her arms out to her sides to maintain her balance.

"Might I ask my laird's indulgence to allow me to be seated?"

It was difficult enough to deceive Torquil on her

most clever days, without the distraction of wondering whether her legs would stop supporting her at any moment.

"I've no inclination to provide for yer comfort. No with treachery such as yers hanging heavy over yer head. Now answer my question. Why did you betray me?"

As a child, Christiana had often spied on her father's warriors as they'd trained, admiring their skill and dedication, envying their freedom to come and go as they pleased. The words so often intoned by the old listmaster returned to her now.

You canna depend on defense alone, lads. That's a ploy what leads to a sure death. Distract and attack. That's the path to victory. Distract and attack.

Praying the old warrior had been correct, she gave in to the weakness dragging her down and crumpled to a heap on the hard stone floor. Behind her she heard a flurry of movement, but the steps halted as quickly as they'd begun. None here would defy her brother's will to come to her assistance.

"How long was I . . ." She paused, lifting her gaze to again meet Torquil's glare as she allowed the words to linger in the air around them. "How long was I lost to the—"

"Clear the chamber!" Torquil bellowed, lurching up from behind his table as his startled men rushed from their laird's solar.

She'd suspected that her brother didn't want to share the knowledge of her Visions with everyone.

"Have a care to yer tongue, Sister," he warned in a low growl as he loomed over her.

Christiana nodded, waiting until the door closed behind the last man before speaking again. "I canna seem to put my mind in a straight line, Brother. I dinna even ken how I came to be here. My last memory is of a quiet forest clearing where I lay down to seek guidance from the Visions. Then, in the next moment, yer men were pulling me from my room and bringing me here."

"Hardly a moment," Torquil snorted. "We've waited three days for you to awaken."

"Three days!" Little wonder she felt so weak and disoriented. "The Visions have never kept me so long."

"That little fact has no escaped me. Along with an explanation of yer behavior, I'll be wanting a full accounting of what you saw as you traversed Skuld's world."

She'd like to know that accounting herself. Her memories of the Vision were clouded and merged, as if she'd been presented with too many options mixed together, and she'd experienced them layered one on top of another, all occurring simultaneously.

"You've every right to be angry with me." She paused to gather herself, picking her words with care. "It's only that I've never had a sister before, and I wanted Orabilis to meet Danielle. I should have asked yer permission to take her with me to visit Orabilis, but it was my belief you would deny such a request, so, selfishly, I dinna ask it of you."

"Indeed?" Torquil stared at her, no doubt weighing the truth of her words. "Is that also yer reason for assisting in Malcolm's escape? Because you dinna think I would agree to it?"

Christiana's heart pounded. Her next words could well determine whether she lived or died.

"In spite of what you may think, I dinna assist Malcolm into that wagon. When we came to the edge of the forest and he emerged from that barrel, it was the first I'd seen of him since my visit to the cell where you held him prisoner."

Every single word she uttered was technically true, as anything she said had to be. She honestly had wanted Orabilis to meet Malcolm's wife. No need to add that she'd known when they left Tordenet Castle that they'd never reach the old crone's home. Just as there was no need to add that from the moment she'd helped her brother escape from his cell, she'd made sure she stayed ahead of him and never looked back, specifically so that she wouldn't see him. She'd even stood with her back to the wagon as the others helped him climb into the barrel and covered him in flour, for she had known that this moment would come.

Torquil's eyes narrowed, distrust rolling off him in great, heaving waves of emotion so powerful that she felt their energy wash over her.

"You expect me to believe you had nothing to do with our brother's escape?"

"I expect nothing of you, Torquil. You ken as well as I do that the price I pay for the gift of Vision is my inability to speak a falsehood. How many times have I shared with you that which I dinna want to share? How many times have I given the answers I dinna want to give?"

Too many times to count, before she'd learned the key lay in her intent, not in her words. The line between truth and deception was thin enough to be obscured by a carefully chosen word.

"So you have, my gentle Christiana."

Torquil reached down to grip her upper arms, his hands like iron bands as he lifted her to her feet. His eyes, hard and cold, locked on hers when he pulled her face close to his, filling her with a fear that would have sent her once again to her knees had he not supported her.

"I want yer promise, yer sworn oath, that you'll no ever try such as this again."

Easy enough to promise. It wasn't as if the same situation would ever present itself again.

"I will never again attempt to take someone to Orabilis without first asking yer permission."

She was forced to her tiptoes as he pulled her closer still, his head dipping next to hers.

"Swear it," he insisted, his hot breath fanning over her skin as his mouth hovered next to her ear.

Fighting the fear, she forced her lips to move. "I so swear."

"Good." He moved back from her, his expression triumphant. "If no you, then who was it who aided Malcolm in his escape? You must have seen someone."

"What?" Foolishly, she hadn't anticipated that question.

"If no you, which of my men betrayed me by helping Malcolm in his escape?"

Rauf's long, thin face filled her mind and she fought to push the vision away lest her brother somehow read her thoughts. "None of those loyal to you would ever—" she began.

"I've no time for yer word games," Torquil interrupted, his voice as sharp as the look with which he pierced her. "Obviously none loyal to me would have helped our brother. I ask you again, which of my men is a traitor?"

"I . . . I have no way to answer you. I am no aware of any of yer men who would dare to cross you."

A truth, though only by the thinnest thread. Rauf was not one of Torquil's men. His loyalty was to her father, the old laird. He'd been tasked with watching over her younger brother, Dermid, but upon her father's death he'd become her man, as her father had instructed him. She would die before she would expose him for his part in Malcolm's escape.

"As you say," Torquil murmured, obviously weighing her every word. "Since it appears I'll learn nothing of this matter from you, I'd have yer account of what you saw while you traveled Skuld's world. I want to know everything."

He would not like what she had to say.

"I have no words to describe what I remember. I'm left with memories of feelings, more than of specific events."

"I've no interest in yer feelings. I want to hear of yer time in the Visions. Try harder," he hissed, one hand moving up to grip her throat. "Try as if yer life depended upon it."

She had not a single doubt that her life *did* depend upon it.

"It was unlike anything I've experienced in the Visions before. Always before I've seen the choices Skuld affords us laid out ahead of me like trails I could travel, though many were shadowed in the Myst of Choice. I've always known that each of those paths has many branches, each representing the choices we are free to make along the way. But in the past, I've traveled only one pathway to its conclusion. Always the one where the Myst has lifted."

"And yet"—his fingers tightened ever so slightly, digging into her skin—"you've warned of all those choices that I should avoid."

She nodded as best she could, her movement constrained by his grip. "I was always granted glimmers of the consequences of other trails, of other decisions. Spots along the way where the Myst had cleared. Sometimes the end of a path. But never the fullness of all those paths. Never until now."

His fingers loosened but didn't leave her throat. "And this time?"

"This time it was as if I was being shown every possible outcome, all at once. So many choices, so many paths, intertwining, entangled, one layered upon another until I could not tell where one ended and the next began. I felt splintered, shattered, torn in so many directions, each an endless multitude of intersecting corridors, like some intricate web woven by a crazed spider."

So much information laid out before her, yet she'd come away with almost nothing.

"What did you see of my plans?" Again Torquil's eyes narrowed.

"I saw at least one pathway leading to yer defeat."

"And my victory? Did you see the pathway leading to that possibility as well?"

"I saw that possibility. It exists, but only with the correct combination of choices."

Fear knotted her stomach again as Torquil dipped his head next to hers. His hair teased against her cheek even as his hot breath feathered over her ear when he spoke.

"I've decided to have mercy upon you, little sister. For now, at least. You'd no be wise to disappoint me again."

He held her there for a moment longer, her heart beating wildly, and then, just when she was sure he could taste her fear, he dropped his hands from her and stepped away.

"May I return to my chambers now?" Her voice shook, far beyond her ability to control it.

"You may."

Christiana had taken barely two steps before her brother spoke again.

"I send riders forth even now to recruit more men to my cause. In the spring, I will ride against Castle MacGahan. You have seen this?"

"I have. There are bits and pieces of it in my memories." He wanted more from her, as he always did. But in this she must move slowly.

"And building my ranks, bringing in new men—is this one of the correct choices?" Irritation crept into his clipped tones even as he kept his back turned to her.

"It is an absolute necessity." She paused, weighing the importance of what she would say next. "There will be one among them who is essential to the desired outcome." Essential to the outcome *she* desired, that is.

He turned in her direction, surprise and interest warring in his expression. "You've seen a warrior who will champion my cause?"

"I've seen a champion, yes." Though not of Torquil's cause.

"You will recognize this man on sight?"

"I've seen him only in a haze, never clearly enough to identify his features." And yet, she couldn't imagine not recognizing the sound of his voice or the feel of his touch when he finally arrived. So familiar they had become to her, she often had to remind herself the man was nothing more to her than her rescuer.

"He was a part of yer Visions and yet his visage remains a mystery to you. If you'll no recognize him, how am I to distinguish him from all the other newcomers?"

"I canna say how you will pick him from the others. I ken only that he will be different somehow. The Vision was quite clear that he alone will determine the difference between success and failure."

Torquil nodded slowly, beginning to pace back and forth in front of the fireplace, his hands clasped behind his back. At last his footsteps halted and he turned a narrowed gaze back in her direction.

"And this man of great importance to me, this champion of mine, will he have any interaction with you, little sister?"

Her heart skipped a beat, but she answered without delay. "He will."

"Do you think to lie with him?"

Christiana gasped, unable to hide her shock at such a personal question. "No!"

It wasn't as if this were the love of her heart she awaited. If that were the case, surely the Visions would have given some hint in that direction. True, she felt a strange elation each time he appeared in the Visions, but that made sense: he was the one who would deliver her from her captivity.

"That had best be the case, little sister. You are my property and I will permit trespass from none. Champion or no, if this stranger thinks to bed you, I'll have his head on a pike over my gate and serve up his entrails for buzzard feed. Is that clear?"

She could only nod, terrified by the strange glitter in his eyes and the vehemence in his voice.

"Very well, then. I will think upon all you have told me this day. Best you pray to the Ancient Ones that they send my new champion quickly. Now, leave me."

"As you bid me, my laird, so shall it be."

With a dip of her head, she made her way to the door and outside, breathing deeply only after she'd traversed the wide entry hall and stepped into the fresh air.

With renewed purpose, she hurried across the bailey and into the small tower at the far edge of the castle wall. Her quarters. Her refuge.

She set about building a fire in the cold pit before filling a small pot with water and tossing in a few well-chosen herbs. The warm tonic would soothe her nerves and mellow the worries plaguing her heart.

As she waited for the water to bubble, her thoughts drifted to her brother's edict.

Best you pray to the Ancient Ones that they send my new champion quickly.

He had no idea that she wanted that more than anything else. She'd been sending those prayers up to the Ancient Ones for many months, with a new twist added now.

A prayer that the Elf who'd accompanied her new sister would keep the promise she had made in the glen. For without her aid, all would be lost.

Three

"YOU BEST SKEDADDLE on over to the mess hall, greenhorn." The old cowboy reached out to take the reins Chase handed over. "The way them cowboys was eatin' when I was there, it's a good chance won't be nothin' but bones left by now."

Chase grinned at the old man. "That would be a shame, missing out on Miss Fern's cooking."

Whitey returned the grin, displaying a gap where his front top teeth should have been. "Damn straight. It's roast chicken tonight and she's made corn bread and chili beans, too."

Though the main dish varied from day to day, the old cook made corn bread and chili beans so often, it had Chase missing the MREs he'd carried in his army pack. Not that he'd ever give voice to that thought. Everyone on the Lazy J knew how Whitey felt about Miss Fern. The two of them had been an item for the last forty years.

A twinge of envy flickered through Chase. He couldn't think of too many things he wanted more from life than to find his own Fern.

Chase headed out of the barn and into the cold night to do exactly as Whitey had suggested.

The familiar smells of the dining hall filled his nostrils as he opened the door, assuring him he wouldn't go hungry after all.

No thanks to the wild horses he'd hunted since early morning. They'd made sure he'd earned his pay this particularly cold and blustery winter day. Still, he felt good about bringing them in. They were destined for a new home in Colorado with a fellow who'd made himself a name for his excellent care and breeding of horses.

These ponies that would end up at the Seun Fardach Ranch were some of the lucky few. Chase just wished some of their luck would rub off on him.

Inside the door he remembered the hat he wore, pulling it off his head to stuff under his arm.

"You're sure pullin' a late one tonight, Chase," Miss Fern called from behind the serving table. She looked up as he neared. "What the hell happened to you?"

His hand flew to his forehead. He'd almost forgotten the incident.

"Paying more attention to one of those ponies I was chasing than to the land I chased him through. Low-hanging branch got me." Chase shrugged, feeling foolish.

"Don't look all that bad up close, I guess." She peered over the top of her thick reading glasses. "Grab yourself a plate and fill 'er up, boy. I was just getting ready to put stuff away for the night."

Chase hurried along the table. "Thank you, ma'am. Smells wonderful, as always."

Miss Fern beamed and plopped an extra-large helping of chili beans on his plate. He might be grateful for the job, the two square meals a day, and the honest, friendly people, but he'd be a seriously happy man if he never saw another chili bean again.

Chase took a seat across the room, his back to the wall as usual.

The opportunity to work here had fallen in his lap just when he'd needed it most. Two months working in construction outside Seattle had convinced him he needed a more solitary occupation. He hadn't minded the hard work; far from it. That had been the only part of the job that had kept him sane. What he'd hated was the congestion of the city, the cars, the noise. It wasn't where he belonged.

Then Jay Jones had entered his life, recruiting cowboys. Jay had hired him in spite of his lack of experience, and he was determined not to disappoint the Lazy J or its owner.

Ranching wasn't where he belonged, any more than construction or the army had been, but it was as good a place to be as any while he waited for his destiny to find him.

After he finished eating, he stacked his dish with all the others, nodded to Miss Fern, and made his way back out into the night, more blustery now than it had been half an hour earlier. The damp, biting promise of snow was definitely in the air.

As he stepped onto the porch leading to his room, he glanced up just in time to see a shooting star pierce the inky black of the opening between banks of clouds.

"Good sign," he murmured to himself as he mounted the two steps and entered his room.

Soon, the breeze whispered back.

His imagination was playing tricks again, likely because his father had always claimed shooting stars were signs of a Faerie promise kept. He shook his head at his flight of fancy as he tossed off his rain slicker and then went into the bathroom for a nice, hot shower.

If the Faeries intended to set him on the path to his destiny, they'd better get a move on. After all these years, all his searching, he was close to losing faith it would ever happen. Had his father really promised him his life would be changing soon that day at the Fairy Falls? Or was it only his imagination promising what he wanted to hear?

The things he sought were no more than any man would want: a home where he belonged and a woman to share it with him. Not just any woman, but his own SoulMate. It was what his father had promised awaited him. And if those promises ended up being nothing but a dream, then it would be up to him to make that dream come true.

He got into the shower, allowing the hot water to wash away the long hours spent in a saddle. The bump on his head stung as the water hit it, but not bad enough to worry him. His mind was still filled with thoughts of what he should do next in life. The world was a big place and he wasn't getting any younger. Sooner or later he'd need to let go of the dreams his father had given him and pick a course on which to steer his ship.

That was perhaps the biggest drawback to his solitary occupation: too much time spent inside his own head.

"Not a tidy place to be at all," he mused, tipping his head back and scrubbing his fingers through his hair.

When he was done, he dried off and then wiped the steam from the mirror. One glance confirmed the limb had left him quite a colorful reminder of their meeting. And that he needed a shave and a haircut.

He ran his fingers over the bump, knowing he'd get a shitload of ribbing from the other ranch hands over how he'd managed to miss seeing a whole tree out in the pastureland. That was okay. He could handle their good-natured teasing.

The shave he'd deal with in the morning, and as for the haircut, well, that would have to wait until his next trip into town. After the years he'd spent in the military, he couldn't remember the last time his hair had been long enough to cover his collar. Might look a little scruffy, but it felt kind of nice. If he let it grow a little more, it might help to keep his ears warm this winter.

For now, all he needed was eight hours of uninterrupted rack time and he'd be good as new.

He could hear the wind picking up outside as he climbed into his bunk, but his little room was warm enough that he needed nothing more than a pair of boxers and a thin blanket. The Lazy J bunkhouse was nicer than most of the motels he'd stayed in over the years.

IT FELT AS if he'd just laid his head on the pillow when Chase awoke to a gentle breeze brushing over his chest. His groggy confusion told him he'd been sleeping deeply, but it did nothing to help him identify the source of the insistent green light flashing in the room.

He sat up and scrubbed his hands over his face, scanning the room for evidence of entry.

His door was closed and he certainly hadn't left any windows open. It made no sense at all, a breeze blowing in his room like this. No more sense than the brilliant shots of light sparkling around him.

Tossing his covers back, he climbed from his bunk and struggled to stand as the floor heaved under his feet.

"What the hell?" he muttered, completely awake now.

Arms outstretched for balance, he attempted to cross to the door as the floor rolled like an angry sea beneath him. Earthquake? They had them up here, but he'd never experienced anything like this.

He'd barely made it two feet before a gust of wind whipped past him, battering at his bare skin. The lights changed to a brilliant green splattered with a million colored twinkles, sparkling and dancing, shooting around the room like angry shards of rainbow.

A second heavy gust toppled his chair and knocked him from his feet, battering his ears as if with words shouted from afar. He held up his arms to cushion his landing as he fell, but the floor he expected to hit had disappeared.

Instead, he felt himself tossed into the air and slammed forward into an endless void, the incessant chant of "Now, now, now!" ringing in his ears as his mind faded to black.

Four

COLD GNAWED AT his skin like a starving animal, and voices buzzed angrily in his ears. Chase struggled to open his eyes but it felt as if his eyelids had been glued shut.

"Best you keep to your saddles, lads, if you value your heads upon your shoulders, that is," a deep voice said.

The words made no sense. From what Chase remembered before he'd blacked out, he must have been right at the epicenter of the biggest earthquake in Montana's history. Had rescuers arrived? That had to be it! He needed to let them know he was here.

He struggled to call out to them, but all he could manage was a grunt.

"What's happened to that one?" another voice asked.

"Set upon by thieves, I'd say. His mount, his weapon, even his clothes are gone. They left him with naught but a nasty bump on his head." It was the first voice again, filled with authority and tinged with an odd accent. "Could even have been the two of you, for all I know."

A bump on his head. They were talking about him! They thought him a robbery victim? What was wrong with these guys? There had been an earthquake and—

"Here, now, we'll be hearing none of that from the likes of you. We're about our good laird's business, seeking men to his employ. We've no a need to be robbing strangers along the road."

Chase struggled to move, but couldn't, and realized that he was bound by some rough cloth as if he were a mummy. Bandages, perhaps?

"And who might this great laird of yours be, this man who seeks to hire strangers to his cause?"

"Torquil of Katanes," one man said, his voice hushed. "Laird of the MacDowylt."

At last Chase's eyes cooperated with his brain's commands and opened. Not bandages but a woolen blanket covered him, wrapped around and under him. With a superhuman effort, he rolled himself from his stomach to his back, lying still when he finished, unable to do more than breathe through the weakness gripping his body.

"Yer lad over there is moving around."

"So he is," the original voice agreed. "Am I correct in assuming we'd be well paid if we were to choose to throw our lot in with this Katanes of yours?"

"For yer service, he offers a full belly and a roof over yer head. He offers a home at Tordenet Castle."

The original speaker chuckled. "I'm quite capable of finding my own food and shelter, lads. That's precious little incentive to raise my weapon in battle on your great laird's behalf."

"He also offers silver," a third voice added. "The amount of which will be dependent upon yer usefulness with that weapon you brandish about."

"Done, then," the first man boomed. "How do we find our way to this Tordenet Castle of yours?"

"You follow this trail. Two days' ride to the northeast and you'll come upon her. You canna miss her, for she gleams in the sunlight like a white jewel in the distance. Tell the guards that Artur, right hand to Ulfr, sent you."

"That I will, Artur, right hand to Ulfr. Go in peace."

Chase's heart pounded as he lay there, his eyes blinking against the light. This was insane. Everything he'd heard was utter gibberish. He needed help, not some bad reenactment of Shakespeare.

"So, you're back from Hela's clutches at last. Strong enough to sit up, are you?"

The hand that grabbed Chase's was massive, fitting for the massive man it belonged to.

"Don't try to stand yet, lad. Get your wits about you first. You've been out for quite some time. How is it you come to be here?"

Excellent question.

"Depends on where 'here' is," Chase managed, his voice cracking as he looked around the clearing.

Because wherever "here" was, it sure as hell wasn't the least bit familiar.

The big man poked at the campfire with a long stick before he sat down next to it. "'Here' is an easy day's ride from the coast. Does that help?"

The coast. How was that even possible?

"Washington?" Chase croaked, reaching out to accept the flask the big man offered. Couldn't be. That was over eight hundred miles from the Lazy J.

He started to say as much but the drink burned down his throat in a cold rush, shutting off his breath for a moment, leaving him to suck air in between his teeth.

"Not as I've heard it called, lad. Pictland it is. Or was, I suppose. Scotland, they call themselves now."

Scotland? A second drink hung in the back of his throat and he choked, coughing as the big man laughed and reached over to pound on his back.

"Easy, lad. The mead is bit strong, but always good for what ails you."

He must be dreaming. None of this was possible, no matter how real it felt. The last thing he remembered was standing in his room, in the middle of an earthquake, his skin glowing with that crazy green light like some kind of . . .

Chase's mind froze as if he'd taken a slap to the face, an old memory shoving its way to the front of his thoughts.

Green light exactly like his father had always described accompanying a burst of Faerie magic.

Another memory followed on the heels of the first. The pounding chant of *"Now, now, now!"* in those last moments before he'd blacked out.

A thrill of excitement tightened his chest. That shooting star had been a message sent for him, his father's promise to him fulfilled. He just hadn't been smart enough to realize it.

"Not an earthquake," he muttered, lifting the flask to his lips again. He was prepared for the burn this time, and the heady liquid flowed much more smoothly down his throat, warming his chest and belly. "But perhaps, at long last, where I'm supposed to be."

His companion took the flask from his hand and tossed back a swallow of his own. "Where you're supposed to be, I cannot say, only that here is where you are. What are you called, lad?"

"Chase. Chase Noble." He stuck out his hand to shake. "And you?"

"Halldor O'Donar, at your service." Halldor rose to his feet, a wide grin lifting his features. "Ah, yes. Noble, it is. By fidelity and fortitude, eh?"

Chase shrugged, having no idea what the big man meant. "It's just a name." Though the "fidelity and fortitude" line did appeal to him, sounding very much like something his father might have claimed.

"That's an interesting mark you wear upon your arm." Halldor ran his fingers down his beard, scratching idly like a man who had something more to say. "I've not seen its match worn so before."

Chase had never seen one like it before wandering into that little dive of a tattoo parlor on a whim and letting himself get talked into getting inked.

"Yeah. It was supposed to be something else entirely. But I kind of like it now."

"I carry naught but this one spare tunic," the big man said, digging in a large leather bag and pulling out a roll of cloth, which he dropped in Chase's lap. "It'll no doubt be a bit large on you, but it'll do until we make our way to our new laird's castle, eh? You can use the plaid there, too. Neither of them so new or fancy, but a sight better than traipsing around in those strange little trews of yours."

Strange little trews? Chase looked down. His boxers. How perfect was this? Absolutely perfect if you thought like a Fae, with their inherently warped sense of humor. Strand someone halfway across the world in nothing but their underwear. There must be a whole roomful of Faeries laughing their asses off about this one.

Wait. His mind raced in a whole new direction, one that didn't offer the least bit of comfort. Trews? Laird? Castle?

No, no, no. That would be way too wild, even for Faeries. But it *was* Faeries, after all, so he couldn't discount the suspicion.

"Can you tell me the date?"

Halldor paused, the flask halfway to his lips, and stared thoughtfully into the sky. "Let me think. Winternights has passed but it's not yet Jul. I'd say we're in early December, though I've lost track of the exact day."

"Not the day. The year. I need to know the year." Chase could barely push the words past his lips.

His father had told him of the ancient Fae's power to manipulate time. But surely those were nothing more than stories of days long gone.

Just like Faeries were supposed to be stories?

Surely they couldn't. They wouldn't. Not after he'd faithfully waited for so long.

"Twelve ninety-four," Halldor answered, his brow wrinkling in concern. "That blow to your head must have been harder than I thought. Best we find ourselves a healer in the next village we pass and get some herbs to put on that swelling."

"Twelve ninety-four," Chase muttered. "Twelve freakin' ninety-four."

They could, they would, and they had.

Damned unbelievable Faeries. His father had been right. Even when they gave you what you wanted, they always had to add their own screwed-up twist to it.

Five

TROUBLE HOVERED AROUND her like a swarm of midges on a summer's eve.

Syrie knew she should never have done something like this. Then again, how could she not? She had given her solemn promise.

She rolled her shoulders in a vain attempt to relieve the apprehension weighing her down and strode to the big door, stopping with her hand poised above the wood.

The MacGahan laird on the other side of this door would be, in all likelihood, quite upset with her news. The fact that she could already hear the murmur of angry voices coming from the chamber behind the door didn't lend any comfort. It would have been her preference to find him alone and in a good mood.

Her hand dropped to her waist, where her fingers locked together with those of her other hand.

"By the goddess," she muttered, remembering only as the words left her mouth that the goddess was perhaps the last being she should call upon.

Danu would be even more displeased with her actions than Malcolm MacDowylt could ever consider being. And the wrath of the goddess was a far more formidable threat than any tantrum the MacGahan laird might pitch.

She sighed, glanced down to her clasped hands, and forced them to her sides.

"Ridiculous," she huffed under her breath.

She was no timid girl to be wringing her hands over her laird's anticipated tongue-lashing, even if that was the part she'd allowed herself to be coaxed into playing. She was Elesyria AÍ? Byrn, a full-blood Faerie at the height of her magical strength.

"Though for how long I'll remain that way is another matter all together," she muttered, the nagging guilt washing back over her. Once her goddess discovered what she had done . . .

She clamped her lips together and lifted her hand once again to rap upon the wood, but the door opened before her knuckles made contact. The laird's brother Patrick stood on the other side, wearing his usual stoic expression.

"I'd wondered how long before you'd show up," he whispered, motioning for her to follow him to a spot at the side of the room, and indicating with a finger to his lips the need for her silence.

As if he thought she hadn't the good sense to keep her mouth shut in the crowded room!

With a scathing look, she stepped back against the wall, making herself as inconspicuous as possible.

Six men hovered around the table where their laird engaged in discussion.

Malcolm, his face a mask of obstinate authority, bent toward the young woman across the table from him. Almost as tall as Malcolm, she gave not an inch, standing her ground, her expression matching his.

"I want Jamesy called home," she insisted. "Our father's murder cries out for vengeance, and if yer no going to see to it, then it's up to us." Her whole body radiated her anger.

Curious, Syrie decided having her questions answered was worth the irritation of speaking to Patrick.

"Who is she?" she whispered, stretching up on tiptoe so her words wouldn't travel beyond his ear.

"Bridget MacCulloch," he whispered back. "Hamud's daughter."

The guard who had accompanied them on their journey to Tordenet Castle in their quest to rescue Malcolm had been a pleasant fellow, kind and helpful. Right up to the moment he'd been hanged on the orders of that abomination from the old gods, Torquil MacDowylt.

"I've already told you, Brie, that I sent word to yer brother," Malcolm said. "He kens by now what's happened to yer da. But it's best for everyone if he stays where he is. He'll do us more good in Edinburgh than he can here."

Again Syrie stretched up on her tiptoes to speak, bumping her nose against Patrick's chin as he leaned down toward her.

"And this brother of hers, this Jamesy, what is he doing in Edinburgh?" she whispered.

Patrick's attempt to answer was lost as Bridget's hand slammed down on the table.

"Best for everyone?" Bridget demanded incredulously. "Best for *you,* you mean. You think by educating my brother you'll have another MacCulloch indebted to you, willing to give his life for you. It was yer life my father gave his own to save. And yer no even going after the bastards what murdered him."

"That's enough, Bridget!" one of the older men in the group cautioned.

"No, Uncle, it's no even close to enough. I've only begun to have my say," the girl fired back. "I'll have their heads with my own sword if there's none here man enough to do the deed."

Patrick took Syrie's arm and quietly edged her toward the door and out into the hallway.

"Why did you do that?" she asked as soon as the door closed behind them.

"Because I saw that look come over yer face. You were but moments away from inserting yer own voice into the fray. You canna leave well enough alone when you think someone the victim."

His assessment of her personal weakness was too

close for comfort. It was that inability to let people deal with their own problems that had resulted in the act of disobedience that brought her here to speak with Malcolm in the first place.

"About that," she began, clutching her hands in front of her to keep them from fluttering around. "I've just the tiniest issue I need to bring to Malcolm's attention as soon as he has a free moment."

Patrick's eyes narrowed. "What mischief have you brought upon us now, Elf?"

Elf, indeed. She cut her gaze up at him, making no effort to hide the irritation spiking through her body. The man was eternally suspicious, especially when it came to her. Naturally he'd think the worst of her, simply because he didn't like her kind.

He met her scowl with no show of emotion, bathed in the obvious calm she always found so arrogant and irritating. His reaction was made all the more annoying by the fact that this time his suspicion was well deserved.

She had caused a problem, and she had precious little idea of how to make it better.

"Out with it, Elf. What troubles you?"

Syrie straightened her back, meeting Patrick's gaze. Though his face reflected none of his thoughts, a glimmer of concern in his eyes gave him away. They were cut of the same cloth, he and Malcolm, both convinced it was their purpose in life to carry the burdens of others.

Neither of them would understand that the larger

part of this burden was hers and hers alone to carry. She'd put herself in this predicament, and she alone must pay the price for her poor choices.

Still, part of it concerned them. And that part was what she needed to share.

"There in the glen, before the battle, before you arrived, I gave my oath to your sister. I have now fulfilled the promise I made." She paused, her gaze flickering away and back again before continuing. "With only the tiniest hint of an issue, I assure you."

She could swear the corner of Patrick's eye twitched.

"What could my sister possibly have asked of you? She has no need and certainly no wish for the troubles caused by the Magic yer kind possesses."

Patrick didn't know his sister as well as he thought. Faerie Magic was exactly what she'd asked for. Insisted upon, in fact.

"Christiana wanted my assistance in locating a man she has seen in her visions, a warrior who is to play a vital part in obtaining her freedom. She asked that I use my Magic to help this man in his quest to reach her."

Patrick's eyes widened. Whatever he had expected, this apparently was not it.

"Well then," he said, wiping any trace of surprise from his expression. "Where is this wonder of a man you've discovered?"

"I have no idea."

"You have no idea," he repeated slowly, adding emphasis to each word. "Yer promise was to find the man, aye? To find him and aid him in reaching Christiana. If you've no idea where he is, that does no sound to me as though you kept yer promise. It sounds to me as if you failed in yer oath."

"It only sounds that way because you don't understand what I'm trying to tell you."

She made no attempt to hide her irritation with him. The thickheaded Northman was missing the whole point of her having come to him in the first place. If it were as simple as merely locating someone and sending a messenger, they wouldn't be having this conversation. If it were that simple, she wouldn't have to live in dread of Danu's discovery of her actions.

"Then perhaps you'll be so kind as to enlighten—" His eyes narrowed in that annoyingly suspicious way he had. "Or is this the 'tiniest issue' you mentioned earlier?"

Perhaps he was a tad quicker than she'd given him credit for.

"Exactly."

"Out with it, Elf," he all but growled. "With yer powers, how could you fail in finding the man? What's gone wrong this time?"

She resented his implication, but arguing was more difficult when he was so close to being absolutely on target.

"I didn't fail in finding him. There was little challenge in that and I located him easily enough." Her hand fluttered into the air as if with a mind of its own and she drew it to her side, clenching her fingers into fists. "It was only when I set the Magic to pull him back through time that everything got a little . . . messy."

Time travel was tricky. Like any unpracticed Magic, it required the utmost of concentration to accomplish. The guilt burning through her fingers as she'd sent the Magic out into the ether had distracted her. The goddess, Danu, had allowed her into the Mortal world with her Magic intact only for the purpose of dealing with her daughter's disappearance, and nothing more. But she'd disobeyed Danu's edict by using the Magic to help Christiana. There would be a price to pay for her disobedience, she had no doubt.

"What in the name of Freya were you thinking, woman? You've drawn another innocent through time? And if that alone wasn't bad enough, you lost him? Have we no enough troubles what with the threat of Torquil's revenge hanging over our heads? Now we've some poor soul wandering around lost in a time not his own."

"I didn't say he was lost," she denied, though in truth, that was exactly what she was saying. "It's more a matter of his being misplaced. Temporarily, of course."

No point in explaining to this one the intricacies of working with Magic. No point at all in trying to tell him how the Magic fought you, always seeking its own end. "My intent was to—"

The door to Malcolm's solar burst open and Bridget stormed out. The men who'd witnessed her confrontation with Malcolm followed more slowly, as if they had no desire to cross her path at the moment.

Malcolm emerged last, rubbing his brow. "Unpleasant, that," he muttered, glancing toward the bodies disappearing down the hallway. "But at least I've one less odious task on my hands now."

"About that." Patrick caught Syrie's arm and pulled her toward the doorway. "I'd no be counting my hands empty just yet if I were you. The Elf here has a little something she needs to tell you."

Six

"GLEAMS LIKE A jewel in the sun, does she?" Halldor muttered. "My arse!"

Chase bit back a grin at his new friend's irritation. That whole sun description thing was of course dependent upon the sun actually shining. If he'd needed anything to convince him he was in Scotland rather than Montana, the weather here was doing its best to accommodate, alternating between plain overcast gray and cold gray drizzle.

Definitely not the semi-arid, sunny landscape he'd ridden through only days before.

"How are your feet holding up?" Halldor asked.

Chase shrugged. "They hurt like hell."

Thanks to the inopportune moment the Faeries had chosen for zapping him through time, not only had he ended up without clothing, he also had no shoes. From his big leather bag, Halldor had produced a couple of thick, furry skins and a length of fine cord for Chase to secure them around his feet. They provided protection and warmth but weren't sturdy enough for the two days of walking he'd just put in. He was pretty sure he'd worn a hole in the bottom of one of them.

"A bother it is that I parted with my spare animal before we met. Should we stop for a rest?"

Though Halldor attempted nonchalance, keeping his eyes fixed to the road ahead of them, Chase could hear the concern in his friend's voice. The man had more than earned Chase's admiration over the past two days. Not once had he pursued any of what he had to see as strange questions that Chase asked. Only once had he remarked on Chase's past, and that was simply to comment on the tattoo emblazoned on Chase's upper arm. Halldor had laughed and joked, had accepted him without question, and had done everything in his power to help Chase. He even walked his own horse behind them, matching Chase step for step when he easily could have ridden.

"No. Let's keep going. It'll be fine."

It would be, too. Of all the skills he'd gained during his tours in Afghanistan, endurance was high on the list.

Halldor nodded and pointed down the trail. "It's not what I'd call gleaming by any stretch, but does that not look like a white tower off there in the distance?"

It did indeed.

Another hour of steady walking and they reached the massive gates.

"Wow," Chase murmured as they at last drew

close. The rock walls stretched out in both directions, encompassing an enormous area.

"Impressive, indeed," Halldor agreed. "Let's see if the MacDowylt laird who rules here is equally impressive."

"State yer business or be off with you," a man called down from the wall above them.

"We're here to see your laird, the Lord of the Katanes. We were sent by one of your own, Artur, right hand to Ulfr."

Chase felt like he'd just fallen into a scene straight out of a Tolkien book. When the heavy chains began to clank and the metal grate slowly lifted, he half expected to see a horde of angry orcs raging out.

He shook his head at his own fancy. That healthy dose of skepticism lasted halfway into the tunnel leading to the castle yard, at which point it deserted him entirely.

A shiver ran down his spine and he took a deep breath, as if some strange, heavy air surrounded them. Beside him, Halldor took a similar deep breath.

Chase slowed to a stop, looking over his shoulder at the metal grate sliding back into place behind them. The bizarre events of the last few days must finally be taking their toll. Either that, or he was headed down the batshit-crazy trail.

"This is where I need to be," he whispered, reminding himself that there was a reason for everything. His father had promised him as a child that one day the Fae would send him to his destiny, and since this was where they had sent him, this was obviously where he belonged. And if he was where he belonged, perhaps *she* was here—the woman he'd waited his whole life to find.

"What is it that troubles you, my friend?" Halldor's footsteps had ceased as well, his expression more serious than Chase had seen it before.

"Nothing. Weird vibe to this place, that's all."

They both began to move forward again, their steps a bit slower than they had been. With the grate clanking down behind them, they were committed to their forward course.

"This 'vibe' you speak of, is it a feeling that crawls upon your skin?"

Chase nodded, glancing up at his friend. Halldor's eyes were fixed ahead of him on their destination. If Chase was on the batshit-crazy trail, at least he wasn't marching down it alone.

Armed warriors ringed the entrance as they emerged from the tunnel. One of their number stepped forward, his hand on the sword at his side.

"I am Ulfr, captain of the MacDowylt's personal guard. Your names?"

"I am Halldor O'Donar and this . . ." Halldor paused, one corner of his mouth twitching up as he glanced in Chase's direction. "This is my brother Chase."

Only years of training allowed Chase to school his expression. Whatever reason his friend had for introducing him as such, he'd honor it. Halldor had given him no cause to doubt him.

"O'Donar, eh?" Ulfr asked, strutting back and forth in front of them, reminding Chase of a shooting-gallery duck. Or maybe a peacock on parade. "Irish, are you? What brings you to Scotland?"

"I did indeed cross the sea from the island," Halldor agreed. "To find my brother." He slapped Chase on the back, his usual big grin returned to his face.

"And now you've come to Tordenet to join us in service to our laird." Ulfr spoke as if their reason for being here was a foregone conclusion. "Orwen will show you to yer quarters in the—"

"Not so fast, Ulfr, captain of the guard," Halldor interrupted. "I would bargain for the price of our service before we commit ourselves. I would meet the man to whom we offer our weapons."

"Impossible," Ulfr huffed. "It is not done in that way at Tordenet."

"Nevertheless, this is the way I do it," Halldor replied, his determination on display with every word. "I would have this laird of yours come out to meet with us. I would look him in the eye to judge the cut of his cloth before we pledge our swords to him."

Surprise danced across Ulfr's expression before he turned away to focus his gaze upward. In the tallest tower, a face peered down at them from a large window. Ulfr lifted an arm and the face withdrew.

"Our laird will join us momentarily."

They waited, surrounded by a contingent of men with their swords drawn. Waited in a silence so uncomfortable Chase wondered that Halldor didn't draw his own sword. Apparently even ancient warriors understood the importance of not letting them see you sweat.

At last a man appeared at the top of the huge staircase at the castle entrance.

He was tall, close to Chase's own height and build, with blond hair similar in color to Chase's. There the similarity ended. This guy was pretty-boy blond, with hair down around his shoulders. After a closer look, Chase saw that two odd white streaks shot through his hair, one on either side of his head.

The assembled men all dropped to one knee as he approached.

"Ah," Halldor breathed. "It would appear, little brother, that we have both found the place we need to be."

Seven

TORQUIL STOOD IN the center of his tower chamber, as he had since before the first light of day broke through the open window: hands pressed together in front of him, eyes closed, back straight. His mind fought to overcome the human weakness he'd yet to eliminate from his soul.

Until he found a way to push aside that small piece of him that had not come from Odin, he wouldn't have the ability to master the spell from the ancient scroll he'd found hidden in his father's things.

His jaw tightened as a wave of anger shimmered through his mind.

As if his father thought he'd never find those things.

His eyes opened and he allowed his arms to drop to his sides. Pain lanced through the muscles held in position for so many hours but he ignored it, envisioning himself scooping the pain into a large wooden chest and slamming the lid shut.

That, he had mastered. That and a million other

little feats of Magic. But those amazing abilities spoken of in the scroll, ah, those were passed down from the ancient *seid*, from the darkest corners of Svartálfheim. The words written on those scrolls represented a dark power. The True power. To be able to disappear in one place and materialize in another excited his imagination in a way none of the other powers had for a very long time.

And that power *would* be his, no matter how long it took him to master it.

"But not, it appears, on this day."

Once the anger slithered into his mind, it robbed him of his concentration. And without concentration, he had no chance at mastering the ancient Magic.

He walked across to the table and ran his hand over the yellowed parchment before lovingly rolling it into its former cylindrical shape and replacing it in the jeweled case where it belonged—right next to its twin and their deadly companion, the Sword of the Ancients.

It was as if his father had planned this misery for his son long before his untimely death. As if the old man had hidden the scrolls for the purpose of taunting Torquil, after he himself was no longer able to, knowing that the act would trigger his son's anger. Knowing that Torquil's anger would prevent his mastering that which he wanted more than anything.

"More's the pity I waited so long to send you

where you belong, Father." He spoke to the sky but he had no doubt his father's spirit was not there. After the way his father had contaminated their ancient bloodline by taking that filthy Tinkler for his second wife, there was no way the gods would have allowed him to spend his eternity anywhere but in the agony of Hela's domain.

Below him, in the courtyard, movement caught his eye. Two strangers stood encircled by his guards.

Likely more new recruits. Strangers had been trickling in to augment his forces for weeks now. Ulfr had returned yesterday bringing several new faces with him, and others had been dispatched to hire as many men as they could find. Come spring, Malcolm would taste the fruits of his revenge when he marched his army south on Castle MacGahan. When he finished with them there would be nothing left behind, and no one to remember his brother had ever existed.

Something about the little gathering below snagged his attention again and held it. Something odd in Ulfr's manner as he dealt with the newcomers. When his captain turned to face his direction and raised his arm, Torquil felt quite strongly that his presence was needed in the courtyard. Perhaps because he'd recently mastered the ability to call Ulfr to him when he chose to do so.

He returned the jeweled case to its hiding spot behind the stones above the fireplace. No one would dare enter his tower chamber without his permission, but neither the scroll nor the sword was an item he'd want falling into the wrong hands.

He made his way to the main entrance of the castle and paused at the top of the staircase to eye the newcomers. He liked what he saw well enough to descend the stairs and approach the gathering of men.

Not the toothless vermin his men usually dragged back to serve him. These two had the look of breeding about them. Both appeared strong and well fed. Though the younger of the two dressed oddly, these were the types of warriors he wanted to fill the ranks of his army.

"My lord." Ulfr rose from his knee, eyes still averted. "These Irish wish to . . ." He paused, looking uncomfortable. "They wish to bargain with you for their service."

"Bargain with me?" Laughter crawled up Torquil's throat, but he swallowed it. He'd rarely heard such a foolhardy request. "Bargain away, warriors. What would you have of me for the use of your swords?"

The larger of the two men stepped forward, ignoring the ring of steel as Ulfr drew his weapon. Supreme confidence. Torquil liked that in a man. Especially in a man who served him.

"My brother was set upon by thieves along the road. He needs proper clothing and a good weapon to replace that which was taken from him, along

with a suitable mount. I assume you have a healer.
We need access to her skills as well, or at least to her
supply of herbs." The big Irishman leaned forward,
grinning as the tip of Ulfr's sword touched his chest.
"And silver, of course. We'll both be wanting plenty
of silver for our efforts, good sir."

"And are you worth such a large investment on
my part?"

"We are," the younger man answered. "All that
he asked for, and more."

The laughter in Torquil's throat burst forth. What
grand audacity these Irish brothers showed! They
amused him as none had in a very long time.

"Then let it be so," he said as his laughter sub-
sided. "Ulfr, take them to my sister and then provide
them with whatever they need."

Turning from them, he strode back toward the
staircase that would lead him inside Tordenet, feeling well pleased. With such bravado, he'd have high
expectations for them. They were certainly different
from any he'd yet seen enter his—

His foot skidded to a stop and he turned to stare
after the men being led to his sister's tower.

They *were* different.

What was it Christiana had said about her Vision
of the man who would determine the outcome of
his plans? That he would be somehow different from
all the others. That he would have interaction
with her.

Access to the healer was among the first requests

these men had made. And even now they were on their way to Christiana's tower.

These two would bear watching. One of them could very well be the man he'd searched for.

Torquil smiled. His plans seemed to be progressing even more quickly than he had hoped. Now he must do his part to be ready.

All the more reason to continue his efforts to master the Magic of the ancient scroll.

Eight

CHRISTIANA RUMMAGED THROUGH her jars of herbs, looking for the exact ones she wanted. So many of them were either close to empty or completely gone. Soon she'd need to seek Torquil's permission to visit Orabilis to restock her supplies. Although, after what had happened the last time she'd received permission for a trip to see the wise woman, he might well decide to forbid her ever going again.

She pushed away the thought. Her stomach already tumbled with nerves gone strangely awry this day. A good, hot tisane of all her favorite herbs was exactly what she needed to rid her of this unexplained sense of disquiet.

A bit of lavender, a pinch of balm, some periwinkle.

"No," she groaned, turning the little pottery jar she held upside down in hopes there might be some small shreds stuck to the bottom. Empty. Completely empty. There would be no periwinkle in her tisane this day. She'd have to settle for a little chamomile and betony instead.

"Oh, bollocks!" she fumed, finding the betony jar down to less than a quarter of its leaves and crumbles.

This was one of herbs she used most, for everything from headaches to wounds. With her supply so low, she couldn't afford to waste it on herself simply because she was feeling jumpy. She'd have to do without its aid this day. She'd be doing without *most* of her favorites for a while, with her stock so low.

The alternative was marching across the bailey and demanding to speak with Torquil.

With a snort, she put the stopper back on the betony jar and crossed the room to place her little pot of water over the fire.

When she considered it in those terms, it was an easy enough choice. She'd rather drink lukewarm water running straight off the muck in the goat pens than face Torquil unnecessarily.

She'd just retrieved her favorite mug when a knock at her door served as the final straw for her jittery nerves. The clay mug tumbled from her fingers, shattering on the hard floor.

Visitors to her tower were infrequent, consisting only of those needing help with a wound or sickness or the men her brother sent when he summoned her.

Taking a moment to compose herself, she brushed a few loose strands of hair from her face and then opened the door to find Ulfr waiting there, accompanied by two men she'd never seen before.

Warriors, from the looks of them. From their massive builds to their sharp expressions, they radiated strength and confidence.

Christiana stepped back into her room, extending an arm to invite them in. It was preferable to having them push her aside when they entered, which they would do if Torquil had sent them, regardless of whether or not she offered invitation.

Her concern waned a bit when the strangers dipped their heads courteously as they entered, a sure sign they were new to Tordenet. Once they observed her place at the bottom of the pecking order, they'd treat her with the same indifference everyone else did.

"These men have requested the assistance of a healer. Our lord has commanded me to bring them to you." Ulfr's gaze wandered around the room while he spoke, as if he hoped to find some sign of illicit behavior that he might report to his master.

"What troubles you?" she asked, looking from one of the newcomers to the other.

Weariness rode their shoulders, evidence they had traveled long and hard to reach their destination. Both men had hair in shades of gold, but there the similarities stopped. The larger of the two wore a neatly trimmed beard, his hair hanging loose around his shoulders, and he dressed in finely made clothing, while the smaller man wore what appeared to be oversize castoffs, and his hair barely brushed his shoulders.

As they passed her on entering her chambers, she realized the second man was hardly what she could consider small, towering over her as he did. He was equal in stature to Ulfr. No, it was only that the first was a great bear of man.

The larger of the two, obviously the one used to being in charge, spoke up first.

"Begging your pardon, my lady, but on our travels here, my brother was set upon by thieves. He's a nasty bump to his head and, with their having taken his boots, he's blisters upon his feet now. We've a need for an herbal poultice to help with the healing."

"It's not all that bad," the second man added. "You don't need to put yourself out, ma'am. I'll be fine."

Something about his words, something in his voice, tickled at the back of her mind.

"Sit. Remove the bindings from your feet," the first one said as if his brother had never spoken. "Allow the healer to see for herself."

Christiana pushed away the odd feeling, attributing it to the strange disquiet and worry she'd battled all morning. "Here."

She pulled a small stool forward for the man, regretting her choice as soon as he bent down to perch awkwardly upon it. She dropped to her knees on the floor next to him, pushing his hands away to loosen the bindings herself before he lifted his foot for her to examine.

The animal skin he'd worn had rubbed against

the bottom of his foot until liquid-filled blisters had risen and, some of them, burst. The knowledge of the pain he endured knotted her stomach.

"I can help you," she assured, looking up to find him staring down at her with a gaze so intent, she floundered for her next words. "I've a . . . a balm," she began. What was it about him that so put her off her comfort?

"It's a poultice what he'll be wanting, my lady," the one standing interrupted. "Made of good herbs."

"My balms are made from good herbs," she explained, her eyes still held by the man in front of her. "But if you prefer a poultice, I can see what—"

Her words froze in her throat as her fingers brushed over the man's skin. A prickle of awareness ran the length of her arm and she jerked her hand away.

Only his hand darting out to grasp her elbow saved her the embarrassment of toppling backward onto her bottom right there in front of them.

"Steady," he advised.

What had that feeling been?

"A . . . a poultice," she managed, pulling away from him to rise to her feet. Steady? Not with that man's hand upon her. "Herbs, yes. Of course."

"Of course," the standing man agreed.

"For wounds," she murmured to herself, turning her back on her visitors as she moved to the wall shelves to search among her dwindling stock.

She ran her hands over the jars to gain time to recover her senses.

He had felt it as well, she was sure. The dark centers of his eyes had widened in acknowledgment of what had passed between them, like polished jet rising from a churning green sea.

"Comfrey," the big man advised. "And Jupiter's Beard. Yarrow. I don't suppose you have calendula?"

"Calendula? No." It surprised her that this man knew his herbs so well, especially when he named one she'd never heard of. "But I have others I would use, if they meet your approval. Agrimony and betony are two I like for wounds."

At his nod, she dumped the various herbs into a stone bowl and ground them with the pestle before adding a splash of whisky she kept on the shelf for exactly that purpose.

"Good," the big man muttered from his spot by the door.

Of course what she did was *good*. She'd learned from the best. She'd like to see him dare to lead Orabilis through this process, as he had her.

Dropping back onto her knees in front of her patient, she kept her eyes on the work in front of her, rubbing her hands together to force away the tremors that rippled through her fingers.

"I'll do my best to avoid causing you any further pain, sir," she said, daring a glance up.

"Don't worry. You won't hurt me," he said quietly. "And my name is Chase, not sir."

She glanced up just as he smiled. Only a tiny lifting of one corner of his mouth, but it was enough. His eyes captured hers and she caught her breath as a wave of recognition broke over her.

It was *him*! How she had not known it from the moment he'd entered her door was beyond her. She'd never clearly seen his face, but those eyes! She'd been lost in them too many times not to know them now. Her whole body tingled with recognition, a physical reaction to their first meeting she'd never foreseen or imagined possible.

"And I am Halldor O'Donar," the man next to the door boomed, laughter rolling in his voice. "Clearly, in the care of such a lovely healer, my brother has forgotten any manners he might have once had."

"You've no the need to waste yer time on introductions to Mistress Christiana. Our good laird's sister is no one you'll be talking to again, I can assure you," Ulfr said.

She flinched, almost having forgotten her brother's hound still stood in the room.

"You have another healer here, do you?" Halldor questioned, waiting only for Ulfr to shake his head in answer. "No? Then I suspect we'll be seeing this good lady regularly until my brother's wounds have healed. That poultice she's wrapping around his foot will need changing soon enough."

Halldor was right about that. Unfortunately, some of the jars she'd selected for her mix were close to empty. She had enough for two, perhaps three more treatments.

After that, she'd be forced to seek Torquil's permission to visit Orabilis.

"That poultice and bandage will want changing in two days' time," she advised Chase, watching his hands as he retied the straps around the furs covering his feet. "And best you find some proper footwear, aye? Or all the herbs in the world won't help you."

She risked a look up just as a full grin split his face. It was as if her heart had forgotten how to beat.

"Yeah. Proper footwear. I'll do what I can about that. Thank you for your kindness . . ." He paused, that half-smile tugging at his mouth again before he finished. "Christiana."

She nodded, and the three of them filed out, her knees so weak she leaned her back against the door as she watched them walk away.

Chase's voice was deep and rich and his words had such a strange sound to them, befitting a man who came from a faraway land. With joy, she could listen to him speak for hours on end. And if the only word he chose to say over and over again was her name, she'd be well pleased.

It was only as they crossed the bailey toward the soldier's lodgings that she remembered what she must do.

"Ulfr!" she called, stepping outside as the sun broke from behind the clouds where it had hidden all day. A good omen. "I'd ask you to carry a message to our laird. I'd seek an audience with him, if it pleases him."

Ulfr nodded his acknowledgment and strode off, leading the strangers to their new quarters.

No, she reminded herself as she hurried back inside her tower. Not strangers. They were much, much more than that. They were her savior and his brother.

Nine

BRIDGET MACCULLOCH PACED along the wall walk, a favorite spot since the first time her father had allowed her up here.

Her beloved father. Her murdered father.

Wild anger shafted through her grief-ravaged heart. After her mother's death, Hamud had cared for her as both mother and father. Now it was time for her to pay back the debt of love she owed the man who had given her life.

You've no a need to fash yerself over Jamesy, her uncle had said. *We'll find you a husband to fill yer days as yer father should have done long ago, and you'll forget this vengeance business soon enough.*

Brie spat on the ground beside her. *That's* what she thought of her uncle's idea. How could any man who shared her father's blood be so daft? How could her own uncle know so little about her? If these men thought she was simply going to accept her father's murder, sitting in her little cottage, mourning away her life, or devoting it to the upkeep of some slovenly bastard they chose for her, well, they were all badly mistaken.

Through her mother, Brie was a daughter of the House MacUlagh, descended from the Ancient Seven who'd ruled over this land when not even the Roman invaders had dared challenge all the way to the northern sea. Her father had honored her mother's bloodline, training Brie with weapons even as he'd trained her older brother. Warrior ran in her blood as much as in Jamesy's.

Except that in her blood, temper ran in equal parts with warrior. Her da had always claimed it was that which kept her from being her brother's equal. She drew in a deep breath, fighting to tamp down the anger as her father had often instructed. Fighting to wrestle it to the ground and bury it in a deep, dark hole.

As always, she was only partially successful.

When Jamesy returned, the foul MacDowylt laird of the northern clan would be made to pay, even though Malcolm would do nothing to avenge her father's death.

Jamesy *would* return. Any day now. He would.

"If," she hissed into the wind, her fists clenched at her side. *If* Malcolm had told her the truth. *If* he had actually sent word to Jamesy of what had happened to their father.

But what if he hadn't? What if Malcolm had lied

and Jamesy had no knowledge of their father's murder? It was a possibility she had to face. If her brother didn't return, it was up to her to set the grievance right on her own. Whatever it took, she'd make her way to Tordenet Castle and seek vengeance against the vile Torquil herself. One way or another, he would be made to pay for the crime he had committed against her family.

"By the Seven," she vowed, stopping as her attention fell to the clanging of the heavy chains raising the gate to give someone entrance to Castle MacGahan.

Could it be? Her heart pounded as she rushed to the opposite side of the wall walk to peer down to the road below, holding back her disappointment at the sight greeting her eyes.

Not her brother, but a distraction nonetheless. Tinklers!

She raced back across the wall walk to look down on the courtyard. As if word had spread by magic, inhabitants of the castle streamed from the keep and outbuildings, all hurrying to reach the Tinklers' wagons as they pulled into the bailey.

Though this was the first visit Tinklers had made in the year she'd lived at Castle MacGahan, she'd heard the stories of how they'd long been refused entry to the castle grounds. But all that had changed thanks to Laird Malcolm's first wife, the Lady Isabella.

These days the Tinklers and the wares they carried were welcomed. One who appeared to be their leader, a man by the name of William Faas, if Brie remembered the stories correctly, jumped down from the lead wagon before reaching up to assist a woman to the ground beside him.

Cook weaved her way through the gathering crowd to speak to the man. With Cook's silver tongue, there'd likely be new pots in the keep's kitchen before day's end. The Tinkler woman did not join in the conversation with Cook, but hurried away from the wagon, directly toward the stairs where their laird and his lady waited with Lady Danielle's friend, Mistress Syrie.

As soon as the Tinkler reached the group and made her greetings, she and Mistress Syrie moved away from the others, their heads bowed close together in conversation.

Fair odd, that. But from what Brie had seen of Mistress Syrie since her arrival at the castle, she shouldn't be surprised. That woman was fair odd, herself. Every bit as odd as her aunt had been, before she had left to be replaced by Syrie as Lady Danielle's companion.

Brie would have loved to be close enough to hear the conversation shared by those two, but she had little time to dwell upon that curiosity, because more visitors climbed down from the second wagon. Visitors who did not dress the same as the Tinklers. It wasn't so much the people themselves that interested her as what they carried. One man held a drum, another a set of pipes and within the blink of an eye, the men began to play while a woman danced behind them.

That was enough for Brie. Down the narrow stairs she ran, not stopping until she reached the edge of the crowd that had gathered. To her disappointment, she'd no more than arrived when the music ceased.

"A taste, good people, only a taste. We'll share the full of our talents this very night in yer own hall. All we ask is a few paltry coins to cross our palms in payment for the pleasure of our talent."

Murmurs of the crowd buzzed in Brie's ears as Laird Malcolm himself made his way through the people gathered around the newcomers.

"Welcome, friends. I'm sorry to say there's none here what can afford to cross yer palm with anything, minstrel. Though yer welcome to take yer night's rest within the safety of these walls and we'll gladly share our evening meal with you."

"Done!" William Faas agreed. "And perhaps these minstrels who travel with us as our guests will agree to repay your kindness with a few songs!"

It didn't look as if the minstrel standing next to William was any too pleased with that idea, but the cheers of the crowd perhaps encouraged him to relent.

"As you will it, Master Faas," he agreed. "Our journey north continues on the morrow only due to your kindness. A small performance for these people tonight seems a price well paid for the transport you provide us."

They journeyed north on the morrow? Brie's mind churned with a fast-forming plan. It was almost too perfect to believe.

North was exactly where she needed to go if she was to avenge her father's murder.

Ten

THIS WILL NOT do." Halldor slapped the mare on her hindquarters and stepped back from the stall. "Not at all. This horse is no better than that reject from the peat bogs Ulfr thought to pass off as a sword."

As promised, Ulfr had provided Chase with new clothing and boots on the first day, soon after assigning them their spaces in the barracks. A weapon and mount had been much slower to come. Days, in fact. And when Chase found the weapon Ulfr had left, even he thought it must be a joke of some sort.

The sword he carried on his back was really a weapon in name only. It looked as if it had been dug up from under a rock somewhere or, as Halldor liked to claim, out of the peat bogs. Rusted and chipped, it would do him little good in battle.

The horse, though, wasn't all that bad.

"She looks to be a healthy animal." In much better shape than many of the wild horses Chase had rounded up back in Montana.

Back in another life. The knowledge that Faerie Magic had transported him seven hundred years into the past still rattled his brain if he thought on it much.

He tried his best not to think about it at all. Very quickly, he'd learned that ignoring his past made facing each morning easier. If this was where he belonged, then this was where he'd make the best of being.

No, the horse wasn't all that bad.

"She's a gentle one, too," he added, almost as an afterthought.

Halldor's response was a rude snort.

"Gentle is the last thing you want in battle, my friend. This is a woman's beast. A palfrey. What you want under you when you ride against a field of men is a destrier, like my own."

Point well taken. The difference between the horse Ulfr had picked out for him and a war horse like Halldor's would be the equivalent of a moped versus an armored Humvee.

"I suppose that means we'll need to speak with our friend Ulfr."

Halldor snorted even louder than before.

"That we will. And I suppose it goes without saying that it would be a mistake to think Ulfr our friend. He's not a man to be trusted."

"It goes without saying," Chase agreed, exchanging a grin with Halldor as they left the stable.

Some things didn't change, no matter what century you were in. Brownnosers and backstabbers weren't confined to any particular period in time. People were people everywhere. Everywhen.

They made their way around the animal pens and past the men training in the lists in time to see a familiar figure hurrying across the courtyard toward the keep.

"Isn't that your little healer?"

It was indeed Christiana. Funny how just seeing her at a distance could bring a smile to Chase's lips and set his heart racing. It was as if the sun shone a little brighter for her.

The woman had been extraordinary over the past few days in treating his blistered feet. He'd always healed quickly. His mother had claimed he could thank his Faerie blood for that, but he'd had his doubts about the process without the benefit of modern medicine. If he didn't know better, he'd be tempted to claim there were magical powers in those herbs she'd used.

The only drawback to her skills was that now that he was better, he had no reason to visit her. And visiting her was something he very much wanted to continue to do.

"Looks like she's headed into the keep," he observed. "Hey. Didn't Ulfr say that was where he was going, too? To meet with Torquil?"

"I believe he did, at that," Halldor responded, a wide grin spreading over his face. "And since we absolutely need to get this horse business settled so that we might attend to other matters, it appears to me as though we've no choice but to follow the lady."

"No choice whatsoever," Chase agreed, his steps already leading him in that direction.

At the bottom of the stairs, Halldor cleared his throat.

"I should mention that I have sensed a . . . what did you call it before?" His forehead wrinkled and then smoothed. "Yes. A vibe. A vibe that the Lord of Katanes may not welcome the intrusion into his keep of two lowly soldiers such as ourselves."

Chase snorted this time. He didn't care what century it was, his personal code didn't change. "First off, Torquil is not my lord. He's just my employer. And if I'm not good enough to pass through his doorway, maybe I'm not good enough to wield my sword in his name. Maybe that means I'm outta here."

Though the thought of never seeing Christiana again bothered him a little more strongly than he would have expected. "As soon as I'm sure my wounds are completely healed, that is."

Halldor slapped him on the back. "Then we go together," he said, leading the way up the stairs to the massive doors. "As soon as the little healer has finished with you, of course."

Why Chase's face heated was beyond him. It just made good sense not to set out into the world until he was sure there was no residual chance of infection. He was only thinking of the logic of the situation.

The door ahead of them opened to two guards, swords held at the ready.

"What business have you here?" one of them asked.

"We're here to see a man about a horse," Chase answered, catching up to Halldor's side.

When his friend lifted an eyebrow in question, Chase shrugged. It was a line he'd always wanted to use and there would likely never be a better time than right now.

"We seek Ulfr," Halldor clarified.

"And there he is," Chase pointed out, pushing past the guards and into the entryway where Ulfr stood beside Christiana, his hand gripping her elbow. And not in a good way, from where Chase stood. "Are we interrupting something?"

"Yes," Ulfr barked, drowning out Christiana's quiet denial. "What do you want?"

"We're here to see a—" Chase began, feeling quite pleased that he could use the catchphrase twice, when Halldor interrupted.

"We've a problem that could prevent our being able to remain in service to the MacDowylt."

As Halldor spoke, the door next to Ulfr opened and Torquil stepped into the hallway.

"There's a problem?" he asked.

"No, my lord," Ulfr hurried to answer.

"Begging your pardon, Laird MacDowylt, but I'm afraid there is." Halldor stood his ground, ignoring Ulfr's angry glare.

Torquil studied each of them in turn, then stepped back inside the room. "I'd have you join me in my solar so that we might get to the bottom of this. All of you."

"My lady?" Halldor offered his arm to Christiana, nudging Ulfr aside as she accepted.

Chase swept his hand in invitation for the captain of the guard to enter ahead of him.

No way he wanted that man at his back.

Inside, his eyes immediately sought out Christiana, as he found himself doing each time he was in a room with her. She stood apart from the others, her hands clasped at her waist. Perhaps it was only the swords and scabbards hanging on the high stone walls that made her appear so small and out of place, but he found himself fighting the urge to go to her side and reassure her. She looked every bit as uncomfortable as he felt in here.

From the moment he'd entered, it was as if the walls were closing in. Not that the room was small by any means. It was more a matter of the feel of the room, as if something in it weakened him and sucked the air from his lungs.

"Show him that piece of bog trash you carry on your back."

Chase's attention snapped away from the woman, and he found Halldor and Torquil staring at him.

"Go on. Hand it over to the laird."

"It mayhap need a wee touch of a polish by the metalworker," Ulfr offered, his voice trailing off into the oppressive silence.

Chase pulled the rusted weapon from the scabbard he wore on his back and stepped closer, dipping his head respectfully as he passed it to Torquil. Once the other man accepted, he stepped away, his own gaze once again sweeping the room, lighting on Christiana only briefly before he forced himself to study the weapons hanging on the walls instead.

This wasn't the twenty-first century, where a man could gawk at a woman with impunity. Things weren't done that way here. Now. No matter how much he was drawn to her.

"A *good* weapon was the terms of our agreement," Halldor reminded. "This does not fulfill those terms, any more than the palfrey they've tried to give my brother fulfills our agreement for a suitable mount."

Torquil barely glanced at the sword before dropping it to the table next to him.

"It does little good to spend my silver in hiring talented swordsmen if they're ill-equipped," Torquil murmured, his eyes boring into his captain.

Chase almost felt sorry for the man. Almost felt compelled to speak up in his defense. Almost.

Then he spotted something hanging on the wall he never thought he'd see again. A sword so like the one his father had owned it could have been the same weapon. He was drawn to it immediately, crossing the room to run his finger down the blade.

"Here now, O'Donar!" Ulfr called after him. "Dinna be thinking to handle the artifacts what belong to Clan MacDowylt."

"You've a good eye." Torquil had moved to stand beside him. "That is a weapon of distinction. An ancient weapon forged by some long-forgotten MacDowylt ancestor, hung upon this wall for who knows how long."

"My apologies if I offended, my laird." Chase dipped his head once more. "It's only that this sword bears a remarkable resemblance to the one my father had when he first taught me the use of such a weapon." Such a remarkable resemblance, in fact, he half expected to see his father stroll into the room at any moment.

"No offense taken, I assure you. Please, take the weapon into yer hands if you like. Test the feel of it." Torquil moved behind his table and took a seat, very much like a man waiting to be entertained.

Chase lifted the sword down from its mountings. In his grip it felt different from his father's, but good all the same. He laid the sword across his palm to feel its weight. Admiring the fine balance, he peered at the markings on the blade. Made in the fires of the ancient Celts, his father had claimed of his own. Holding this one, Chase didn't doubt it.

"Ulfr!"

Torquil uttered his captain's name like a man commanding a trained animal and Chase looked up to find Ulfr charging him, teeth bared, his sword leading.

Instinctively, Chase raised the weapon he held, just in time to meet the downward blow of Ulfr's sword. The leaf-shaped weapon felt natural as metal clanged on metal, as if it were an extension of his own arm. The lessons with his father rushed back to him. His vision tunneled on the man in front of him and he twirled, dodging the next attack, blocking from his mind Christiana's scream and Halldor's shout as the big man threw himself in front of the healer. Chase pivoted under Ulfr's strike, slicing upward at the last minute. A thin red line appeared on his opponent's forearm as he glided past.

Ulfr screamed, backing away, his free hand tightly clenched over the dripping wound.

"Excellent!" Torquil rose from his seat, clapping his hands in appreciation. "Expertly done, indeed. You wield that weapon as if you were born to it, O'Donar. The sword you hold is meant to be used, no to decorate a wall. It's yers to keep, and the sheath, as well. As to a horse, take yer pick of any from my stables. Satisfactory?"

Chase's heart pounded in his ears from the adrenaline pumping through his system. It had been a long time since he'd felt the rush that accompanied hand-to-hand combat.

"Satisfactory!" Halldor boomed.

"Noble," Chase corrected quietly, turning to face the MacDowylt laird. This part of their charade had come to an end. Dishonesty didn't sit well on his shoulders. He didn't like pretending to be something or someone he wasn't. He never had.

"What did you say?" Torquil stared at him, his lack of expression concealing his thoughts.

"My name is Noble, not O'Donar. Chase Noble."

"My brother speaks truly. We do not share the same father," Halldor interrupted with a shrug before throwing an arm around Chase's shoulders to usher him from the room. "Why else would I have had to come all the way to Scotland looking for this one, eh?"

Chase considered refusing the offer of the weapon, but only for a moment. Torquil was correct. The sword was never intended to be a decoration gathering dust on a wall. It was meant for the hand of a warrior, and it fit his as if they had been made for each other.

He pulled away from Halldor's grip and turned to face Torquil, lifting the sword in salute.

"My thanks, Laird MacDowylt. I pledge to use this weapon to the best of my ability."

"If you use it half so well in yer service to me as you did a moment ago, I'll consider it a gift well given."

Chase dipped his head one last time and walked out of the room.

He'd pledged to use the weapon to the best of

his ability. But he wasn't yet completely sure that would mean using it in the service of Torquil Mac-Dowylt.

IT COULD BE either one of them.

Torquil stared after the departing men, frustrated by his inability to read which of them carried the fate of his destiny on their shoulders.

"I asked for a moment with you, my laird, because I have need of—"

"Silence!" He held up a hand to stop Christiana from speaking. His interest was not in what *she* needed but in what *he* needed, a fact she so often failed to remember. "It's one of them, isn't it?"

A flare of irritation sparked in her eyes when they met his. Irritation and . . . was that defiance he saw there? Foolish girl. She had neither the ability to lie to him nor the intelligence necessary to trick him. For his part, he had neither the time nor the patience to indulge her in playing her usual word games.

"I want a straight answer. Is one of them the man you saw in your Vision? Yes or no, little sister. Don't parse your words with me. I'm in no mood for it."

Her lips straightened to a thin, hard line. "Yes."

Good. Progress at last. Though it was like pulling nettles from the skin one by one to get the information he wanted from her.

"Which of them? Is it the elder brother, Halldor?"

That one certainly appeared the logical choice. It was he, after all, who'd rushed to escort her into the room; he who'd thrown himself in front of her like a shield when the swordplay had begun.

"I cannot with any certainty say it is he."

The muscles in her jaw worked as if she tried to prevent herself from giving the answers he wanted. Pathetic Tinkler spawn. Had she any sense at all, she would have accepted her place—and her fate—long ago.

"But it is definitely one of them." He stated the obvious, seeking her confirmation. "Is it no?"

"It is." She bit off the words as if in an attempt to hold them back.

Leaving him with the challenge of determining which of the men he needed and what role that man would play. Torquil could think of only one way to accomplish the task quickly.

"I must know which of those men will be responsible for my success. I require you to retire to my tower immediately. You will travel to Skuld's world for me, seeking a very specific Vision of the future from her." She had the ability. He'd seen her do such a thing before. That it was difficult and dangerous for her to challenge Skuld's will was of no importance to him.

"I canna do as you ask."

"What?" He turned on her, roaring his anger, allowing the beast within to rear its head. "I dinna *ask* it. I *ordered* it to be so. You'll do what I say, when

I say it. You'll no be about refusing me if you value keeping yer daft head upon yer shoulders."

"I'm no refusing you, my laird." She spoke without flinching despite his threat. "I simply canna do as you order. I tried to tell you earlier. It's the reason I came here, the reason I've requested an audience with you for the past week. My supply of herbs is gone. To travel in the manner you require, I must have the tonic Orabilis brews for me. Without the herbs to prepare it, I have no control over where the Visions take me."

Deep inside him, violence stirred. Control of the beast had become so much more difficult since that day in the forest when he'd unleashed its power. Even now, the beast clawed its way up from his bowels as his rage flared, demanding to be free, to wreak vengeance on those who would oppose him. To taste blood again.

But giving himself over to the beast meant relinquishing intellectual control, and that he could not allow. Now, of all times, his wits must remain keen.

"No," he forced out between gritted teeth, his internal battle rampaging within.

"Then I dinna see how—" Christiana began.

"Silence!" he yelled. Or perhaps the command had come from the beast within him; he couldn't be sure.

She backed away from him, her clutched hands held over her heart, her eyes filled with fear.

Fear that only strengthened the beast.

Torquil labored to close his eyes, finally turning his back on her, hoping it would be enough. An unearthly howl filled his mind as the beast shrank back into the depths where it lived, taking the bloodlust that colored his sanity with it.

He straightened his back, breathing in the sweet smell of control once more. Clarity of thought returned, he wiped the spittle from the corners of his mouth before turning back to face those waiting for his next move.

No alternative was left for him but to allow Christiana to visit her witch. But having this forced upon him didn't mean he couldn't use it for his own ends.

"Very well, I will consider your request. Leave me."

"I will need to take flour along to trade." Her voice shook and she took a step backward, away from him.

"I said I would consider it. Now do as yer told and leave me!"

He had but to raise his voice only a little and she complied. Complied? He clamped his jaw shut to keep himself from laughing out loud. She scuttled from the room like a terrified mouse.

A mouse who had no need to know his decision had already been made.

At last he turned his attention to Ulfr. The idiot stood, dripping blood to a puddle on the floor, his eyes round as loaves of bread.

"You will accompany my sister to trade with her witch. You personally, Ulfr. Not someone you assign to the task as you have in the past. Do I make myself clear?"

Had Ulfr done as he was told last time, Malcolm might not have escaped, although the women who helped him did so with a Magic of their own that even Ulfr would have been helpless against.

"Yes, my lord. As you say, it will be done."

"Good. I want those two new men, O'Donar and his brother, assigned to accompany you. You are to observe their every interaction with Christiana and report it back to me. Observe, but you'll no interfere with either of the men. This is of the utmost importance to me, Ulfr. I'll no take well to yer failing me in this task."

"As you will it, my lord."

The man bowed his head, but not before Torquil saw the fear in his face.

"Now go. And send someone in to clean up this mess." The odor of fresh blood made it all the more difficult to restrain the beast.

Ulfr nearly ran from the room, reminding Torquil of Christiana's retreat.

Perhaps the time had come to replace Ulfr as captain of his personal guard. Noble had certainly defeated him easily enough. Perhaps that was the role the man from his sister's Vision was destined to play. Champion to the Lord of Katanes in title as well as in deed.

He rather liked the sound of that.

Ulfr, meanwhile, would have this one last chance to be of good use. With some well-placed suggestions, he might even be able to instigate the actions that would point to his own replacement. And after he returned, whether through his observations or through Christiana's Vision travel, Torquil would name his new champion.

Eleven

SHE HAD INVADED his dreams every night since the gates of Tordenet had first closed behind him. Though tonight was no exception, the dream itself was altogether different.

Chase peered down into the face of the woman clasped against him, her body warm and willing under his.

"Christiana."

He breathed her name, savoring the feel of it on his lips. Her eyes opened and he plunged into their depths. Falling, falling, adrenaline pumping, the air rushing past his ears. He'd experienced this feeling before, every time he'd jumped from the belly of a Chinook copter, and again during the earthquake that sent him hurtling back . . .

As though a bucket of cold water had hit him in the face, he was suddenly wide awake, his breathing heavy, his body aching with unfulfilled need.

No way he'd be able to get back to sleep now.

As quietly as possible he stood and slipped his feet into his boots, then wrapped his plaid around him. With his shirt clasped in his hand, he slipped through the door and out into the night.

The cold stung his senses, which was exactly what he needed right now.

He slid into his shirt and wrapped the end of his plaid over his head and shoulders, thinking, not for the first time, about the practicality of the garment.

His gaze was drawn to the far side of bailey, to the tower perched in dark relief against the stone wall. A tiny shard of light wavered from the top window.

Was she awake? Had she dreamed of him, as he'd dreamed of her? He could no more put her from his waking thoughts than he could from his dreams.

This was what he'd come to. Lusting after a woman he barely knew. He rubbed a hand over his face, unable to pull his gaze from the orange flicker in the distance.

That limb must have hit his head a whole lot harder than he'd thought, as Halldor was so fond of saying. Either that or getting jerked through seven hundred years had seriously messed him up.

"A warrior who cannot sleep is a warrior who cannot fight."

"I can always fight," Chase responded, somehow not surprised that Halldor had joined him.

"There's a change on the wind tonight," his friend said quietly after a time. "Is it that which keeps you awake?"

"Maybe." He'd much rather let his friend think

that was the problem, than confide his fantasizing over Christiana MacDowylt like he was some thirteen-year-old who'd just discovered girls. "You expect it to snow?"

"Snow?" Surprise sounded in Halldor's voice. "I suppose that is possible as well, though that was not where my thoughts carried me."

The tower window went dark and Chase finally turned to face his friend. "Then where are your thoughts?"

"They are in this place, little brother. Things are not as they seem here."

Chase shook his head, wondering exactly what his friend meant. "They are as they seem if you believe this is a powerful man gearing up for war. Over half the men I've spoken to are newly hired mercenaries, just like us. Our employer is planning to take someone down. Hard."

"I do not speak of that. At least not just that. Look around you. Feel this place. There's a great violence dwelling here."

"It's a violent time." Chase opted for a cavalier note as he turned his gaze up to the starlit sky, but he knew as soon as he uttered the words they were meaningless. He had personal knowledge that people would always be so. "We're a violent race."

"Open your eyes, little brother. Open your heart. There's more than the violence of men in this place. Evil dwells here."

More than most, Chase understood that there

was a modicum of truth in many of the strange beliefs held by ancient peoples. That didn't mean, however, that he was a practitioner of those beliefs.

"Not one of my talents, I'm afraid. I don't 'feel' things." At least nothing other than a warning tingle up the back of his neck that had more than once saved his life.

"You must believe me when I tell you that there are men who possess extraordinary gifts of power. Gifts such as the ones that live deeply trapped within your own soul. You've but to tap into them and set them free. Our first day here, you spoke of the 'vibes' you felt when we entered this place. You credit yourself far too little."

"No, my friend, you credit me far too much. Don't get me wrong. I do believe there are people who've been gifted with extraordinary powers." His sister Leah's face danced through his mind, but Chase pushed those memories away. "I just don't happen to be one of them. I'm nothing more than a warrior, Halldor. A warrior plain and simple." It was all he was ever meant to be, and apparently he'd been put in the place he belonged in order to be exactly that.

CHRISTIANA SAT CROSS-LEGGED on the stones in front of a flickering candle, her head cradled in her hands, despair gnawing at her innards.

What would she do? If Torquil refused her passage to visit Orabilis again, what could she do?

Nothing.

She would be his prisoner here forever, her fate at the mercy of Skuld's every whim. Trapped here without either the knowledge or the ability to steer her own destiny. Watching helplessly as the man whose destiny she had interfered with suffered whatever fate the future might bring. That fear, more than anything else, pained her.

For without access to the herbs Orabilis provided, she hadn't the ability to search Skuld's world for the information she needed to find. She'd spent the last several hours attempting unsuccessfully to make her way into the Visions. Not only could she not target what she wanted to find, it seemed as though she was no longer able to step foot in Skuld's world of future possibilities at all.

She couldn't even focus on the pathway to reach her desired destination. Each time she closed her eyes it was Chase Noble that filled her mind. Chase's strong shoulders, straining at the cloth of his tunic as he practiced in the lists, his easy smile as she bandaged his foot, the sound of his voice as he spoke her name, the way her skin heated each time they touched. She could only imagine what it might feel like to have him hold her close; to have his lips hovering over hers as they shared a kiss.

A shiver ran the length of her spine and she forced the image of him away. It was completely improper for her to harbor such fantasies about him. It was a rescuer, not a lover, that she had seen in her future, and that was what the Elf had sent to her.

She couldn't fault Chase for her inability to reach the Visions. There must be some other reason. Something she was overlooking.

Had she spent so long in Skuld's world the last time that she'd worn out her welcome? Or was it as simple as the disquiet she carried in her soul after her meeting with Torquil?

Her half brother had long worried her. Better than most, she saw that the power he took into himself changed him. Corrupted him. Blackened his soul. But today, for the first time ever, she'd known true fear in his presence. When he'd turned to order her from the room, the eyes that had looked back at her from his face, red and glowing hot, had not belonged to him. It had taken all the courage she could muster to speak to him again before fleeing.

Rising from the floor, Christiana picked up her candle to carry it with her down the winding stairs. Cold licked at her ankles as she reached the bottom step, where only the soft glow of embers remained in her fireplace to greet her. She bent down to stir them before adding wood to encourage the fire back to life.

Her stomach growled as she pulled her bedding close to the fire, reminding her she'd missed her meals in her effort to travel on the wings of the Visions.

"And all for naught," she sighed. She was no closer to knowing what was to come than she had been at first light, when she'd rolled these blankets up to store them for the day.

Sitting down, she pulled off her shoes and dropped them to the raised hearth next to her. The fire crackled and spit, releasing a spark that floated away on a current of heated air. Her eyes followed it as it danced upward like a living thing seeking its freedom, until it reached the level of the mantel. There it touched upon her bag of runes, just as its heat faded and it disappeared into nothing.

Her runes!

Had the gods called her name aloud, they couldn't have made themselves heard any more clearly.

"Thank you," she whispered, not sure which of the gods might have smiled upon her this night and unwilling to annoy any of them by choosing the wrong one to honor.

The bag was small and dark, made from the softest of leathers. Her father had claimed that it had been passed down through generations of their family, and she had no reason to doubt his word.

She sat on the floor again, loosened the ties, and pulled forth a square of embroidered linen before allowing the contents to spill out into her hand. Twenty-four bits of carved wood, darkened and worn smooth by untold years of use.

Her runes.

With the linen square flattened out in front of

her, she closed her eyes and dropped the runes from her hand.

With her Visions of the future withheld, she asked for guidance from the Ancient Ones. Some clue as to what was to come. Some clue as to what she needed to do to save herself and the man she'd forced the Elf to send to her. One false step on her part and Torquil could well bring the world as they knew it to an end. The world and Chase Noble.

Eyes still shut, she concentrated on the two of them—her and Chase, together, his arms entwined around her. With the vision in her mind, she reached down and chose two of the runes at random, closing her fingers around them, savoring the feel of the old wood against her palm.

One for her, one for the man whose arrival she'd awaited so long. One for Christiana, one for Chase.

Within her palm, the little coins of wood nested together, face-to-face. With a shaking finger, she pushed them flat to see what message she had been given.

Tiwaz, the warrior, and *Berkana,* the birch tree. The first advised courage and strength of conviction, while the second portended new beginnings and birth. Or rebirth.

Only as she stared at the old carvings did her mistake occur to her. She should have chosen them one at a time. One clearly for her, one clearly for him.

Too late for that now. The Ancient Ones had already spoken.

She fisted her fingers around the runes and lay back on her blankets. Snuggling down into the heavy woolens, she clutched them to her heart.

The answers she'd sought were here for the taking. She had but to interpret their meaning properly. Which of them was to be the Warrior and which one was to be Reborn?

Twelve

As feelings went, this was a new one.

Chase stroked his hand along the neck of the large horse he'd chosen last night, surveying the activity in the courtyard around him.

Being here felt right. Him, the horse, his friend Halldor at his side—all of it. He basked in a new-found sense that this was where he was supposed to be at this moment in time.

At this moment in time.

Thinking the words still sent a shiver down his neck, though not the jolt to his system it had a few days before. It seemed that whether he was boarding a C-17 in the States and offloading in a desert half way around the world or slamming through seven centuries, his brain adapted and compensated, keeping him on course like the autopilot on an airplane.

"How amazing is the human mind?" he muttered, tugging on his horse's lead as he headed across the bailey toward the waiting wagon.

"Most amazing, indeed," Halldor agreed, keeping

pace with him. "It's a man's mind, not his brawn, what will most often save him in a battle."

Chase spared a look at the big man, grinning in spite of himself. He wondered, for perhaps the thousandth time, how he'd been so lucky as to have this man be his first contact in this world.

"Is it not a fine day for a jaunt into the countryside?" Halldor boomed, returning the grin. "A hearty meal in our bellies, a sky filled with the promise of good weather, and friends to share the day. What more can a man ask from life?"

Ahead of him, Christiana waited by the wagon, her cloak fluttering in the cold breeze. She lifted a hand to brush a lock of hair from her face, revealing cheeks stained pink by the cold.

With scenery like that, a man didn't need anything more.

"Not a single thing I can think of," Chase responded. "It looks like I have everything I need for a good day."

Any day he could find an excuse to spend with Christiana was a good day. The only thing that could make it better would be if the two of them were spending that day alone together.

A few more steps brought him close enough to realize it wasn't the cold that brought color to Christiana's face.

"Ignoring me will gain you nothing, Ulfr." Her voice was raised beyond its normal pitch. "One barrel is no nearly enough."

"Enough or no, it's all yer witch gets from our stores. Now get in the wagon before our good laird changes his mind and refuses to send anything at all."

Ulfr waited, arms crossed, making no attempt to assist Christiana.

The whole scenario struck Chase as odd. He would have expected the captain to show considerably more respect to his laird's sister.

"If that's yer final word, then so be it." She stepped back from the wagon, crossing her arms to mirror Ulfr's stance. "Unless we take the full complement to barter, I've no reason to go."

They faced one another across the space of three feet, neither appearing willing to back down.

"Lord Torquil will no be pleased if I have to fetch him here." Ulfr leaned closer toward Christiana. "I'd no suppose our laird's displeasure is something you wish to bring down upon yerself, now is it?"

That Ulfr pulled the threat card didn't sit well with Chase. Not well at all. Couple that with the way he'd been holding her arm when they'd followed her yesterday, and Chase's hand itched for another go at the man.

"Is there a problem here?" He pasted an easy smile on his lips as he stepped within reaching distance of the two.

"No problem at all, good sir," Christiana answered, not taking her eyes off Ulfr. "Though I fear you've wasted yer time in preparing for a journey that will no be happening now."

"We'll see how brave you sound after I speak to yer brother." Ulfr turned his back and strode off toward the main keep.

"Four barrels, Ulfr!" Christiana called after him. "I'll travel with nothing less."

An uncomfortable silence settled around them, broken at length by Halldor.

"So it's a witch we're off to see, is it?"

Christiana blinked several times as if she tried to process the question. Whether it was the words themselves that surprised her or Halldor's speaking in the first place, Chase couldn't be sure. What he was sure of was that she wrestled with her answer before responding.

"Orabilis is no witch, no matter what Ulfr or others might say. She's but a wise woman, a healer." She stopped, like a woman who'd said her piece, her lips drawn into a thin, straight line. Then, with a deep breath, she lifted her chin as if daring them to argue with her and continued. "She is also perhaps the kindest, most intelligent person I have ever known in the whole of my life."

"As you'd have it, my lady." Halldor dipped his head respectfully. "Though there's naught in your words to refute her being a witch."

"Is it no enough that I vouch for her? That I tell you there's no reason to fear her? Have I given you any reason to doubt that I speak the truth?" The color on Christiana's cheeks deepened.

"Let it go," Chase cautioned his friend before turning to face Christiana. "We are more than satisfied that you speak the truth."

It was obvious that the woman was already upset enough without Halldor carrying on about witches, of all things. Though, in the man's defense, Chase was hardly in any position to pass judgment on whatever fantasies his friend might believe to be true. He was living proof that real life actually did harbor a host of the bizarre and unusual.

"Apologies, my lady." Halldor dipped his head once more. "It was not my intent to question the truth of your words. It's only that you defend this woman as if being a witch is a bad thing. It's not. They have their own roles to play in the web the Norns have woven for us. I've no fear of them, only a healthy respect."

Chase cast an annoyed glance to his friend, preparing himself for Christiana's angry response.

Instead, she surprised him with a small smile. "Yer words sound like something my father might have said. I'd offer up my own apologies for making assumptions without first listening. It's only that Orabilis is—"

Her words were cut short by Ulfr calling out to Chase and Halldor as he approached them.

"Mount up and lead the lady's wagon around to the door of the kitchen's storeroom. It seems we'll be adding barrels to our wagon."

Every trace of Christiana's smile disappeared, her chin once again lifted defiantly. "Four barrels in total?" she asked.

"Four barrels in total," Ulfr confirmed, reaching for his horse's reins. Turning his back to them, he led the way without waiting for further comment.

Christiana placed one foot upon the step of the wagon and Chase was instantly at her side, his hands around her waist to lift her up. No sooner had his fingers grazed against the cloth of her gown than a bolt of excitement shot through him, setting his heart pounding.

Beneath his touch she tensed, turning her head to look up into his eyes. She placed a hand on his forearm as he lifted, and time seemed to stop as her face came level with his. Her lips, parted and inviting, were so close he needed only to dip his head a fraction of an inch to capture them as he'd wanted to from the first moment he'd seen her.

Behind him, Halldor cleared his throat, breaking the spell.

Chase hoisted her up into the wagon and, as soon as she took her seat, he stepped quickly away, his breath coming in short, ragged pants. The urge to hold her close was so strong, he'd had to make himself release his grip on her. Forcing himself to concentrate on the task at hand, he did his best to push the feelings away as he climbed onto his horse, but they were too strong to be ignored.

Un-freaking-believable.

It was need that overwhelmed him. Need, pure and simple, and every bit as vivid as if he were caught in another dream of her.

Thirteen

"WHAT ARE WE to do with her?"

Brie backed against the side of the Tinklers' wagon, refusing to cower before the people gathered around her. She straightened her back and squared her shoulders, meeting their accusing stares. She'd known this moment would come, when they'd discover she'd hidden herself in their wagon and confronted her for her actions.

But knowing didn't make it any easier. And it certainly wasn't her fault that pitiful little minstrel dancer had been frightened enough to jump from the wagon and hurt herself.

"Return her. She belongs to the MacGahan."

Brie cut her eyes to the woman who'd spoken and the woman took a step away. As she should. Brie belonged to none save her own self.

"There's no silver to be made in backtracking. I say we leave her here and go on," one of the minstrels said.

Not exactly a caring man, that one. And people

claimed it was the Tinklers who were not to be trusted.

"I say we punish her." The minstrel girl sat on the ground several feet away, her eyes wet with tears, a cold, wet cloth held to her face. "Beat her with a stick and leave her here by the side of the road."

Brie lifted her chin and stared the girl down. She'd like to see any of them try what the weak little scold dared suggest.

"Hush, Eleyne. Yer face and foot will heal." The Tinklers' leader spoke up at last. "What say you, lass? Why have you hidden yerself in our wagon? What are you running from?"

"Yer mistaken in yer question, William." His wife, Editha, moved closer, her hand outstretched as if she caressed a passing breeze. "It's where she's running *to*, no from, that puts her here with us. Is that not so?"

Brie studied the other woman's eyes, searching for any sense of accusation, but she found no malice there. No judgment. Nothing to draw her ire.

"It is true that I have a need to travel north. When I learned that yer wagons headed in that direction, I decided to join you."

The woman who wanted to take her back to Castle MacGahan responded, "Hiding in a pile of woolens is no joining us. Yer but a shameless woman who's run from her home, leaving us to be heaped with the blame for stealing you away against yer will. We must return her, else they'll send men after us."

"Calm yerself, Esther. The MacGahan is unlikely to think us responsible for—"

"Leave her and be done with it," the minstrel interrupted. "She's but a witless, troublesome wench who thinks to gain herself the adventure of a market day in Inverness, hunting for pretties. There's no a single silver to be made in taking her there."

"I've no interest in market day or in Inverness." Brie had contained herself as long as she could. "It's no pretties I seek, but a man. The man who murdered my father."

"Revenge, is it?" The minstrel laughed, his mouth drawn into a cruel, mocking line. "Revenge is the business of men. Best you keep yerself to yer man's warm hearth, woman."

"Have a care for yer tongue, Hugo," William warned. "She's but a lass."

"I belong to no man. I am Bridget MacCulloch, daughter of the House MacUlagh, descended from the Ancient Seven who ruled all this land upon which you trod. I'm more than capable of seeking my own revenge."

"Oh, my apologies, yer highness," Hugo mocked. "I'll grant you appear to be fit enough for a woman. I've no doubt yer chores are but little effort to you, and you obviously had no problem in tossing our poor wee Eleyne out on her arse. But yer hardly a fit match for a man. For a fact you—"

With a speed matched by only a well-trained few, Bridget leapt at the man, unsheathing the knife she wore at her waist as she moved to hold it to Hugo's throat, abruptly ending his words in a sharp, hissing intake of breath.

"Hardly a fit match for a man, am I? Then what are you, minstrel? No a man by yer own definition, I'd say. Here I've bested you, and I'm no even breathing hard for doing it."

"You see? She's wicked!" Eleyne screamed.

"Hold yer weapon down, Bridget MacCulloch," William ordered. "If, that is, you'd have us give any consideration to taking you where you want to go."

"What?" Hugo exclaimed, stumbling away from her, his hand at his neck, as she resheathed her weapon. "By what good sense would you think even once upon allowing this savage wildling to travel with us?"

"You claim birthright from the houses of the Ancient Picts, do you?" Editha approached to stand close to Brie, speaking to her as if no one else were around them.

"I do."

"Then I will rely on the honor of yer ancestors for yer absolute honesty with us. Where is it you'd hope to go?"

"Toward the northern coast." To a place she hadn't seen since she was little more than a bairn. "To Tordenet Castle."

"I dinna ken a place called—" William began.

"Thunder Castle," Editha interrupted. "Gleaming white upon the shore. Deandrea's home."

"A gleaming white castle, is it? There is wealth in this place of which you speak?" Hugo seemed to have overcome his distrust at the mention of Brie's destination.

"There's wealth aplenty," Brie confirmed. If Torquil MacDowylt had stolen from others as he stole from the MacGahan, he must have storage rooms filled to the bursting with treasures.

"We willna go to the Thunder Castle. We would no pass through the gates of Tordenet for a wagon filled with silver." William crossed his arms. "No Tinkler would."

"But you can go near to Tordenet, even if you dinna go inside, true?" That was all Brie needed. She'd find her own way in.

"Indeed," Hugo agreed. "This Tordenet of yers sounds to me to be a place in dire need of the entertainment we can provide. Especially since you say no one goes there."

"Just get me close. That's all I ask." Begging didn't come easily to Brie, but she was willing to make an exception for so important a cause. "I will be in yer debt."

"I suppose we are long overdue for a visit to Rowan Cottage." William looked to his wife, waiting for her nod of agreement.

"It is settled then. We travel to the Thunder Castle."

Fourteen

"YOU'LL STAY WHERE you are until I say it's time to stop, aye? And this is no the time I'm choosing to stop."

Chase had taken just about all of Ulfr's crap he could stomach. Much more of this over-the-top rudeness to Christiana and he wasn't sure he'd be keeping his job with the MacDowylt, regardless of whether the Faeries who'd sent him wanted him here.

Punching out your senior officer was likely as bad now as it would be in his own time.

He glanced to Halldor to see his friend's face uncharacteristically drawn in anger.

Christiana ignored Ulfr as if he'd never spoken, climbing down from the wagon and hopping the final distance to the ground.

"I'm only going as far as the trees. I've a need for a moment of privacy, so I'd appreciate yer no following me."

Seemed a perfectly reasonable request to Chase.

Apparently Ulfr didn't see it that way. He dismounted and started after her.

There was a definite line between acceptable and unacceptable that Ulfr seemed determined to blunder across. With a tug on his reins, Chase moved his horse forward, blocking his captain's path.

"And what do you think yer doing?" Ulfr demanded. "I gave an order and I expect it obeyed. We've precious little daylight left us as it is, especially with the speed at which this storm is rolling in. We've no time to waste."

"Let her have her moment of privacy. Five minutes one way or another isn't going to make that much of a difference now." Chase glanced up toward the dark, heavy clouds roiling overhead. "If we're going to get caught out in bad weather, whether it's here or five hundred feet down the trail won't matter much, now will it?"

Halldor moved his mount closer. "There's no need for disagreement, gentlemen. Here's our lady now," he announced.

Christiana had emerged from the trees, clutching her cloak against the rising wind as she made her way back toward the wagon.

Ulfr stepped around Chase's horse and strode in her direction, grabbing her arm to jerk her forward, causing her to stumble.

That did it. Line was officially crossed and, job or no job, Chase could tolerate no more of Ulfr's behavior.

One moment Chase was sliding from his saddle and the next, his fingers closed around the linen at the back of Ulfr's neck, bringing the man to an abrupt halt.

"If you plan on keeping that hand, asswipe, you better keep it to yourself," Chase advised. "Now let go of the lady and get back on your horse."

Chase led Christiana to the wagon, assisting her up into her seat. Her gasp as she turned had him spinning just in time to avoid Ulfr's charge.

"Son of a—" Chase ducked under the other man's arm, leading with an uppercut to Ulfr's chin that sent the captain staggering sideways against the wagon even as Halldor roared a warning.

Thunder cracked overhead and Christiana screamed as her frightened horses reared and bolted forward. Chase grabbed for Ulfr's plaid, yanking him away from the out-of-control wagon just in time to avoid his being crushed under the massive wheel. He let the other man fall to the ground, running for his mount, urging his horse to a gallop even before he had both feet in the stirrups.

Christiana had fallen backward over the seat into the bed of the wagon. She wrapped her arms around one of the barrels of flour as the wagon pitched perilously over rocks and dips in the trail with the horses gaining speed.

One side of the wagon lifted entirely up off the ground and hit back down with a loud crash of splintering wood as the back wheel gave way. The horses, in full frenzy, dragged the broken wagon off the trail and through the brush.

Chase was so close now, he could see the reins flapping uselessly over the lead animal's back. He tried not to think what it meant that Christiana's body bounced between the barrels like a rag doll. Another few feet and he should be able to reach . . .

The horses darted away in another direction, speeding across an almost dry riverbed, sending the wagon off-kilter. His heart thudded in his chest as he raced toward them, so close he could see Christiana's face but too far to do more than yell, when the whole thing tilted onto its side and rolled completely over.

As if by some random intervention of a benevolent god, the front of the wagon jammed into the riverbank and the rigging broke free, allowing the horses to stampede on, leaving the broken wagon behind.

"Christiana!" he yelled as he jumped from his horse and squatted beside the wreck, reaching into the small, dark opening between the seat and the wet ground. His touch grazed something soft and he tightened his fingers around his find, the edge of her cloak.

"Christiana? Can you hear me?"

He waited, holding his breath, praying for a response. A noise sounded from the dark—a groan perhaps? It was all the encouragement Chase needed.

He was up, his back against the side of the wagon, straining to lift it off her.

"Halldor!" he called, shifting position to put his shoulder into his effort. He couldn't do this alone; the wagon was far too heavy. "Help me, Hall. Hurry!"

"On three," the big man said, landing at his side as he leapt from his horse. "One, two, three!"

Together they pushed the bed of the wagon a few feet up off the ground.

"Move a barrel there." Halldor motioned down with his head. "I can balance this."

Trusting his friend to know the limits of his own strength, Chase reached inside to drag one of the barrels under the edge of the wagon bed.

With the side propped up he could see her clearly now, making not even the slightest movement. On his hands and knees he moved to her side, slipping two fingers along the warmth of her neck.

The pulse he felt there, strong and steady, rocked him with relief.

Short-lived relief, as a crunching sound came from the barrel supporting the wagon's weight.

"Get out of there," Hall ordered.

Ideally he'd check any victim of an accident for broken bones before moving them, but this situation was about as far from ideal as he could imagine.

On hands and knees, he hooked his hands under Christiana's arms and began to back out, but something was holding her firmly in place.

Another splintering crunch from the barrel.

"Hurry, little brother. Our brace is not going to hold for much longer."

"She's stuck."

Chase methodically felt along her body, tucking her arms up onto her chest and following lower to her legs, at last finding the problem. One foot was trapped between two barrels, both of which were firmly lodged under the lower edge of the wagon.

"Goddammit," he growled, ramming his shoulder against one of the barrels without result.

Light blocked out behind him as Hall, on his hands and knees, backed into the opening.

"Back up against the wagon bed. If we push together, we can lift this wooden beast onto her side."

Chase slid into position and, giving it everything he had, pushed, straightening his legs as he lifted up.

Another splintering crack and the wagon rocked back over onto its side. With the weight of the wagon lifted off the barrels, it was now a simple matter to move them and free Christiana's foot.

"She lives?" the big man asked, hovering over them.

As if in answer, Christiana groaned.

"She lives," Chase confirmed, kneeling at her side to brush away the hair splayed across her face.

Another groan and her eyes fluttered open.

"You've had yourself quite the little adventure, haven't you?" he asked, smiling down at her.

"I'm no at all fond of adventure," she managed through gritted teeth, clutching the hand he offered. "I must reach Orabilis."

"She wants her wit—" Hall bit off the word before starting again. "She wants her wise woman. That one will be able to heal our lady's pains."

"In that case, I'm taking her to her wise woman."

"I've captured the runaway team," Ulfr called as he rode toward them, leading the panting animals behind him. "They tired of their escape at last."

Chase was already in his saddle, leaning down to take Christiana from Hall's arms by the time Ulfr reached their side.

"Here now, what's this? What do you think yer doing with our laird's sister?"

Chase had no time for Ulfr's questions. "If I stay on this path, will it lead me directly to the wise woman?"

"Yes, but . . ." The captain looked from Chase to Hall and back again, his eyes narrowing. "We're no going forward now. We'll head back to Tordenet and return with a work detail to repair the wagon."

"No, *you'll* head back to Tordenet. Christiana's hurt. She says this Orabilis can help her, so I'm taking her there."

Chase urged his horse forward to speed down the trail. It didn't matter what Ulfr had to say. He was doing what needed to be done, and he'd deal with the consequences later.

"STRONG BARRELS, EH?" Halldor slapped a hand down on one, still intact in spite of the accident. Turning his back on the quickly disappearing rider, he gathered up the reins of his own animal and climbed into the saddle. "I pray the wise woman's healing skills are good enough to justify our lady's faith in her."

"Good as any, I'd suppose." Ulfr turned his horse back in the direction they'd come from. "Though you'd no catch me putting my own self into the clutches of one such as her. Wise woman, my arse. A witch she is, plain and simple."

It would do little good to point out that a talented witch could often be a valuable ally. Such thoughts would be wasted on the likes of this captain. They rode in silence for the next several minutes, the guilt of not having done enough to prevent the accident preying on Halldor's mind. He should never have lost his temper.

"Unpleasant business, this," he intoned, as much to himself as to his traveling companion. "I suppose our laird will be heartily displeased at news of his sister's injuries."

"Mayhap." Ulfr shrugged. "But like as no, his ire will be tempered by the knowledge that yer brother is the one he seeks."

Halldor tugged on his reins, bringing his horse to a stop. He didn't care for the sound of that. "Explain yourself."

"My lord directed that I should seek to determine which of you it is that fulfills Mistress Christiana's Vision. It was foretold that the rightful man would see himself as her defender."

"Visions? Of future events?"

Now there was a twist he'd not counted on. And if Torquil was so set upon determining which of them had appeared in the good lady's visions, it seemed only wise to hinder that determination in any way he could.

"Aye," Ulfr confirmed.

"And it was for this reason you behaved as you did to the good lady we accompanied?"

Ulfr only nodded, as if he suspected he'd already said too much. Perhaps he had.

"It's not that I want to ruin your plan to tell your laird that my brother is the man he seeks, but I feel that I should be honest with you about one small detail."

"Aye? And that would be?"

"The only reason it was Chase instead of me who ended up defending our good lady against your rudeness is that I was on the opposite side of the wagon at the time."

Ulfr swung his head in denial. "No, yer brother was ready to do battle over Mistress Christiana. It's him, no you, as I figure it."

"Could be you're right. Not having all the information available, I'll be the first to admit I could be wrong." Halldor paused, waiting for his words to lull the other man. "On the other hand, I can tell you this much for a fact. If I ever see you treating our good lady in such an accursed manner again, I'll crush your head between my own two hands like a dried apple between rocks. You follow my meaning?"

Ulfr nodded, this time pulling his horse a few steps ahead of Halldor.

That should give the worm something to think over, and something to pass along to his laird, as well.

The silence hung over them for miles, which Halldor appreciated, since it freed him to consider more important matters.

And chief among them was deciding which he found more interesting: that Mistress Christiana frequented Skuld's world in visions of the future, or that he and Chase Noble somehow figured into those visions.

Fifteen

CHASE TIGHTENED HIS hold on Christiana, berating himself for all his mistakes. Just about everything he could imagine doing wrong, he had done wrong, like some new recruit on his first mission out. He knew better than to be jostling an accident victim cross-country on horseback. Not that he had much choice. He could hardly call for an evac here.

Still, he'd failed his training on the most basic level. He hadn't checked for a spinal injury or broken bones before hefting her into his lap and heading out at a trot, bouncing every bone in both their bodies. Hell, he hadn't even checked for concussion.

You couldn't get much sloppier than that.

Okay. Fine. He'd dropped the ball. But she was still breathing and he would make the best of the situation. He knew for a fact she was in pain, and her ankle had swelled to twice its normal size.

Not that he'd spent an inordinate amount of time studying her ankles, pre-accident. Maybe his eyes had strayed there a few times, but what he saw now was sure as hell no normal ankle.

If the accident had done that to her foot when she hit the ground, there was no telling what it could have done to her head. And since he hadn't had the good sense to verify it one way or another, his smartest move was to go on the assumption that there was a problem and make sure she didn't drift off to sleep before they reached the wise woman's home.

"How are you holding up?" he asked.

"How am I . . . I'm no holding anything." She shifted in his arms, groaning in the process.

He tightened his grip on her. "Just relax. I've got you." Though somehow the Magic allowed him to speak the same language as everyone in this time, "same language" didn't always have the same meaning. "I only wanted to know how you're feeling."

"Ah." Again she shifted, eliciting another groan. "My foot pains me still."

Little wonder, considering how those barrels had wedged against her ankle.

When he felt her relax against his chest, he was tempted to allow her to escape the pain through dozing off, but that would be as careless as his having neglected to check her injuries in the first place.

"We're a long way from Tordenet. How is it you found this wise woman of yours way out here in the first place?"

"I had no need to find Orabilis. She brought me to Rowan Cottage herself many times. She lived in this place long before my family arrived. In the years before my father grew ill and infirm, she and I would travel here to spend time tending her gardens."

"So she used to live at the castle with you, and now she's back out here all by herself. Why would she choose to do that? Seems to me like Tordenet would be a much safer place for an elderly woman." Especially in this day and age.

"Things are not always as they seem."

"Fair point." He of all people knew that to be truth. "So, you're saying that she is safer out here on her own. Is that because people like Ulfr accuse her of being a witch?"

"People like Ulfr are little more than an annoyance to Orabilis. Tordenet's danger lies more in people like my brother. People who'd gladly see her dead."

And why would a powerful laird like Torquil want to harm an old woman? He was about to ask when Christiana spoke again.

"We're close now," she said. "See the small trail there into the trees? Down that way just a piece and we'll be there."

He did see the trail, now that she'd pointed it out. But had she not been with him, or had she been unable to direct him, he could easily have missed the cutoff.

The trail, perhaps—but not the signs that someone lived around here. He sniffed the air, ripe with the acrid scent of burning peat. He should have picked up on those clues some time ago. Instead, he'd been captivated by Christiana, completely ignoring his surroundings.

What was it about this woman that so put him off his game?

"Through those trees there."

As they cleared the stand of trees, the location of the cottage became evident, though without the smoke curling from one end of the roof he might have missed it, set behind a rise in the land as it was. A ring of trees surrounded the house, spaced far enough apart that there was no mistaking a human hand in their placement. Ten minutes ago he would have sworn that landscaping for the sake of pleasing the eye didn't exist in this day and age. The cottage and trees he approached now told him a very different story.

"She's there!"

The words escaped Christiana's lips on a breath, as if without her conscious thought.

An old woman stopped midway between the door of the cottage and a large earthen mound, her arms piled high with squares of peat.

"Christiana?" she called, as if she doubted her own eyes. "Christiana! Oh, by the gods!" She dropped her load to lift her skirts, enabling her to run in their direction.

Waddle, actually. Quickly, but she waddled nonetheless, swaying from side to side like a cartoon character.

Chase urged his horse to a trot to save the elderly woman the effort.

"What's happened to her? What have you done to her?" she demanded as Chase reached her side.

"No, no, Orabilis," Christiana pulled herself forward, grimacing as she moved. "It's an accident with a runaway wagon what's put me in this distress. This kind man has brought me to you for help."

"Come along with you, then." Orabilis wiped her hands down the sides of her apron, already waddling toward her open door. "Bring her in. Lay her by the fire. Dinna you dawdle, now. I can see from here that she's in pain."

Chase did as he was told, kneeling to gently deposit Christiana onto a fur the old woman spread out in front of the fire. She lay with her eyes closed, her face pale. One hand clutched at a small cloth pouch hanging from her neck while the fingers of her other hand twined with his, gripping him tightly.

It was only because she was in pain. The logical part of his brain knew that. Something deep in his chest though, some odd twinge-like thing there, didn't want to break that contact. The odd twinge-thing wanted to believe that she held on to him because his touch made a difference—*his* touch, not just the touch of any human being. He chose to listen to the twinge-thing, remaining on his knees, holding Christiana's hand, rubbing his thumb in circles on her palm while Orabilis searched through a shelf overflowing with small clay pots.

At last she found what she wanted and made her way over to the fire. With a grunt, she struggled to her knees. Chase held out his free hand to assist her but she ignored the offer, her watery eyes tracking from his hand holding Christiana's to his face and back down again.

Her unspoken message was clear enough. He untwined his fingers from Christiana's and rose to his feet to stand by the door to wait. To watch. To make sure all was well.

Not that he really believed this old lady was a witch. Or that she would in any way harm Christiana. It was only that he needed to be sure of Christiana's safety before he stepped back outside to deal with his horse.

"I'm so sorry about the flour. I've hopes some of it can still be brought to you." Christiana shook her head as if the accident had been her own fault. "I ken you must be in need of more by now."

"Pfft," Orabilis answered, lifting Christiana's head to allow her to drink from the clay pot the old woman held. "Only a small sip now, little one. Dinna you waste another thought upon the flour. I'll make do. Surely that's no the only thing what's brought you all the way out here, is it?"

"My herbs are gone. Skuld willna allow me entrance without them, and I have desperate need to see the path she's woven for me."

"Why would you . . ." Orabilis paused, turning her pale stare in Chase's direction. "You. Dinna you be standing there, wasting what's left of this day's light. Best you go collect those peat turves you made me drop when you came riding up here on that great beast of yers. Scared the very life out of me, you did."

"My apologies," he began.

"I've no need for yer apologies, lad. Only for those turves, if I'm to keep this fire burning through the night. Now, get along with you and do as I asked, aye? And there's food and shelter for yer animal in the shed out back. See to it."

With a nod, Chase escaped into the fresh air. The looks on the faces of both women made it quite clear that his presence was no longer necessary or desired. That old woman had all but tossed him out on his ear. In a whole different century, he could easily picture her as a retired drill sergeant.

Christiana didn't appear to be in any danger from Orabilis, though the desperation in her voice when she spoke of the "herbs" she'd come after bothered him a little. He didn't remember much of the history he'd learned covering drugs in the Middle Ages, but there was probably a whole lot the history books didn't cover. It was definitely something he planned to ask Christiana about later on. Just as he'd be asking Orabilis what was in that little jar she'd given Christiana to drink.

For now, he'd do as he'd been told and let the wise woman do what she could to alleviate Christiana's pain.

"THANK YOU." CHRISTIANA lay back on the heavy fur, giving in to the throbbing pain she'd felt for the past few hours. Without Chase holding her hand it seemed to hurt worse. "I wasna thinking properly to be bringing up such things in front of Chase." Especially not in front of Chase.

"Chase, is it now? Yer on a given-name basis with this man?"

Heat suffused Christiana's neck and cheeks. The pain robbed her of her concentration and had allowed her words, always so carefully guarded, to flow like spring runoff. Fortunately, Orabilis was the one person in the world with whom she had little need to guard her tongue.

One glance to the doorway to assure herself that he was well and truly not within hearing distance, and she was ready to voice her confession.

"It's him, Shen-Ora." The name she'd called Orabilis in her childhood slipped easily off her lips, as if it hadn't been so very many years since she'd uttered it last. "The one I've been waiting for."

"Ah, the man of yer dreams."

"No *from* my dreams," she corrected, trying to lift the precious bundle she wore at her neck to prove what she said. "But from my vishes . . . vitches . . . visions. He's the one I saw in my Visions." Her tongue grew thick and heavy, just like her lips. And her eyelids. They were almost too heavy to lift open. "He's why I need the herbs. I must travel the proper path. I canna let him fall to Torquil. There is so much I must learn. I told you of him on my last visit. Told you he's the only one who might have me. No! The only one who might *save* me. That's what I meant to say. Save me."

"So you did, little one." Orabilis chuckled, her words drifting somewhere in the distance. "And save you, yer fine warrior will. You'll have yer herbs soon enough, but for now, we must concentrate on you and yer injury. Give yourself over to the potion, Christy. No need to stay here and do battle with the pain. Just drift for me."

Orabilis's voice seemed to come from a dream, floating past Christiana's ears in a most soothing way. And then, just as her mind slipped into a warm, safe place, the old woman touched her ankle and a scream ripped up her throat, the pain so intense it was as if a thousand demons stabbed her with their spears.

Stabbed her and dragged her down into a black abyss of agony.

Sixteen

Odd that she could have forgotten how intimidating Tordenet Castle really was.

Not intimidating, Brie quickly corrected herself, as if denying the thought might untie the knot in her stomach. *Impressive* was the word she'd wanted. That was it. An impressive castle.

And not odd at all that she would have forgotten the place. She'd been barely able to walk when her father had followed Malcolm MacDowylt from here, his wife and children trailing behind with the other camp followers. Brie hadn't been back since. She wouldn't be here now, if the monster living behind those gates hadn't murdered her father.

Mathew, Hugo's younger brother, whistled between his teeth. "This far away, and already you can see the gleam of her walls. Bollocks, but she's one damned intimidating structure, is she no?"

Brie shot him a look, wishing his mouth were sewn shut. Little good it did her to correct her own thinking if those around her were determined to erode what little confidence she had left.

"With the sun setting on her that way, she looks like a tower of gold to me." Hugo laughed, rubbing his hands together.

"Like you've ever seen gold," Eleyne sniped from her perch on the wagon, her swollen foot propped on a bed of woolens in front of her, watching as everyone else prepared their campsite for the night.

"I've seen it, fair cousin, never you doubt. And I intend to have some of it for my very own after our visit to yon distant lovely towers."

"But only if the wildling can do her part, aye?" Mathew looked from his brother to Brie and back again. "The men behind those gates willna part with silver, let alone with gold, for our music only. It's the beauty of the dance what greases their palms."

"The dance and the drink," Hugo agreed.

"She's no ready," Eleyne grumbled. "And I can be of no use, no with my foot so swollen and my face all scratched to here and back again. Thanks to her."

The knot in Brie's stomach grew. "It's no much of a challenge to wiggle one's hips to the beat of a drum. I'm ready enough."

She had to be. The minstrels held her responsible for scaring Eleyne the night she'd been discovered. Scaring her so badly when the idiot woman had seen Brie moving beneath the pile of woolens that she'd thrown herself from the back of the wagon to escape the ghostly fiend she imagined hiding there, injuring herself in the process.

Since Brie was responsible for their loss, to their

way of thinking, they expected her to take Eleyne's place. It had taken her only a few moments of consideration to agree to their demand.

Not that she cared whether the minstrels made a single copper coin from their upcoming performance. Once she carried out her careful plan, the minstrels would be lucky to escape with their heads still attached to their shoulders.

Replacing the annoying Eleyne would get her through the gates of Tordenet and inside the great hall. It was the perfect opportunity to seek her revenge. The perfect opportunity to get close enough to Torquil MacDowylt to slice him open and bleed him dry.

Seventeen

CHRISTIANA'S SCREAM VIBRATED in the air, pounding against the ribs in Chase's chest.

He dropped the peat piled high in his arms, drawing his sword as he ran across the open ground to burst through the doorway. Whoever had harmed Christiana would meet their end on the sharp edge of his blade.

"What happened?" he demanded, his voice inexplicably breathless.

"Nothing's happened. She's fine," the old woman assured him without turning, her hands busily wrapping a fine, white strip of linen around Christiana's foot. "She fought the pull of the potion but she sleeps now."

The bandage wound up and around Christiana's ankle in a thick, heavy-looking bundle, reminiscent of a cast.

"Is it broken?" Even as he asked, he doubted the wisdom of the question. It wasn't like this old woman was a real doctor with access to an X-ray machine in the back room.

"No. Only badly bruised. As you should have known yer ownself." She turned her gaze on him then. "You've too little faith, lad. And where's my peat turves? Did I no tell you I need them to keep the fire going? I canna be expected to do everything myself, can I?"

The damned peat lay all over the ground outside where he'd dropped it when he'd heard the scream. "I'll have them right in."

By the time Chase returned to the house, Orabilis was nowhere to be seen. He stacked the peat on the floor beside the big fireplace before kneeling beside Christiana.

She appeared to sleep, her soft lips slightly parted, delicately moving as if she carried on a conversation in her dreams. Only the frown wrinkling her forehead confirmed that, even in her sleep, the pain of her injury still reached her.

He ran his thumb over the furrows in her brow, as if he could drive away her troubles.

If only he hadn't allowed himself the luxury of confronting Ulfr back there on the trail, he might have prevented this. Had he not been off his horse, bent on proving himself to be some macho-man warrior, he might have had a chance to reach the out-of-control horses before they'd sent the wagon crashing upside down, pinning Christiana underneath. But no, in that moment he'd been more interested in her impression of him than in her safety.

And Christiana had paid the price for his pride.

"If you really want to help, perhaps you might carry her in here."

Chase jerked his hand from Christiana's brow, feeling a little like a child caught with his hand in the cookie jar. "Where were you?"

Some warrior he'd turned into, when even a shuffling old woman could sneak up on him.

"Preparing a bed for my guest. Now, if you'll be so kind . . ." Orabilis stepped aside, holding an arm out to indicate the open door behind her.

He scooped Christiana into his arms and rose easily to his feet. In his embrace, she moaned and turned her face into his chest. If he didn't know better, he'd swear she snuggled against him.

Her warm breath penetrated his heavy linen shirt in a way none of the sharp, cold winter winds had done, setting his heart pounding.

Inside the little room he leaned down to lay her on the pallet spread out on the floor, but Orabilis stopped him.

"No, on the bed, I told you. I'll take the blankets beside her for this night."

The old woman hardly looked able to climb in and out of a bed, let alone up and down from the floor, but he did his best to blank any doubt from his face.

"Are you sure?"

"I told you so, did I no?" She shook her head, her disgust clearly evident. "Young people today. No appreciation at all for the abilities of their elders."

Apparently his face had been more expressive than he'd intended. "I'm sorry. I didn't mean to offend you."

He could have said more, but chances were good he'd only end up with his foot farther down his own throat. He laid Christiana onto the narrow bed, surprised when he had to peel her fingers from the grip they held on his shirt.

Orabilis motioned him outside the room and followed shortly after, shutting the door behind her.

"She'll rest through the night and feel much better when she awakes." The old woman pointed to a chair as she made her way to the fireplace, pausing to pick up a small clay jar. "As for us, I've a pot of stew on that will be ready soon enough. Have yerself a seat and we'll visit for a piece as we await our meal."

Chase did as he was told, pulling a seat out from the table as Orabilis scooped a handful of something from the jar and tossed it into the bubbling pot.

"What's that?" he asked, settling into the hard chair. It was a good bet the floor would be equally comfortable.

"Just a bit of this and that. A mixture of herbs I favor for seasoning my food."

He wasn't sure how it would taste, but his growling stomach could attest to the fact that it smelled like something from a five-star restaurant.

For the next few minutes Orabilis busied herself drawing up two large mugs of ale. Surprisingly fine ale, as the first sip disclosed.

"This is good."

"Of course it is," she said dismissively, but he caught her fighting off a smile. "It's the honey. The bees love my herbs when they flower, and the herbs flavor their honey. I'll return in a moment. You just sit back and enjoy yer ale, lad."

Chase briefly considered whether or not he should have more of the ale. She might have put something into the drink to knock him out as she had with Christiana. But, since he had no reason to mistrust her, he decided his concerns were foolish.

She returned soon enough, her arms wrapped around the biggest bowl he'd ever seen. When she set it on the table, he could see it was filled with what looked like dried weeds. As soon as she began crunching down on the bowl's contents with the large pestle she held, the aroma assured him it was herbs, not weeds.

After a few minutes of watching Orabilis struggle with her task, he couldn't sit still any longer.

"Here. Why don't you let me do that for you? You've been on your feet ever since we arrived." And for someone who looked like she could easily be a hundred years old, she could probably use the rest.

"I think I will at that," she agreed. "But mind you, lad, I'd have you put some muscle into it. No lazing about."

"Yes, ma'am," he responded, grinning in spite of himself.

"Ah, now I see." She downed a large swallow from her glass and returned the grin, revealing a full set of straight, white teeth, completely at odds with everything else about her. "It's that smile of yers what encouraged my Christy to trust herself to you."

My Christy. The old woman's words alluded to a close history between the two of them. Closer than he'd realized from what Christiana had told him.

"What was it you gave her to drink earlier? The stuff that put her to sleep. Narcotics of some sort?"

"I'm no familiar with this 'narcotics' you ask over. It's a dwale I use, of course." She gave him a look that said she thought him slow-witted. "Dangerous, it is, but helpful in small amounts to alleviate suffering. I keep some mixed at all times. You never can tell when you'll need someone to drift away quickly."

"What's in it?"

She shrugged and lifted her tankard. "The usual. A bit of bile, some bryony. A touch of hemlock. Opium. Henbane. All steeped in wine to preserve them."

"Jesus! That sounds like one potent mixture."

Hemlock? Opium? For someone who claimed no knowledge of narcotics, she was this century's version of a pharmacist.

"Aye. I told you it's dangerous. You canna allow but a sip to pass yer lips. Just enough and no more."

"Is that what Christiana came here to get, this dwale?"

"No," Orabilis rose to her feet and hobbled over

to the bubbling pot to give it a stir. "Though I'm sure she has a batch of her own on hand for treating the wounded. She is the healer at Tordenet. Surely yer aware of that, are you no? She's here because she's in need of all the regular herbs she uses for her healing. Most important of all her needs is that which yer grinding up for me right there."

Chase looked down at the mixture in the bowl. A deep sniff of it told him very little. It smelled of mint and busy kitchens more than anything else. Not even a pinch on his tongue revealed anything other than what he could pull out of a spice rack.

"That's a good job, you've done there, lad. Well mixed and finely crushed, it is. Here is the bag to fill for Christiana. Mind you doona spill. There's none to waste this time of year."

He accepted the big cloth bag but held off on transferring the contents of the bowl into it, curious about what these herbs were supposed to cure.

"What does she use this for? Why is this particular mixture so important to her?" *What's in it?* was what he really wanted to ask, but he doubted the old woman would be so forthcoming with an answer on that one. Since Christiana had to come all the way out here to get it, chances were the old woman kept the ingredients as closely guarded as an old family recipe.

Orabilis seemed to consider his question, her back to him as she stirred her pot of stew. "If you doona already ken my Christy's use for this, then I suspect that's for her to be telling you, no me. Her secrets are hers to share, no mine."

That Christiana had a secret use for this mixture piqued his interest even more.

"Go ahead," Orabilis urged, motioning with her spoon. "Put that into the bag. There's nothing in there what will harm her, so you can put yer mind to rest on that question."

That was a good first step, though it was far from satisfying his curiosity.

Holding the bag up to the side of the bowl, he carefully slid the contents inside, tapping the bottom to encourage every bit out. Almost every bit. When Orabilis turned her back, he slipped a handful from the bowl and tucked it away in the pouch hanging from his waist.

Orabilis might not think there was anything harmful in the mixture, but he'd like to know that for a fact. While he might not know one herb from another, his friend Hall knew more about them than anyone he'd ever met, these two women included.

There was only one way he could think of to discover Christiana's secret that might be better than asking Hall's help.

He could ask Christiana.

Eighteen

"WHAT IS THAT?"

Halldor strained in his saddle to focus on the tiny colorful dot outside the walls of Tordenet. If not for the evil dwelling inside those walls, he'd swear it was a wagon belonging to . . .

"Tinklers," Ulfr answered, his disgust showing through clearly. "Though I canna imagine why they've come to Tordenet. They're no welcomed inside *our* gates."

"You say that as if it's something to take pride in. Tinklers bring luck to man's home. If they're welcomed, that is."

"Bah." Ulfr turned his head to spit on the ground. "They're naught but filthy thieves and whores. Our lord Torquil has forbidden them entry."

Halldor doubted their exclusion was because they were thieves and whores. No, he'd guess Torquil had other reasons for avoiding the Tinkler folk.

"Old tales say they're favored by the Fae. What say you to that? You'd willingly anger the Faeries?"

"No such thing," Ulfr mumbled, but the wild fear dancing in his eyes belied his claim.

The captain ended their conversation with a kick to his mount's sides, forcing the animal to a run, telling Hall all he needed to know.

Ulfr knew, just as Torquil did. Tinklers weren't just the Fae's favored people. More often than not, where you found Tinklers, you were likely to find the Fae themselves. They were as real as the Norse gods the MacDowylt clan claimed to honor. As real, and every bit as vindictive.

If Torquil was what Hall suspected him to be, it was little wonder that Torquil forbade Tinklers entrance to Tordenet Castle. They, too, would recognize what lived inside those walls.

"Here, now! What's this?" Ulfr called from ahead of him, his horse already disappearing into the open gate at a gallop.

Hall urged his own mount to greater speed, easily reaching Ulfr's side as they entered the inner courtyard of Tordenet.

"Why have the gates been left open?" Ulfr demanded, sliding down off his mount.

"To allow the minstrels access," Artur, the one who claimed to be Ulfr's right hand, answered. "Our lord Torquil has bade it be so."

"But the Tinklers—" Ulfr began.

"No, my captain. The Tinklers are but a means of travel for the minstrels. Our lord Torquil has bade the minstrels to remain here to perform for the return of his sister. . . ." Artur's words faltered as he looked around. "But where is—"

"Keep to yer own business. Where is our lord? I've urgent need to speak to him." Ulfr didn't wait for an answer, already hurrying off toward the main keep.

"Minstrels, eh?" Halldor asked.

"Aye. Come see them. They've brought out their instruments for our inspection. And"—excitement rolled off Artur in great, palpable waves as he leaned in closer—"they've a woman who dances while they play."

"Indeed? Well then, lad, take me to them. I'd very much like to see these amusements."

Artur led the way, pushing through a throng of men circled around the newcomers. Two men stood in front of a display of instruments, along with two women. One of the women was seated, a small harp held in her arms, while the other hung back, her eyes scanning the crowd.

Warrior. The description reverberated inside Hall's head as if he'd said the word aloud. She was tall and lithe, her brown hair gathered into a long braid hanging down her back. Doubtless this was the one who danced, though she hovered in the background like a guard set to attack rather than a performer for the crowd's amusement.

A beauty by Halldor's standards, though too

young for his tastes. But a beauty who would bear watching.

"You simply let them ride away, unchaperoned, without making the slightest effort to stop them." Torquil hardly knew how to respond to the news Ulfr had brought him.

What if Christiana's injuries were fatal? What if she managed to escape? What if the man who had taken her ended up being the very one he needed for his own plans? Christiana would know that, and could easily enough prevent his return just to thwart Torquil's desires.

Everything, *everything,* hung in the balance and Ulfr had let them simply ride away.

"Fool!"

Frustration clawed at Torquil's gut. He was no closer now to determining which of the brothers he needed than he had been before they'd left. Further away, in fact, since he no longer had control of Christiana or her Visions.

"I'd thought to prepare a contingent of men to recover and repair the wagon, and to follow Noble and yer sister to the witches'"—Ulfr paused and cleared his throat before continuing—"to the lodging of Orabilis to bring our lady home. If that meets yer approval, my lord."

"Go. Bring my sister back where she belongs! And Ulfr." He turned a hard stare on the man, holding his next words until he knew his captain had grown uncomfortable with the waiting. "Dinna fail me in this, or you'll find yer next lodging to be in the oubliette. I want her back without delay. Are we clear on that?"

Ulfr nodded, all but running from the hall.

As he should, the incompetent fool. His days were numbered.

Once the sun settled onto the horizon, Torquil would see for himself whether Noble had indeed taken Christiana to Orabilis, or if she'd convinced him to aid her in an attempted escape.

For now, though, he needed to check on the strangers he'd allowed entry to Tordenet. What had possessed him to acquiesce to his men's pleas was beyond him. This sort of indulgence rankled at his very core. But his father had always professed that the best way to tie your men to you was to win their hearts. Though his father had become a disloyal embarrassment with his marriage to Deandrea, the one thing he had been good at was building loyalty among his men. And loyalty was something Torquil would be counting on heavily come spring, when he led his men against Malcolm and Castle Mac-Gahan.

For that reason alone, he'd welcomed the minstrels, despite the irritation of having Tinklers camped just beyond his walls.

He stepped outside, immediately spotting the crowd of men gathered in the courtyard. His guests would likely be at the center of that throng.

Descending the great staircase, he breathed deeply of the cold, crisp air and noted that clouds already gathered in the sky, a sure sign heralding a moonless night. And a moonless night was exactly what he needed to wing his way sightlessly across his lands.

Nineteen

CHRISTIANA SWAM IN the dark green pools that were Chase Noble's eyes. She splashed and rolled, the water heating her body with its wet caress.

And then there was no water, only his strong arms holding her, his head dipping close to hers as they floated weightless together. He spoke her name, his warm breath fanning over her face, and it was as if they were the only two people in the world.

His mouth hovered over hers and she thrilled that at long last she would taste those full, smiling lips.

And in that instant, he was gone, evaporating in front of her as her foot touched down on a familiar gravel path.

"What are you doing here?"

Christiana froze in her tracks, staring straight ahead at the three women squatting in the shade of an enormous green tree.

She knew where she was. Her wonderful dream had carried her straight to the world of her Visions.

"You can see me?" she asked.

It was the first time any of the Norns had ever spoken to her. In fact, since none of them had ever even appeared to notice her presence when she'd traversed the Vision world before, she had assumed they couldn't see her.

Skuld, Keeper of the Future, her face hidden in the folds of her veil, snorted her disgust. "Do I look to be blind? Of course I see you. What do you want here?"

"I come to travel the Vision world. I have a great need to see what I must do."

"You've no right to see what's to come." The beauty in the middle—Verthandi, Keeper of the Present—spoke. "Live it. You will see it as it happens, as everyone is meant to do."

"She has the right." The eldest of the three, Urd, was Keeper of the Past. "In ages long past, Odin paid the price for such knowledge, and he's chosen to pass it along to this one."

"But she's already seen that which is to come." Skuld kept her head down, her fingers busily working at the loom in front of her. "I've nothing more to show her."

"Please, there were so many paths the last time I was here." How could she know what to do? How could she possibly make sure Chase walked the proper path?

"So many paths?" Verthandi laid aside the yarn she held, turning her gaze toward her sister. "You allowed her to travel the Maze of Possibility? What's to be accomplished by that? Nothing. She might as well have wandered in the Paths of Possible Pasts. She could have been lost in there forever."

Skuld shrugged. "She's the one who pushed her way into that maze. I didn't force her."

"Now that you know the danger, why are you back?" Verthandi turned her gaze toward Christiana.

"Yes, why?" Urd echoed.

Guilt pooled in Christiana's stomach. But feeling guilty was ridiculous. She had every right to be here. It wasn't as if she were searching out something to aid only herself. It was the common good she sought. A way to stop Torquil from committing the evil he planned.

"I know why she's here." Skuld's head swung her direction. "It's because of *him*."

Verthandi nodded as if now she understood. "She's willing to risk the dangers of losing herself in the Maze again for the love of a man."

"Love?" Christiana squeaked. "Absolutely not." Love had nothing to do with any of this, despite the dream that had brought her here. Chase was the one who could save her from Torquil. She'd seen it. All that existed between them was a rescue—nothing more.

"And because you saw it, you forced it." Skuld chided as if she'd read Christiana's thoughts. "You bargained with the Elf to bring him to your world. You placed him in danger for your own benefit. Best you search your heart before you return here again, youngling. Best you consider why you deny your feelings so vehemently, lest you end up here forever like us."

With that, Skuld pulled the hood from her head, revealing herself for the first time.

Christiana recognized her instantly.

It was her own guilt-ridden blue eyes staring back at her that sent her running from the Norns screaming, their cackling laughter following her in her frenzied escape.

CHRISTIANA'S SCREAM SPIKED fear in Chase's chest and had him on his feet, headed for her door.

"No need to get yerself all in a tizzy," Orabilis assured him from the pot where she stood stirring. "Naught but a bad dream. The dwale does that now and again."

Bad dream or no, Chase wasn't taking any chances. Not with the potent combination of drugs she had flowing in her system.

"I think I'll go check, all the same."

"Do as you like. I canna leave the elixir I'm working on. No at this stage of boil."

Chase pushed open the door and hurried to Christiana's bedside. She lay on her back, the light of the fireplace glinting off the side of her face.

He dropped to his knees and, without thought, reached out to run his thumb over the shiny spot on her cheek.

Wet with tears.

She turned toward him, her eyes wide open.

"You screamed. Are you in pain?" The idea of her lying here in the dark, alone, hurting, was almost more than he could stand. "I can go get you some more of the dwale that Orabilis gave you before."

"No." She placed a restraining hand on his forearm. "It's no my leg but my Visions that trouble me now."

"Visions?"

She tightened her grip on his arm. "I have little hope you'll accept what I say. It's a leap of faith for any man. But you must hear the truth, whether or no you believe me."

"I'm all ears." At her frown, he tried again. "I meant to say, I'm listening. Tell me whatever you need to."

She scooted up to sit on the bed, her expression serious in the faint flicker of firelight, her arms crossed protectively in front of her.

"I've the gift of prophecy, come to me through my father's bloodline. I have Visions of what's to come. At least, I do when Skuld permits it."

"Who is Skuld?"

"One of the Norns, the three goddesses who weave the tapestry of our fates. Skuld determines what it is to be, and it is within her world that I travel the Visions to see what is to come."

Chase's first instinct was disbelief. But he, the son of a Faerie, living seven hundred years out of his own time, knew better. The world was filled with Magic beyond mere man's ability to imagine. And only accepting that fact saved his sanity.

"So it was one of those visions, something you saw happening in the future, that frightened you as you slept?"

Christiana shook her head. "I'm no sure whether what I saw was Vision or merely a phantom brought on by a nightmare. Traveling to Skuld's world has been difficult since . . ." Her words stopped as if she changed her mind partway through the thought. "It's why I came to see Orabilis. I needed the herbal elixir she prepares for me in order to control the Visions. I canna seem to manage them on my own anymore."

"Maybe it's whatever is in that elixir that makes it difficult for you to concentrate."

Again she shook her head. "It's no a matter of concentration. It's much larger than that. And as to whether or not it was a true Vision that awoke me, it's of no import to what I must say to you. Although, that which I just experienced did confirm that I canna in good conscience hold my tongue any longer."

He waited, allowing her the time she needed to collect her thoughts.

"Yer in danger here."

"In danger? From what? That little old woman in the other room?" He seriously doubted that.

"No, I dinna mean here in Orabilis's home. For

a fact, this is the safest place for you to be in all the land." Her hands tightened around her upper arms, her fingers visibly biting into the tender flesh there. "It's yer presence at Tordenet of which I speak. Yer in danger as long as you remain there. You and yer brother both. Yer in danger, and it's my fault for bringing you there in the first place."

She looked close to tears and she shivered as if she were freezing.

"Listen to me. You just had a bad dream." He rose to his feet and pushed her gently back down onto the bed, pulling the covers up to her chin. "What you need right now is to sleep to allow your body time to heal."

"I must warn you," she began.

"Then consider me warned. And believe me on this, you didn't have anything to do with my being at Tordenet. Hall and I made that decision on our own." Or Hall had, anyway. He'd just tagged along because what else was he going to do but go where the Faeries sent him?

"But I did," she protested. "You dinna ken the whole of it."

"Then tomorrow, when you're all rested, you can fill me in on the whole of it. But for now, you need your sleep."

"I dinna want to sleep. I dinna want to see those apparitions again this night." Already her eyelids drooped, belying her protest.

She reached out a hand and he took it. Soft and

smooth, it fit his grasp as comfortably as if it were meant to be there.

Again he dropped to his knees, meeting her gaze at eye level.

"Don't you worry about a thing, Christy." The name Orabilis had used fell easily from his lips as if he'd known it always. "I'll stay right here to guard you while you sleep. Whatever came after you before has no chance of getting to you with me here. I promise."

She smiled, her eyes closing even as the corners of her mouth curved up and he was lost, determined to spend the whole night right here, protecting her from the hallucinations that plagued her dreams.

Twenty

SUNSET, AT LAST.

Torquil carefully laid the old scroll on his desk, glancing at the open wooden chest that held its twin. Another fruitless afternoon of chasing the elusive Magic had eaten away his hours. When he returned, he would replace the scroll on its silken bed where it lay with its companion, one on either side of the ancient sword. He hadn't the time to roll it properly now. He had overly much that required his attention this night.

He began the process of clearing his mind as he removed his clothing, folding each piece and placing it in a neat stack beside the bed of pillows. Lowering his body to the pallet, he ignored the aches and pains of a day spent trying to force the Magic to work. It would come. It would be his. These spells were more challenging than anything he'd done before, but he would master them just as he had the others.

With a glance to the door, he dismissed any concerns about being interrupted. Ulfr usually guarded his lair when he set out on a spirit journey, but he had nothing to worry over. No one in the entire castle would ever consider entering his tower chambers without his express permission. No one but his sister, and it was her absence that instigated the need for what he was about to do.

Still, caution was his ally. He spared an extra moment for a spell of protection before turning his attention to the task at hand. Now, his only concern was to concentrate, a task made more difficult by the beast within, demanding its freedom. He wrestled the beast back into the dark corner where it lived and reached once again for the concentration this task demanded.

Focus on the breathing. See the shape of what he would be. Will his spirit to take that shape. Feel the great owl claiming him. Become one with the great owl.

In an exhale of breath he rose above his body, taking no time this night to admire the shell that housed his spirit. There was no time for such small pleasures.

Onto the ledge and over it. With a swoop he was airborne, his great wings beating against the cold, damp air.

He circled the courtyard, where the castle's activity had begun to settle down for the night, and allowed the air current to sweep him up and over the massive walls that protected his keep. Just below and off to the right, the Tinkler wagons camped. He circled, but as he'd expected, the pale green glow of Faerie Magic hung over the encampment like a shroud, all but obscuring the people themselves.

Unexpectedly, a movement within the camp stood out. A glow of red spiked from the canopy of green, like a ruby tumbling through sluggish waters.

What had the Tinklers got their hands on? Some new trinket they'd likely stolen from an unsuspecting host somewhere along the way, he'd guess.

It intrigued him, and at any other time it might bear further scrutiny. But not on this night. He had too many miles to cover, and after a day spent pushing his mind to its limits, he could already feel his energy flagging.

With a flap of his enormous wings he turned west, following the trail he knew all too well.

All sorts of small creatures made their way across his lands this night, but none of them the human prey he sought. He came across Ulfr's party camped in a small clearing near a stream, their fires burning brightly. Nothing out of the ordinary there.

Torquil lowered his head against the wind and flapped his wings, covering great swaths of ground. Ahead on the right was the wagon his men had abandoned. He circled, dropping lower to inspect the scene more closely. The wagon lay on its side, one wheel clearly broken. From what he could see, only one barrel of flour had been lost, its contents spread all around. The others appeared to be fine. His sister and her witch would have to make do with those because he had no intention of sending more.

Not much farther to go, now. He could already see the glow up ahead.

He couldn't fly any closer. The dome of color covering Orabilis's home prevented his approach. Not the soft fuzzy green blanket that masked the Tinklers' encampment, but a hard, emerald green shell dominated here, with random sparks of color shooting out into the sky. Sparks that could, and had in the past, singed his feathers.

It was the damned rowan trees ringing her property like a chain of sentinels on guard.

He'd known he'd see nothing there, but from here, he'd begin his search, spreading out in everwidening circles, covering all the distance a mortal on horseback might have covered in the day since Ulfr had last laid eyes on Christiana and Chase.

If they were anywhere but inside that ring of emerald, he would know it. He would find them.

He would find them and make them pay for their disloyalty.

A GREAT WHOMP of wings overhead had Brie scanning the dark sky above her. There was no moon, but she possessed the excellent night vision of a born hunter.

High above her, an enormous bird circled against the backdrop of clouds. If only she had her bow she could easily pick it from the sky. A creature that size could feed the Tinkler families she traveled with for a good two days.

But her bow was neatly stored in her room at Castle MacGahan, and her sights were set on larger prey. Tonight she foraged for information to help her in her quest for revenge. Tonight she tracked Torquil MacDowylt. Once she had a feel for his routine and habits, then she could formulate a plan to make him pay.

She pulled the cloak she'd borrowed from Eleyne closer around her face. It was too short by far, but in her experience men didn't waste time looking at a woman's feet. It was her face she wished to hide. If she slumped down a bit and kept her face to the shadows, she stood a chance of being mistaken for one of the old women who lived here at Tordenet.

If she were careful enough, she just might manage to avoid contact with everyone.

Though the iron gates had been shut for the night, the small wooden entrance to the massive castle wall had been left open. She could thank the small but steady stream of women from the castle out to the Tinklers' wagons for that. Women everywhere loved an opportunity to inspect the Tinkler wares, even if their laird did not approve.

She crossed the empty courtyard and made her way up the main staircase, expecting at any moment to be challenged as to her intent.

But not even when she slipped into the dark entry hall inside did she see anyone. Her luck was holding! And luck, as her da had been fond of saying, could often save a man. Or, in her case, a woman.

If the little kitchen maid had told her true, the stairs toward the back of the great hall should lead her where she needed to go. The young woman had been adamant in her claims that though the lord and master of Tordenet slept in the laird's chambers on the second floor, he spent all his days in this tower.

If this was where he spent the better part of his time, this would be where she would learn the most about him.

Brie's feet slowed as she reached the heavy wooden door at the top of the narrow staircase. What if Torquil MacDowylt had not yet retired to his chambers? What if she walked in on him? It would be the end of her schemes before they'd even begun.

No! No more *what if*s. She was here and she would go through with it.

The door opened easily, allowing her entrance into a tiny room illuminated only by dying embers in its small fireplace. This hardly looked to be a place for the great Torquil MacDowylt to spend his days. Castle MacGahan had storage rooms larger than this. This room, with its solitary chair, presented itself more as a guard's outpost than a room a laird would use.

Brie turned in a tight circle, scanning the walls until she spotted a narrow door. A door with a slit of light splashing out where the wood didn't quite meet the stone floor.

Her breath caught in her chest. A light that bright could mean he was in there. She crossed to the door and positioned her ear against the wood. Holding her breath, she listened for any sound coming from the other side. Nothing. Perhaps with his great wealth, MacDowylt thought nothing of leaving a fireplace burning in an unoccupied room.

Only one way to know.

Squaring her shoulders, she leaned against the door, pushing it ever so slightly open. A space large enough for nothing more to enter than her fingers. She waited, breath held, for the sound of boots against stone.

Not a single noise met her straining ears.

Another push and she slipped inside.

This room, many times larger than the one before it, was more like what she had imagined the laird of the MacDowylt might occupy. A great table, strewn with papers and a jeweled wooden chest, sat directly across from the door, an enormous candle burning brightly on either end. Two more candles blazed on the stone shelf behind the table, illuminating the bound manuscripts stacked there.

She stepped slowly across the empty floor, curious as to what might occupy the days of the beast of Tordenet.

Like many elder sons, Torquil appeared to have been well educated. Scrolls and manuscripts littered his table. One, apparently more special and obviously older than the others, lay neatly rolled in the wooden box next to the most fantastic sword she'd ever seen.

Her fingers itched to lift the weapon, to feel its heft balanced in her palm.

She resisted, though it took great self-control, satisfying herself with a stroke of her finger down the length of the engraved blade. The symbols there were unlike any she'd seen before, though they seemed similar to those on the unrolled scroll lying next to the box. Not numbers, not any letters she knew of, these were entirely foreign markings.

Only with a great force of willpower was she able to step away from the intense lure emanating from the box. She wasn't here to steal from the laird, she reminded herself. Only to kill him. She might travel with Tinklers, but she was not one.

The thought had barely formed before a wave of guilt washed over her. Nothing she'd experienced of the Tinklers supported the rumors she'd heard her whole life. They'd been nothing but kind to her, and they'd certainly done nothing to make her think they were thieves. If anything, the minstrels were more likely to fit that mold than the Tinklers.

Another step back from the table and the pull of the sword weakened enough to allow Brie to collect her thoughts.

She was here for information, not treasures. Information that could help her determine the best way, the best time, the best place to gut the beast who'd murdered her father.

She turned her attention upward, to the tall ceiling and the unshuttered window high on the wall. Her eyes trailed down, to the landing under the window and the four stone stairs leading down to the floor where, on a pallet of pillows, lay the naked body of the fearsome laird of the MacDowylt.

Her breath sucked in between her teeth as if some other being were responsible for the action. Or perhaps it was only the natural result of her heart pounding so hard within her chest, likely trying to push the contents of her stomach back down where they belonged.

She waited, heart pounding loudly enough to wake the dead, expecting at any moment he would open his eyes and cry out for his guards to take her away.

Instead, he lay unmoving, eyes closed, as if he were the very dead she feared awakening.

Panic bubbled in her chest as the sounds of breathing assailed her ears . . . until she recognized that the breathing was her own.

Fool!

She was warrior born, not some dewy-eyed milkmaid to scurry away at the first sign of danger. Repeating that in her mind, she approached the body for a closer inspection.

What was wrong with him? It was as if he were a carving of a man, not actually the man himself.

And a beautiful carving, at that.

She'd seen him from a distance, on the landing of his great staircase, possessively surveying his courtyard. Up close, so close she could reach out and touch him, he was the very definition of beauty. Golden hair flowed out around his head, highlighted by two pure white streaks, one leading back from each temple like stripes on some exotic animal. Taut muscles shaped the skin of his arms, his legs, his torso, forming a perfect ripple along his chest, leading her eyes down to his—

Brie jerked her gaze back to his chest, her thoughts in turmoil. His manhood was not for her investigation, no matter how handsome he might be.

She needed to know if he slept, or if someone had already done her work for her. Did his heart beat still?

She could wonder, or she could be certain.

Against her better judgment, her hand stretched forward, hovering over his chest. Would his skin be warm with life or as cold as the statue he resembled?

As if she'd been snared in some invisible web, she waited, unmoving, transfixed by the man in front of her. He was beyond handsome. He was magnificent. He was perfection.

Pain radiating up her arm brought her to her senses and she shook her head in an effort to rid herself of whatever it was that had held her back. For how long she'd remained there, she couldn't say, only that it had been long enough that her arm ached from the strain of holding it out.

Her will once again her own, she dipped her

hand, allowing her fingers to rest lightly on the perfect stretch of muscled skin.

Not beauty, not perfection, but pure evil incarnate waited under her touch.

Brie jerked her hand away, her fingertips burning as if she'd placed them in the flames of the fireplace.

Panic drove her steps backward until she stumbled and fell to sit, her legs stretched out in front of her, her back against a tapestry-covered screen.

Could some powerful Magic surround the laird? Powerful enough to confuse her purpose and steal her strength of will? Something certainly had and, given more time, she might devise a way around such intense feelings. But such time was not a luxury available to her at the moment.

A noise, like the beat and rustle of a great pair of wings, sounded from the open window, sending her scuttling on hands and knees to hide behind the screen.

Brie huddled on a tiny seat, pressing the heels of her hands into her eyes as if the self-imposed dark might aid her in regaining her courage.

Some semblance of calm returned and she leaned her forehead against the wood of the screen, realizing as she did she could see through the tiny slit between the pieces of wood.

An owl, the largest she'd ever seen so close, perched on the sill of the opening, his head cocked first to one side and then the other as if he scanned the room for intruders.

For her.

Another wave of panic washed over her and she fought the overwhelming need to step from behind the screen and surrender herself. She held her breath, terrified when she heard a great gasp for air that the sound might be coming from her.

Not from her, she realized, but from the laird, sucking in air as if he'd been holding his breath as well, but for much, much longer.

Her eyes tracked back up to the empty window. Where the owl had gone, she had no idea, nor did she have time to spend in wondering.

Torquil MacDowylt had risen to his feet.

He placed a hand to his chest, cocking his head from side to side, much as the owl had, before striding to the table where he slowly and with great care worked the open scroll into a tight roll and placed it inside the wooden box.

With the box under his arm, he crossed to the great fireplace, only feet away from her hiding spot.

Brie concentrated on maintaining her silence, picturing herself in the trees on a hunt, invisible to her prey.

His hand moved from one stone to another below the mantel until at last he pulled one stone free and shoved the box into the opening, before returning the stone to cover any trace of the hiding place.

Again he paused, his head swiveling back and forth, before he turned to cross back to his resting spot. Rather than lying back down, he lifted his clothing, one piece at a time, shook each one, and quickly dressed. With one last look around the room, he lifted a hand and all the candles were extinguished at once as if snuffed out by a chorus of maids in unison.

Magic! She'd suspected it before, but what she'd just seen was proof. She'd heard her father's stories of the MacDowylt having descended from his people's ancient gods, but she'd never believed them.

She didn't move, not even when she heard the laird cross the room and shut the door behind him. She waited on her little stool, realizing only after her legs began to cramp and she at last stood, that the stool was in fact a pot, apparently used as the laird's own private privy.

An almost hysterical giggle formed in her throat, contained only with a great reassertion of self-control.

Brie continued to wait for what felt like hours, but in reality was much more likely minutes. Her sense of time was as skewed at the moment as her nerves.

At last, after she felt sure MacDowylt was well and good away, she silently stepped from behind the screen and crossed the room to slip out the door and pull it shut behind her.

Once it was closed, she leaned against it, gulping great draughts of cold air to steady her resolve before she sprinted from the tiny anteroom.

Never before had she experienced the likes of what she'd encountered behind that door.

Dinna trust yer eyes, lass. Looks can be deceiving. Her father's warning rang in her mind as she raced down the narrow staircase, desperate to get outside the gates of this wretched place.

Never had her father's words made more sense. For all Torquil MacDowylt's beauty, one touch had stripped it all away, confirming what her eyes had doubted at first sight of the man.

The laird's body housed naught but pure, unadulterated evil Magic.

Twenty-one

IF THERE WAS anything Orabilis owned that he hadn't spent time repairing today, Chase couldn't imagine what it could possibly be. From the rickety fencing meant to keep her chickens out of the garden next spring to the chair turned upside down in front of him right now, the old woman had kept him busy from the moment he woke up.

The only bright spot in his day had been Christiana's limping after him as he'd moved from one chore to the next.

Funny, how she could be both the best and the worst parts of his day. Best by virtue of her conversation and the rare reward of her quiet laughter that had made his day go by so quickly. Worst by virtue of what he suffered at her hands right this very moment.

He reached for the mug of ale at his elbow and downed a great swallow before continuing to work on strapping the chair leg.

It wasn't fair to hold her responsible for his current discomfort. He had only himself to blame for this predicament. Himself and his overactive imagination.

It had been *his* suggestion, after all, that a long soak in a hot tub would likely soothe her aching muscles; *he* who had carted bucket after bucket of water from the fire to the tub in the back room; and worst of all, *his* imagination that couldn't seem to think of anything but her sitting in that tub, bare-ass naked at this very moment.

Something sounding suspiciously like a growl crawled up his throat.

"What's that you say?" Orabilis looked up from the pot she stirred. "Is that yer stomach announcing hunger yet again?"

He grunted, a thoroughly noncommittal noise meant to allay her questions without his having to tell her an untruth.

"I've been out here by my ownself long enough that I'd forgotten how much a braw young lad like yerself could eat. Pardie!" she huffed, after reaching into the jar in which she kept her cooking herbs. "I'd forget me own head, I would, were it no so firmly attached."

With an ongoing series of ever-louder grunts, she hoisted herself up to her feet and waddled over to the stack of cloth sacks she'd prepared for Christiana to take back to Tordenet with her. She quickly untied the one on top and dipped her clay jar inside, filling it before retying it and returning to her stool by the fire to toss a handful into the bubbling porridge she cooked.

"Wait a minute." Chase couldn't quite believe what he'd just seen. "Why are you putting that in our food? Isn't that the special mixture you prepared to send Christiana on her little vision quests?"

He'd heard of weed brownies, but this was ridiculous: Was the old woman senile?

"You pay attention to yer own hands there, lad. I ken well enough what I'm doing here."

Chase dropped the tool he used and moved to stand over the old woman and her bubbling pot.

"We need to get something straight between us right now. I can toss back a couple of pints or a shot of whisky with the best of them." With his Faerie constitution, he could polish off a whole damn barrel and it would have no effect on him. "But I don't put that stuff in my body. No chemicals. No dwale, absolutely no opium or hemlock or any of that other shit. And, just so we're on the same page, I'm going to do everything in my power to see that Christiana stops using it, too. It can't be good for her, visions or no visions."

Orabilis stared up at him, one eye squinted against the smoke from the fireplace.

"Oh, do sit yer righteous self down and stop yer fashing, aye? There's no a sprig of any of those things in this mixture. None of it. If you must ken the truth of it, those bags I've set aside for Christiana to take with her are filled with naught but good cooking herbs. You should ken that yer own self since yer the one what mixed them for me." She stirred the pot before fixing him again with her stern frown, shaking her porridge-covered spoon for emphasis and sending little globs of porridge flying in all directions. "But yer no to be telling my Christy about this. No a single word, you ken?"

"No, I don't understand. Not one damn bit of it. How can harmless cooking herbs send Christiana on these wild-ass trips to the future she says she takes?"

The old woman made a clicking sound of disgust with her tongue. "I expected better of you. Of all people." She shook her head and lowered her spoon to the pot in front of her. "Though I've a spell or two up my sleeve, this is no one of them. Those simple herbs work because she believes they work. She has the power all on her own to travel the Vision, but she doubts her own abilities. She's no like us, laddie."

That he could believe, since he sincerely doubted there were an overabundance of Faerie descendants walking around out here. Which meant even Orabilis wasn't like him. What he wasn't sure of, however, was that he swallowed her story about harmless cooking herbs being some kind of security blanket for Christiana. And he definitely wasn't falling for the "spell or two" garbage she was spouting.

"Don't you even try to suck me into the whole witch thing. It may work with those people back at Tordenet, but I know better. Witches aren't real. They don't exist." He gave her a look he hoped was suitably withering.

Her responding grin was not at all what he expected.

"No? So witches dinna exist, eh? No more than, oh, let's say Faeries exist? What have you to say to that one, young lord Noble?"

How could she possibly . . . He closed his mouth when he realized it hung open, sitting down heavily on the hearth as the old woman cackled, sounding every bit the witch people claimed her to be.

Orabilis was right. He of all people should know better than to question what exceptions existed in the world. It was only that, for some reason, his driving need to protect Christiana kept pushing common sense right out of his reach.

Behind them, the door to the little bedroom opened and Christiana emerged on a cloud of fragrance and steam, her face breaking into one of her rare smiles.

"What have you said to so amuse my Shen-Ora?"

"Only that, should yer brother's men take another day to arrive, this one will gladly start the digging on a new waste pit for me." The old woman returned Christiana's smile, hoisting an eyebrow when she turned to face Chase. "Did you no agree to that, my sweet lad?"

Trapped, he nodded, his mind a blank.

"You should see to yer beastly big animal, Chase, dearling. Before the sun goes down and you lose the day's light."

Again he nodded, heading for the door. Only Christiana would fail to see how transparent her old "Shen-Ora" was in trying to get him out of the house and away from her.

"I'll accompany you, if I might." Christiana joined him at the door, lifting her cloak from the hook on the wall. "Keeping my body moving has helped me this day. And after the long soak, I'm feeling quite supple."

Supple? He swallowed hard, hoping neither woman noticed his reaction.

"A good idea," Orabilis agreed. "Oh, and Chase, dearling, would you mind seeing to my goats and chickens while yer in the shed? Their feed is by the door. Christy can show you where it is if you canna find it on yer own. And by the time you finish, I'll have yer meals waiting for you."

"Of course," he answered. What else could he say with Christiana beaming up at him, her eyes shining like those of a child on Christmas morning?

Though, seriously, the "dearling" stuff was laying it on bit thick.

"Is it no wonderful here?" Christiana asked as the door closed behind them. "This place has such a feel to it. It's as if I'm breathing in pure life." As she turned away, he took her hand to steady her walk.

"Sounds daft when I say it aloud, I suppose, but I do love my visits here."

"It doesn't sound daft."

Nothing she said sounded anything but beautiful, her voice lilting like a melody written just for him.

Inside the shed, he helped her take a seat on an old wooden bench before beginning the task of feeding the animals.

"Thank you for yer kindness to Orabilis. Many find her to be fair intimidating at first, but she's a dear, kind woman and very special to me."

That much was clear to him, though not the reason why.

"You called her 'Shen-Ora.' What does that mean?"

Though the light in the animal shed was low, he could almost swear she blushed.

"When I'm here, I fall to old habits too easily, I fear," she said quietly, almost as if she were confessing. "It's a name my mother called her and I used it, too, as a wee bairn. I'm no sure it has a true meaning, though my mother said it was an endearment, something akin to saying 'my mother's mother.'"

Chase stopped in the act of tossing the straw around the stall where he stood.

"Your grandmother? Surely Torquil wouldn't send his own grandmother out into the middle of nowhere to fend for herself."

Christiana shook her head slowly. "I dinna ken whether or no Orabilis and my mother were truly related to one another. I do ken that I could love no one of my own blood any more than I do her. It was she who cared for me after my mother's death. She who led me out of my days as a child, and onto the path of being a woman. It was she who taught me all I ken of the ways of healing. And were she truly of my mother's blood, it would only be more reason for Torquil to despise her, as he despised my mother above any other. You see, Torquil and I share our father's line but we've different mothers. He alone was the issue of our father's first marriage."

Things were starting to make more sense to Chase now.

"So this is why Torquil prepares for war against your brother, Malcolm? Because Malcolm is your mother's son?"

He and Hall had learned that much already. Knowledge of who their enemy was had fallen into the "Are we fighting on the wrong side?" conversation more than once.

"Aye. He's long hated my brothers, Malcolm and Patrick. He sees them as a threat to his power. And make no mistake, Chase Noble, my brother is a very powerful man. Wickedly powerful."

He stared at the top of her head as she fixed her gaze on the floor.

"Why does Torquil keep you around, then? If he hates all your mother's children so much?"

"Because he has use for me, of course. He uses

my gift of prophecy, and he's made no secret that he'd see me dead before he'd allow that gift to be used against him."

Her words were so simple, her voice so matter-of-fact, his heart felt the power of her plight more powerfully than if she'd railed against Torquil.

He dropped the straw and went to her, kneeling in front of her and grasping her hand. When she didn't look up, he placed his forefinger under her chin and lifted, bringing her gaze up to meet his.

"That's just wrong. Brother or not, he has no right to hold you against your will. If you want to leave, you just say the word and I'll see to it that you go wherever you want to go."

"It's no so simple as that."

She reached up, her soft fingers stroking down the side of his cheek, and he was lost. Nothing else mattered but the swirling skies he saw in the depths of her eyes.

"I'll tell you what, Christy. We'll *make* it as simple as that. Your brother is just a man. And there's not a man out there, not even your brother, who I will allow to harm you."

Where that vow had come from, he had no idea, but he meant it from the depths of his soul. Perhaps this was why the Fae had chosen to send him to this time. To this place. To rescue the woman he was meant to spend his life with.

Perhaps Christiana was why he was here.

He could carry out a mission like that with his

eyes closed. A simple rescue op, a snatch-and-grab where the target was a victim, rather than the enemy.

Chase leaned back, surprised to find he'd been steadily leaning in closer toward Christiana as they spoke, as if his mouth were on an independent mission all its own.

"You dinna ken what you say," she denied, her eyes widening in surprise and her mouth forming a perfect little *o* as she stopped speaking.

A perfect little *o* that he would like to—

The force hitting his back sent him hurtling into her, toppling her and the bench over backward.

A red haze of anger filled his mind as he grabbed for the sword from its sheath on his back, finding neither sword nor sheath but clearly seeing in his mind's eye the weapon as it stood in the corner of Orabilis's home next to her fireplace.

"Damn it," he hissed.

Christiana's peals of laughter melted the haze, as surely as salt on ice, allowing him at last to focus on the bleating sound behind him.

"Homer did no take so well to waiting for his food, aye?" Christiana managed. "You see? He's eyeing you even now. Sizing you up to see if you've taken his hint, or if you'll be needing another reminder nudge in the right direction."

The goat? That puny little piece of ragged mohair had barreled into his backside like a two-ton truck?

Okay, he could see the humor here. And once

he realized he was stretched out, full-body-contact on top of Christiana, he even considered giving the animal bonus feed.

She seemed to come to same realization, her laughter drying up abruptly.

"You okay? Did I hurt you?"

She shook her head, her eyes wide in the deepening gloom of evening.

And then, before he had time to think about it, it just sort of happened. His lips were on hers, his hands cradling either side of her face.

Her mouth was soft under his. Warm. Sweet. And when her lips parted he took full advantage, sweeping his tongue inside. The scent of mint and flowers drifted around them as if they lay in a summer field.

Her fingers tangled in his hair, holding him close, as her breath huffed in short, shallow pants.

He rolled to his back, kicking away the bench as he pulled her on top of him, praying she didn't come to her senses and shove him away.

She straddled him and he knew immediately he'd made a serious tactical error. He'd been without the tender mercies of a woman for far too long to withstand such as this.

He wanted her. He wanted her here, now. He wanted her badly enough to take her on the hard, cold, dirt-packed floor of this filthy shed.

Thank the fates the goat had more gumption than he did. Its teeth nibbled at the side of his head, tugging on a clump of his hair until he returned to his senses and did the hardest thing he'd ever done.

"Good God," he murmured, pulling his lips away from Christiana's. "Good, holy God." He couldn't remember ever having lost his composure so thoroughly with a woman.

"My apologies," she murmured, pushing up to sit, tucking the little pouch she wore on a string around her throat back inside the dangerously lowered neckline of her dress.

When had that happened?

She moved again and he grabbed her waist, holding her still.

"Wiggling on top of me is not the best idea at the moment. Not for either of us, I'm guessing. Just . . . be still. Just for a second. I need to . . ." He breathed through the moment, coming out the other side with his control and his pride intact. "Okay."

"Should I move now?"

Her voice wavered with the question and he felt like steaming horse crap, positive that ladies of her station did not find themselves in situations such as this in this day and age.

"Yeah. Yes. Move," he agreed, remembering her injuries only as she attempted to untangle her leg from the cloth of her cloak. What an insensitive jerk he was. "Do you need help?"

"It seems as though the ends of my cloak may be caught beneath your . . . um . . . bottom."

He rolled up to sit as she pulled on the cloth, very nearly sending herself sprawling, but he captured her within his embrace for a second time, somehow pulling her close in the process.

Heat rolled off her cheek onto his. Whether she blushed from embarrassment or excitement he couldn't be sure, but his ego reigned in the moment and he decided to consider it a good sign.

He stood, pulling her up to her feet to stand next to him before he bent to right the bench for her to once again be seated while he finished spreading feed for the animals.

Homer first, of course. If nothing else, Chase was a quick learner.

EVERY NERVE IN Christiana's body tingled with excitement. And her heart! By the Norns, it beat as though it intended to escape her very chest.

Oh, but what Chase must think of her! Her face heated even more, if that were possible. She'd acted like a common strumpet, straddling him as she had, seating herself upon his manhood.

The excitement trilled through her body again, pooling low in her stomach, and she knew without a doubt that no matter what he thought of her, given the opportunity she would do exactly the same again. This would remain in her memory as perhaps the best day in her entire life.

"Okay," he said, in his unique way of speaking. "I think that's all of them."

He dusted his hands against the side of his plaid as he approached her, not stopping until he towered over her. When he reached out a hand to help her stand, she found herself wanting him to take her in his arms as he had before.

Instead he stood his ground, holding her hand as his wonderful lips curved into that smile of his that seemed to reach down into the depths of her innards and tug at them.

When he stroked the side of her cheek with his big, warm finger, she wondered if she might have died in that accident, for surely this had to be her own personal piece of Valhalla.

"In spite of my little indiscretion back there," he said, again with the grin, "I want you to know I meant every word I said. I'm here for you. Whenever you want to leave Tordenet, just say the word. I'll take you away, wherever you want to go."

His reaffirmation of his vow shot fear through her heart, replacing the wispy yearnings floating there. She couldn't let him return to Tordenet with his eyes so blinded. That would be like swinging him from Torquil's gallows with her own two hands, since she bore the responsibility of having brought him here in the first place.

"You've no understanding of the power you challenge. My brother may look like any other man, but he is no mere man. He is more. Much more."

"I'm no mere man, either, Christiana. I, too, am more."

She did not question his manhood or his valor, but she had to make him understand. Even if it meant she would have to tell him everything.

"Perhaps *more* is the wrong word. Perhaps I should have said he is . . . he is *other*. Though my father's blood gifted me with prophecy, the preponderance of our ancestor's powers flowed to Torquil as firstborn son of our line. He's *other* than man. And lately I've begun to fear he's possessed of more than just the gifts of Odin." Those red glowing eyes staring back at her in Torquil's solar had not belonged to her brother, or to anything she had ever seen in this world.

"Odin?"

"Aye. Has the soldiers' gossip no covered that bit of family lore? I carry the bloodline of the Tinklers on my mother's side. Some would say of the Faeries as well, but I can neither confirm nor deny that. On my father's side, though, there's no question of our heritage. Our line extends back to the halls of Asgard. Whatever power we house within our bodies all descends directly from the Allfather, Odin himself. What you must accept of this, Chase, is that Torquil's purpose is not merely to eliminate every trace of my brothers from this world—but to take back the world for the glory of the ancient gods, with him enthroned in Odin's seat."

Any hope she had that her confession might convince him to the side of caution disappeared in the cynical curve of his mouth.

"So Torquil plans to rule the world, is that it?" He shook his head. "Listen to me. Better men than him have tried and failed. He doesn't frighten me, Christiana. The world's a much bigger place than he realizes. He'll soon discover there are those with greater powers than his with which he'll have to reckon. As for you, all you need to remember is that your freedom is as close as I am."

She would have to try another tactic.

"Very well, then. I will accept your pledge of assistance, if you will promise to accept the danger you face at Tordenet. Accept it and prepare yerself against it."

It was the best she could do without confessing that she was responsible for bringing him here to do exactly what he was offering now. She and the Elf. Of course, that had been before she had known him. Before she had considered what could happen to him. Before she had started having all these *feelings* for him.

"We have a deal, then," he agreed, stepping back from her and tugging at her hand. "Come on. We need to get you back inside before your Shen-Ora comes out blaming me for keeping you out in the cold after dark."

It would have to do, that little concession of his. At least until she could convince Skuld to allow her back into the Norns' world to travel the Visions. Only there could she see what path Chase needed to follow to keep him safe.

Christiana started forward, but stumbled as her ankle gave way. Wrestling with the cloak wrapped around it had obviously been a bit more than her healing muscle could take.

"Whoa, hold on." Chase grabbed her arms, supporting her. "Here, let's not push our luck anymore."

One second she was smiling up at him, grateful for his strength and sensibility, and the next she was airborne, lifted up into his arms, her head tucked against his broad chest as he carried her back to the house.

If she'd known that was all it took to get back into his embrace, she would have stumbled much, much sooner.

Twenty-two

THE *THWANG* OF metal striking frozen ground reverberated up Chase's arms and into his shoulders. No wonder the old woman had wanted him to dig her waste pit for her. He doubted she could lift the spade he held, let alone dig the damned hole.

He hoisted the pitiful excuse for a shovel and slammed it down once more, digging into the earth a quarter of an inch.

"Bullshit," he muttered, tossing the spade down in favor of the miniature pickax Orabilis had brought out for him. A *dolabra*, she'd called it. *Ancient toy pick* would have suited it better. This thing looked as though it must have been old when Orabilis was born.

"You've no made much in the way of progress, have you, lad?"

The old witch wobbled in his direction, one hand held above her eyes against the sun.

"You do know that the ground is frozen, right?"

The old woman shrugged one shoulder. "Aye. But I dinna expect a big, strong lad such as yerself to be giving up so easily."

If he clenched his teeth any harder, he suspected his jaw would crack.

"Did I say I was giving up? I'll get your damn hole dug."

One swift move and the blade of the dolabra dug into the ground. Maybe half an inch this time.

Orabilis cackled, obviously taking way too much pleasure from his performance of the task. "Rest for a moment, lad. I've brought you a drop of the good ale to wet yer throat." She held out the small flask she carried, digging in the pouch at her waist after he took it from her. "And this." She held out her hand.

"What's this?" he asked, taking her offering, turning it over to inspect it.

A carving strung on some kind of twine, perhaps the most rustic version of a necklace he'd ever seen. The wooden animal pendant was easily half the size of his hand and the feet had been whittled down to sharp little points.

"A token. A goat formed from the wood of the rowan for luck and protection. To thank you for all you've done, both for me and for my Christy."

"Well, thanks." He hardly knew what to say. Just when he thought the worst of her, Orabilis surprised him. "I appreciate that."

"Dinna go to blubbering now," she cautioned. "And put the thing on. It'll do no good lest it's hanging round a neck."

Chase slid the twine over his head, grinning

at the old woman's retreating back. Her ugly little ornament, and the intent behind it, made him smile.

As did the sound of horses approaching.

Ulfr and the men from Tordenet came into view, hauling the repaired wagon with its precious cargo of flour. Fine, strong men, at that. Strong enough to finish this little chore of his easily if they all divided the work.

Now, wasn't that a stroke of good luck? Maybe Orabilis's charm was already working.

"They've come."

They were the words Christiana had dreaded for the last two days and, from the look on Orabilis's face, her old nurse was no happier about the prospect than she was.

"You could refuse to return with them." Orabilis looked out the open door, her back to Christiana. "But you must decide now, before they come too close."

"No." She couldn't stay here. That option hadn't been shown to her on any of the future paths she'd seen. "Torquil would see to all our deaths if I chose such an action."

The old woman snorted, turning to fix Christiana with a stare. "You ken he has no way to get in here if we dinna allow it."

"And we've no way out. He'd remain outside the circle until his last breath, waiting for starvation to drive us into his arms. You ken that as well as I do."

She would never risk the lives of those dearest to her. Besides, Skuld had already shown her there were bigger things waiting for her. She had a part to play in preventing Torquil from carrying out his despicable plans.

She also had a part to play in keeping Chase alive . . . if she could only figure out exactly what she needed to do in order to keep him safe.

"It's him what puts worry in yer eyes as you gaze toward the future, is it no, little one?"

Orabilis knew her much too well for her to hide anything.

"I suppose it might be. The Visions have shown me he's to play a part in my escaping Torquil's hold. What I haven't seen is what comes after that. I won't go down that path if it leads to his destruction."

Orabilis nodded, scratching her chin thoughtfully. "Do you love him?"

Christiana hadn't expected that.

"How am I supposed to answer that? I canna say for sure what love looks like."

Orabilis chuckled, sitting heavily down on a stool. "Oh, little one, love has many faces through its life. In its infancy it builds low in yer belly like a fire, and sends you crawling into a man's bed to find a way to quench the need it's wrought. At times, it brings you happiness in simply sharing the silence with one another. But at its best . . ." Orabilis lifted her spoon from the pot over the fire as if to demonstrate her point. "At its best, it becomes as the porridge, filling and nurturing and life-sustaining, with each of you more concerned with the needs of the other than with yer own needs."

"I want that," Christiana whispered, as much to herself as to Orabilis. "I want to see the way to find that."

"And so you will have it, little one. You must remember, though, to trust yer heart as well as yer head."

"Perhaps." When she traveled once again to Skuld's world, she would seek out that path to see for herself. "I've no the least clue on how to ken who my porridge is without seeking the knowledge from Skuld."

"Oh, you'll ken, little one." Orabilis chuckled again and dropped her spoon back into the big black pot. "And without any interference from the Seeress, I promise. When he holds you close with his lips covering yers and you've no the desire to push him away, you'll ken well enough. The fire will rage and there will be only one way to tamp down a blaze such as that. Now go and get yer things ready for yer journey back to Tordenet. Yer brother's men will reach the house soon and I canna think they'll be wanting to linger."

Christiana hurried to the bedchamber, grateful for the excuse to escape. Her cheeks flamed with the memory of what had happened in the shed last night. The fire had burned then and, in truth, it burned even now as she remembered the feel of

Chase's lips upon hers. But was it the same fire of which her Shen-Ora spoke?

She gathered the bags Orabilis had prepared for her, taking her time in order to calm herself before she returned to the main room. There, a clay jar waited for her on the mantel above the fireplace, holding the precious elixir that would allow her to see whether Chase might indeed be the man her Shen-Ora had described.

At the doorway she stopped and closed her fingers around the small pouch that rested against her skin. Inside were the messages from the gods.

One to be Reborn, one to be a Warrior.

Was what she felt for Chase love, as the crones in her life all seemed ready to claim, or was it simply duty? She was prepared to give her life in order to save his. But that wasn't because of love, surely. That was only because it was as the gods had foretold.

After all, she could hardly expect to be Reborn without first preparing for death.

Twenty-three

BRIE SMOOTHED HER hands down the soft material of the brightly colored overdress. In all her years, she'd never worn anything so beautiful.

Her hair, braided around her face, interlaced with sprigs of dried lavender, hung shining down her back. *To flow around you like a curtain when you dance,* Eleyne had said.

It did indeed flow when she twirled. She'd tried it. Twice already.

For perhaps the first time in her life, Bridget MacCulloch felt beautiful.

"I've checked through all the goods in both wagons and it's no use." Eleyne limped toward her, a small bundle clasped in one hand. "You'll have to perform without shoes. There's none here what has slippers to fit those great feet of yers. You can take those ugly things yer wearing off once we reach the great hall. Oh . . ." The annoying woman stopped, unwrapping the bundle in her hand. "I do have this, though you must swear on all that's holy, you'll use it with great care."

"This" turned out to be a fine chain of silver, so intricately delicate, Brie could easily believe it had been spun by Magic from the Faeries themselves. Tiny crescent-shaped discs hung from it and made a tinkling noise when Eleyne lifted it to show her.

"It's beautiful," Brie said, sounding like some moonstruck maiden.

"Aye. Lean yer great head down where I can reach you and we'll fasten it in yer hair."

Brie could easily hate the petite blonde, if not for Eleyne's occasional lapses of kindness.

When Brie stood, the chain draped in a loop across her forehead, warm against her skin, giving off tiny little melodious notes with each movement of her head.

Perhaps Eleyne wasn't the worst person in the world, after all.

A long, low whistle of appreciation sounded as Mathew and Hugo rounded the wagon to join them, the younger man pulling a small cart filled with their instruments.

"Quite nice," Mathew complimented.

"Dinna you get carried away, cousin," Eleyne cautioned. "You can adorn a cow with all the pretties you can find, but in the end, all you've got yerself is a dressed-up cow."

No, Eleyne was indeed the worst person in the world.

"We're ready then. Come along with you," Hugo said, heading out, leaving Mathew to pull the little cart. "We've tonight to warm them up and then tomorrow's performance when the laird's sister returns. I can fairly feel the silver MacDowylt has promised in my pocket already."

"No to mention whatever coins the soldiers might toss our way. Perhaps the laird's sister will be delayed." Mathew lifted his cousin up to sit in the back of the cart with their instruments before hurrying forward to walk next to Hugo on their short trek to the castle. "Perhaps we'll have even more performances here."

"I'd no mind that," Hugo answered. "No at all, considering this laird's generosity."

Brie tempered her steps, walking next to the injured Eleyne, ignoring the woman as she went on and on with last-minute reminders about pointing your toe and feeling the beat of the music.

Instead, Brie cleared her thoughts, searching for the center she needed to inhabit before battle. Tonight would be her best chance. The laird would be lulled by drink and the performance would allow her close access to him. With his guard down she would strike, swift and deadly, claiming her revenge.

A shiver traveled up her spine as she remembered her earlier encounter with the MacDowylt. Even now, she chastised herself as she'd done a thousand times or more since that moment in his tower.

She should have killed him then. That fancy sword of his had been at hand and he'd been defenseless, lying there naked and vulnerable. Like a great witless fool, she'd passed up the perfect opportunity.

Yet, there had been something, some force in that room that had felt as if it stalked her, driving fear in her heart that prevented her from taking any action against the MacDowylt.

Force, my great arse, as her father had liked to say. She knew there could be only one acceptable truth of that encounter. No force but fear had stalked her in that tower. Her own fear. Like an untested warrior, she'd allowed it to get the better of her. It had to be that. If she were to accomplish what she needed to this night, she could allow herself to believe in no other power but that of man.

Done and done. She would not make that mistake again.

Entering through the narrow door in the massive gates, she tried not to wonder whether she would ever see the other side of the wall again. She'd tried to prepare herself that she'd likely not escape this place, but it didn't matter. As long as she succeeded in her quest, she didn't care.

The knife her father had given her on her last birthday burned against her breast in a promise of what was to come.

Torquil's men might well take her life this night, even as she would surely take his. But if there was a sword anywhere within reach, she would not pass to the next world alone.

"This is it," Hugo announced, leading the way up the stairs of the keep, a broad smile curving his lips.

"Think on all I have labored to teach you," Eleyne hissed over her shoulder, grabbing her cousin's arm for support.

A twinge of regret for the minstrels who accompanied her sparked in her heart. For their unwitting assistance, they'd likely forfeit their lives, too. The guilt of that knowledge weighed heavily.

"Try not to dance like a great heaving cow."

And just like that, the guilt lifted.

"You can do this. Concentrate on the music." Mathew flashed a smile as they passed into the great hall itself, his young face alight with excitement. "I have faith in you, Bridget MacCulloch."

She would concentrate. But not on the music.

TORQUIL LEANED BACK in his chair, his attention diverted by the arrival of the minstrels but only for a moment.

He had larger worries plaguing his mind than whether his silver was being put to good use.

Something had felt . . . wrong when he'd returned from his foray over his lands last night. Something within his tower chamber had seemed amiss.

Nothing appeared to have been touched. Nothing moved, nothing gone. Had that been the case, there would be heads on pikes decorating his wall today.

At first he'd had some minute concern that one

of the Tinklers had made their way into his lair. His watchers had quickly assured him that, although several of the castle's women had made visits to the wagons camped just outside his walls, not a single one of the Tinklers had left their camp.

He'd been willing to accept those assurances because the residue in his tower didn't feel like Tinkler. That he couldn't identify exactly what it *did* feel like was what concerned him now.

As did the mysterious marks on his chest. Blisters they were, as if he'd been burned. Five small ovals circling his heart, and he had no more clue as to where they'd come from than he had about what had been snooping within his lair.

He didn't like it. He didn't like it one little bit.

Deep inside, the beast raised its muzzle, sending a warning snarl vibrating inside his chest.

Torquil lifted his tankard, motioning for it to be filled. If he couldn't have answers this night, he needed diversion, for he had questions and worries aplenty.

The influx of new men had slowed to a stop as winter had taken hold. At this rate, he'd not have the strength of army he wanted by spring.

Buying men hadn't worked, and since he hadn't yet conquered the Magic that would allow him to force new recruits to his will, he must consider the remaining alternative.

To the west, perhaps two days' ride, the old Sinclair hoarded men and money. With only one son to carry on, it would be a simple matter to capture the heir, and in doing so force the old man to bend his knee to Tordenet. That would have to be his next move.

"More ale, my lord?"

He pushed away the plans and machinations that filled his thoughts to study the woman in front of him. The maid who poured his ale had a familiar look to her. She might have been the one Ulfr brought to him most recently for his pleasure, but he couldn't remember. She had the small stature and the same dark hair, but he couldn't be sure without seeing her eyes, and she kept those fixed on the pitcher from which she poured.

Just as well. If she was the one, she'd been a great disappointment, her and her mud-colored eyes. How Ulfr had ever thought she looked anything like Christiana was beyond his reckoning.

Low in his belly, the beast stirred, as if it feasted on his thoughts of sensual pleasures.

Surely there would be one among these crowds tonight who might meet his needs.

His hall was filled with scores of men and women, all eating his food, drinking his ale, sucking off the teat of his generosity. The tables were lined with them and more crowded around in clumps, laughing and talking with one another.

When the music began, the revelers cleared a space on the floor. One of the female minstrels twirled into that open space, her hair and her skirts flowing out around her, drawing his attention to the musicians in the far corner of his hall.

This festivity wasn't to his taste but his men seemed to be enjoying the performance and that, after all, was why he'd chosen to allow this. He needed the loyalty of these men in the coming days. There would be battles to be fought before his strength grew, and in that time he would be dependent upon them.

Soon, though, he would uncover all the secrets of the scrolls. And when he did, his mastery of their Magic would seal these men and any others he chose to his cause. They would dance to his tune without his needing to work for their petty loyalties. They would belong to him blindly, doing his bidding forever.

He emptied his cup and smiled, catching the eye of another passing server as he lifted the cup for a refill.

His back ached from the hours he'd stood this day, forcing his mind, bending his will to accomplish the next task, the one that would allow him to send not only his spirit but also his body traveling from one location to another through the Magical ether that surrounded everything.

He'd failed again, but he was close. He could feel it.

Deep inside, the beast stirred. The beast could feel how close he was to conquering the Magic, too.

To his left he caught sight of Halldor O'Donar.

Though the big man watched the festivities in the hall, his eyes roamed, always on guard.

Torquil lifted his tankard once more, sparing a thought for how much he hoped that O'Donar was the brother who would become his new champion. He liked the look of that one.

He followed the direction of the big man's gaze, straight to the woman who accompanied the minstrels. Her body moved with the beat of the drums, a slow, fluid extension of arm and leg as if time slowed down in some majestic battle.

Each time she looked up she looked directly at Torquil, with a brazen refusal to avert her gaze from his. No shy, coy maiden, that one.

What could she think to gain by such bold behavior? Surely one such as she didn't imagine she might catch the laird's eye. The thought required his amazing self-discipline to prevent his laughing out loud.

The very idea of a lowly woman such as she daring to hope to wed a man as powerful as he was beyond funny.

"No wedding in yer future," he muttered into his cup, surprised to find it empty so soon.

He lifted his tankard once again, his humor fading as the dancer made her way across the floor in his direction.

No marriage, but a bedding, perhaps? She was a bit overly large for his tastes, but a coupling with one who moved as she did could be entertaining for a night.

She certainly seemed to have caught O'Donar's eye. As she approached the head of the table where he sat, O'Donar rose to his feet and moved in their direction.

Yes, a bedding might be in order with this one. Even the beast within stirred in interest. If she pleased him, and if it came to pass that the big warrior down the table was his new champion, he could gift her to the man. Surely a move such as that would ensure O'Donar's loyalty for a good, long time.

At least for as long as it took for Torquil to conquer the Magic.

Torquil chuckled aloud at the knowledge of his coming power. The woman moving closer obviously thought his mirth was directed at her, because her lips curved in a return smile.

Let her think what she wanted. A whole new set of thoughts would be running through that pretty head when he had her delivered to his chamber later tonight.

HALLDOR DIDN'T LIKE the looks of this. Not one damn bit.

Though a seductive smile curved the lips of the woman who performed with the minstrels, it didn't reach her eyes. The windows to her soul were filled with resolve and determination.

She moved with a grace that would give the warrior queen a run for her money, but this one still carried the blush of youth firm upon her cheeks.

As she danced her way closer to the head table, closer to the dangerous laird of the castle, Halldor continued moving his way through the throngs of men to track her movements. Whatever she planned to do, he would intercede. She was no match for the evil she confronted.

Especially not under these circumstances.

Torquil was well into his cups, not wise for a man who dabbled in the black arts as he obviously did. Whether anyone else noticed the periodic flashes of red in the laird's eyes, Halldor couldn't say. He knew only that he had seen them and knew their origin.

Torquil wasn't the only being who waited for the warrior maiden at the head table.

In an act of singularly bad judgment, which Halldor could only attribute to the amount of ale the laird had imbibed, Torquil leaned across the table as the woman drew near, twining his hand in the length of her hair to drag her close.

Fool!

Halldor shoved people out of his way, frantic to reach the head table before it was too late.

Candlelight glinted off the wickedly sharp blade sliding from her bodice, and he knew his time was up. Dinnerware rattled to the floor as Torquil slammed her back down upon the table, leaning over her as he pinned her arms at her sides.

Halldor leaped upon the table and off the other side onto the floor, reaching the laird as he leaned in against the woman's neck, his mouth opened wide.

"No!" Halldor yelled, hoping to catch the creature's attention, for he knew it was the creature, not the laird, who sought to end the woman's life.

Torquil's head snapped up, his eyes glowing red as saliva dripped from his chin. Beneath him the woman lay unmoving, surprise and fear warring in her features.

"Wait."

The glow receded, replaced by an icy blue that heralded the return of the laird.

"You'd stay my hand against my assailant?" Confusion shadowed Torquil's face, clear evidence that only now did he realize it wasn't his hand he'd been prepared to use against the woman.

"Apologies, my laird, but I fancy this one as I haven't any for a long time. I'll see to her punishment myself if you'll do me the honor of gifting her to me."

He hoped that the request would work, now that Torquil seemed more himself, due to what Ulfr had shared about their laird's belief in his sister's visions of the future. A future that somehow included either him or Chase in some important measure.

It was small comfort to rest upon, but it was all he had.

"Take her!" Torquil pushed away from the table to stand tall, wiping the back of his hand over his mouth. "And when you've had yer fill of her, I'd have her head on a pike and her entrails spread on the wall walk."

"When I've had my fill, aye," Halldor agreed. "Thank you, Laird MacDowylt."

He pulled the woman to her feet, clamping one large hand over her mouth to forestall her protests even as the crowd around them broke into lewd jeers.

"One thing," he added, waiting for Torquil to turn. "Have you a place of privacy where I can take her? I'm not of a mood to share with the likes of these." He tilted his head toward the laughing throng.

"Use Christiana's tower if you like. It's empty until her return." This time it was Torquil's grin that didn't reach his eyes. "And none will be able to hear her screams from there."

Twenty-four

CHRISTIANA HAD FALLEN asleep again, waking only when the wagon bounced in a rut, jostling her against the strong, warm man sitting next to her.

"Okay, that's it. We're done." Chase pulled on the reins, drawing the animals to a stop. "Ulfr! We aren't going any farther tonight. Christiana's exhausted and she's freezing. We need a fire and she needs some sleep."

Ulfr pulled his horse back beside the wagon, his irritation evident.

"We've already wasted enough time digging the witch's pit at yer insistence, Noble. Our lord has bid me to bring his sister back as quickly as possible, and I intend to—"

"As quickly as possible is tomorrow," Chase interrupted. "For now, we're stopping and setting up camp. You can stay here with us or you can go on ahead, but to do anything else is going to mean that you and I are going to dance. And seriously, dude, I don't think you want that to happen."

Christiana didn't blame Ulfr for his look of confusion. Sometimes the things Chase said confused her, as well. But for all his strange words, his meaning was clear enough when he climbed down from the wagon and reached up to assist her in following him.

"Kenneth! How about you take care of unhooking these horses while I escort the lady to the trees over there?" Chase gave orders as if he were the one in charge, ignoring Ulfr's halfhearted protests. "Look at you, Ulfr. You're about to fall out of that saddle. Did you even take an hour to sleep before you started back after us? I didn't think so. Come on, man, give it a rest. Let's bed down for the night and we'll head out at first light. For all I care, you can tell Torquil I'm the one who held us up. It doesn't have to be your fault."

Ulfr appeared almost relieved as he dismounted and led his horse away.

"Come on." Chase grasped Christiana's hand in his, allowing her to lean some of her weight on him. "I'm sure you need to do your lady-stuff before we catch some sleep."

Her "lady-stuff." Christiana muffled the giggle she felt bubbling up in her throat at such an unladylike reference, and tightened her hand in Chase's as he led her limping away from the others.

"I'll wait for you here," he said, releasing her hand once they'd gone far enough into the trees that the sounds from the camp no longer reached them.

When she returned, he was staring up at the night sky.

"I wish I'd spent more time studying the stars," he said. "Because it seems more than a little weird to me that they don't really look any different here than they have anywhere else I've ever been."

"And you would expect them to be different?" She reached out to reclaim the warmth of his hand again.

He pulled her close to him, tucking her under his arm in the protection of the plaid he draped around her, as if it were the most natural thing in the world for them to stand here in the dark together, staring up at the sky.

"Yeah, for some reason, I did. If you could only see the places I've been, I'm guessing you'd think so, too."

Standing here so close to him, she tried to imagine what he would say if he knew she had seen those places. Or at least bits and pieces of them in the Visions she'd had of him. Tiny slices of a world remarkably different from her own. It was that very difference that had led her to seek the assistance of the Elf in bringing him to her.

One day she would have to speak to him of these things. But for now, she simply wanted to revel in this moment as they stared up at the sky. Simply to enjoy without any guilt, without any consideration of the world around them, without any question as to why she wanted this moment to last forever.

But even as she relaxed into the moment, her conversation with Orabilis slipped into her mind, niggling away at her peace and contentment.

Was Chase her porridge?

She certainly felt the burn in her belly every time she was near him. Near him? She only had to *think* of him, to imagine his touch, and the burn ignited.

This moment they shared right now—was this the comfort in silence of which her Shen-Ora had spoken?

The need to know now weighed heavily upon her.

Trust yer heart as well as yer head, Orabilis had advised, and she had never steered Christiana down a wrong path before.

She turned so that they faced one another, with her nose buried in the broad expanse of his chest. His arms tightened around her as if by instinct, enclosing them in the cocoon of his plaid.

"Smells like they have a fire going now." His voice was barely more than a whisper as he gazed down at her. "We should probably be getting back so we can warm you up."

Trust yer heart as well as yer head.

Whether from fear or some emotion she couldn't yet bring herself to admit, the heart she was to trust pounded against the walls of her chest. So loud, so hard, she was sure Chase must feel it as if it were his own. Even as that heart urged her forward, reason called out for her to stop, lest she have to live with the humiliation of rejection.

Trust yer heart as well as yer head.

She needed to know for sure. She needed to know now.

"Kiss me," she demanded, lifting her face up toward his.

He stared down at her for an instant, an instant that felt like a lifetime as she wondered if he'd refuse her.

And then, his mouth covered hers, breathing life into her very soul. She melted into his arms and somehow they turned as one and her back pressed against the trunk of a large tree.

His lips left hers and he whispered her name in tones so beautiful, it brought tears to her eyes.

Her fingers, which were somehow tangled in his hair, tightened and she pulled his mouth back to cover hers, unwilling to end what they had started.

His hands slid down over her breasts and the fire in her belly burned hotter with the pleasure of his touch.

When he lifted his lips from hers, his breath came in heavy, erratic puffs of air, exactly like hers did.

Between them, the little pouch holding her runes seemed to throb with a life of its own, and she knew, as surely as if she'd already walked the paths in Skuld's world, nothing from this moment on would ever be the same again.

"Again," she managed, just before she lost herself once more in the heat of his mouth, spinning away into the wonder that she'd discovered in his embrace.

"Noble?" Ulfr's voice in the distance cut through her haze of pleasure. "Mistress Christiana? Where are you? Answer me!"

Though the moment was entirely ruined, she had discovered what she'd set out to learn.

She had indeed found her porridge.

Twenty-five

"PUT YER TEETH together and come along with me quietly if you want to live."

The warning hissed in her ear halted Brie's struggles and she dropped her fists against the big man's chest. She didn't trust him, but every good warrior knew there was a time for battle and a time to assess your enemy's strength.

This particular enemy was stronger than most men she'd encountered.

Around them, the throngs of men jeered and laughed, many yelling out their disgusting suggestions of what he should do to her. He hoisted her to his shoulder without any sign of effort and strode from the great hall.

Much, much stronger than any man she'd encountered before.

Torquil was nowhere to be seen. Like the coward he was, he'd disappeared from the great hall as soon as he'd pronounced his verdict upon her fate.

As she'd attacked the MacDowylt, something hideous and terrifying had encased her, restraining her knife and blinding her vision, as if a blanket through which she couldn't even breathe had been dropped over her head.

She'd seen the eyes, though. Seen them clearly before her world had gone black. Red and glowing, as if hounds from the depths of the seven hells dwelled inside Torquil's body. She'd seen her own death promised in that glow.

"Be still," the big man muttered as a shiver wracked her body.

He moved quickly out of the keep and across the bailey.

She heard the door of the old tower slam open and a moment later he dropped her unceremoniously on her backside, cutting off the trickle of light by kicking the door shut when she made a move in that direction.

"Don't even think of it," he growled. "His men would take you down before you made the outer bailey."

He was likely right. All things considered, she wasn't exactly working from a position of strength at the moment. It was her wits she'd need to count on now.

On hands and knees, she felt her way to the wall and followed it to a corner, where she huddled. At least here he couldn't come at her from behind.

A thud sounded somewhere in the inky black of the small room, and the big man muttered a curse at the dark just before the flames in the fire pit came to life.

She watched him, wary of what he might do next, as he lit two large candles and set them upon the mantel.

When he turned, his face was a stern mask, his hands upon his hips.

"What do you plan to do with me?" she demanded, putting as much bravado into her words as she could muster.

"Plan?" He all but spat the word. "Of all the plans I've considered, none of them included a nameless shrewling who's too witless to see her own way through the Mortal world."

His burst of anger reignited hers.

"I'm neither nameless nor witless, you great hulking fool," she countered, feeling much more comfortable cloaked in anger than in fear. "Both charges I'd turn back upon you, a beast of a man who'd toss a helpless woman over his shoulder to carry her off and ravage her."

Her verbal thrust and parry might have held more weight had she been on her feet towering over him while he cowered in the corner, rather than the other way around, but she didn't quite have the wherewithal to rise to her feet just yet.

The big man laughed, making his way over to

where she sat. "A helpless woman, is it? Well then, by all I hold dear, rest assured, woman-child, I've no intent to claim your virginity this night."

"For a fact you'll no be doing any such thing. I'll see to that my ownself," she shot back.

He'd be in for quite a fight should he try. Though perhaps, considering his size and strength, she'd be better served by trying a different defense.

"Besides, I am a woman of the world. Whatever would give you the impression that I'm yet a virgin?"

Again he laughed, stretching out a hand to her. "Your own reaction. If I'd had any doubt of it, which I didn't, your reaction would have set me straight enough. Now then, come out of your corner lair, Shield Maiden, and make yourself comfortable over by the fire."

She considered refusing the hand he offered, but the shivers coursing through her body convinced her to do otherwise. Sitting by the fire actually sounded good.

He handed her a blanket that he pulled from a stack in another corner and waited, unmoving, until she had wrapped it around her and taken her seat.

"Since you assure me you have a name, perhaps we should begin there. I am called Halldor O'Donar. And you are?"

He spoke with a deep and oddly reassuring voice, with an accent she'd not encountered before.

"Where do you come from, big man? You've a strange sound to yer words."

"And you've an insolent sound to yours. Let us say that I come from somewhere other than here. A place where we've the courtesy to exchange our names upon meeting."

A flash of embarrassment sparked her mind, along with a twinge of guilt. She looked away from his face for a moment to compose her thoughts. "Well spoken, Halldor O'Donar, and well I deserved that rebuke. I am Bridget MacCulloch, daughter of the House MacUlagh, descended from the Ancient Seven who ruled all this land upon which you . . ." She stumbled to a halt as he rolled his eyes.

"A Pictish princess. I should have guessed from the way you behaved, if not from the way you look." He shook his head and leaned back against the large stones surrounding the fireplace. "Why is it every Pict I've ever met felt the need to recite their lineage back to the beginning of time?"

How *dare* he?

"I'm no a princess but a regular woman. The MacDowylt murdered my father. Hanged him in the courtyard of this very castle, for no reason other than his having followed Malcolm instead of Torquil. I will have my satisfaction from that man, one way or another." Her chest heaved with pent-up emotion.

"I feel for your loss, Bridget MacCulloch. And though there are no words to remove the pain of the loss you feel, I can assure you, your father sits even now in the great hall of Valhalla, surrounded by Valkyries, enjoying the rewards of a warrior's life."

"Bollocks." Her father's people might have believed that was reward enough. She did not. "I'd much prefer him to be sitting here with me."

"We don't always get what we prefer, now, do we? And of all the things you must settle for not having, personal revenge against Torquil MacDowylt will have to top the list."

"I should have ended the bastard's life when I found him sleeping in his tower." Sleeping or whatever that had been. "With that strange sword of his only steps away, I let the perfect chance slip through my fingers."

"A strange sword, you say?" Halldor's head tipped to the side and he leaned forward. "Can you describe it for me?"

"Aye. Fine and shiny it was, with strange markings engraved along the length of the blade." No point in sounding foolish by telling him that the foul thing was likely bespelled, the way it had beckoned to her when she approached it. "Neither letter nor number the markings were, but a match to the scroll lying next to it."

"A scroll? It was open? I suppose it would be asking too much that you've learned to read?"

Could the great, hulking beast of a man not go five minutes without insulting her? She *could* have learned to read. Often enough Jamesy had tried to sit her down to teach her, but the scrawlings in a book had never matched the lure of sword or bow.

"I ken the names of the letters and I recognize a written number when I see it. The markings upon the blade and the scroll were neither of those. They were such as I'd never seen before, all odd squiggles and sharp angled lines." With a demand to be touched she had barely been strong enough to resist.

Halldor stared off into the dark corners, lost in his own thoughts for the next few minutes, almost as if he'd forgotten she were even there.

She cleared her throat to remind him.

With a sigh, he leaned back against the stone, fixing her once again with his unwavering stare. "Nonetheless, I tell you in all truth, you must forgo your quest for personal revenge against Torquil MacDowylt."

She expected as much from Torquil's underling, no matter that he had stepped in to save her life.

"And why is that?"

"Because you're no match for Torquil Mac-Dowylt."

How little Halldor O'Donar knew of her.

"I am a match for any man."

"Well, I can believe that." Halldor smiled, though his eyes held a curtain of sorrow. "But that is the problem, you see. Torquil MacDowylt is no longer a man."

Their conversation was cut short by a banging on the door.

Her stomach twisted with the unwelcome punch of fear, but she rose to her feet. If the MacDowylt had changed his mind regarding her fate, she wouldn't make it easy for him.

Halldor stood too, a deep sigh escaping his lips as he leaned in toward her. "My deepest apologies, Shield Maiden, but I do this for your own good."

Before she could ask what he meant, he gripped the neck of her beautiful colored gown and jerked down, ripping through the layers of cloth to expose her entire body to just below her waist.

She screamed, clasping her arms in front of her in a paltry attempt to cover herself.

"On the floor," he hissed, pulling his shirt off over his head as he made his way to the door. One look around and he quickly but silently overturned the bench by the wall before answering the insistent hammering.

She nodded and dropped to her knees. If he thought to set a proper scene, she would do her part.

"What?" he bellowed, throwing open the door. "Can you not leave a man to his pleasures?"

One of the guards Brie remembered seeing inside the hall waited there, craning his neck to cast a leer in her direction.

"Our lord Torquil would have you attend him in his solar after midday meal on the morrow."

Halldor nodded, holding the door open much farther than he needed to do, supporting her suspicion.

"You may tell him I'll be honored to be there. And now, if that's all you have for me, I've a meal of another kind what wants attending to, eh?"

Both men laughed like drunken fools sharing a vile secret, until Halldor slammed the door shut in the other's face, dropping the bar down to ensure it stayed shut.

When he returned to her side, he dropped a woolen blanket over her shoulders, covering her nakedness before he sat.

She looked up at him, trying to find a grateful smile but failing miserably.

"The good news is, by sunrise, word of your deflowering will have spread to every willing ear on the castle grounds."

"That's the good news?" She could hardly believe how her voice shook. "What, then, could possibly be the bad?"

He reached for her hand, lifting it to his face. "If we're to do this in a way that might be convincing enough to save your life, we must do it right. That means you must be strong enough and clever enough to play your part as well."

Trickles of fear curled in Brie's chest at the look he gave her. She tugged at her hand, feeling a need to put distance between the two of them, but he wouldn't let go.

"Can you do that? Can you be strong enough for what's to come?"

She nodded, and nearly screamed again as he crushed her fingernails into the skin beside his eye, dragging them down the length of face, leaving four ragged trails of blood in their wake.

$\mathcal{T}$ wenty-six

$\mathcal{T}$HERE ARE TINKLERS at Tordenet?" Christiana could hardly believe her eyes. "And you dinna speak of this, Ulfr?"

"There seemed to be no reason to do so. They're no allowed entry through the gates, so it's no as though you'll have any contact with them."

The knowledge struck home painfully. For the first time in many years, she was so close to her mother's people, yet they might as well have been across an ocean for her inability to speak to them.

"You want to visit their camp?" Chase asked quietly from his seat beside her. "Just say the word."

As badly as she wanted to speak with them, to see if they had known her mother, it wasn't a word she would say. Torquil would never allow it, and she wouldn't risk what her brother might do to Chase if he tried to help her.

She caressed the wagons with her eyes as they rolled past, surprised when a woman jumped down from one of those wagons and started toward them.

"Keep yer distance, Tinkler!" Ulfr ordered.

The woman stopped but lifted a hand in greeting, remaining that way until they passed through the opened gates and Christiana could see her no more.

With a sigh, she pushed the woman from her thoughts. Exhaustion from the long ride and from her restless night dulled her senses. What she needed more than anything was a good sleep before she confronted Torquil. A good sleep, and a hot mug of lavender-and-betony tincture to warm her up.

The cause of her restless night nudged his leg against hers, sending a wave of the now-familiar fire coursing through her belly, driving away any need for a hot drink.

As he hopped down to the ground and turned to assist her, she couldn't help but wonder whether he'd gotten any more sleep than she had after they'd returned to the camp last night. Or had he, too, tossed and turned, his mind and body filled with the same longing that had plagued her?

She gave herself over to Chase's hands, holding on to his arms as her feet touched the ground. Even such a small, innocent contact set her wanting more.

"I'll make sure we get the wagon unloaded for you," he offered as he slid an arm around her to support her weight. "You should probably take it easy. You need to rest that foot of yours so it can heal."

She had no desire to tell him it was already all but healed. Healed, she'd have no need of his assistance. No excuse for the strong arm around her waist, supporting her as she made her way toward her door. And for that particular pleasure, a little faking seemed a small enough price to pay.

"Chase!"

Christiana swiveled her head to see Halldor headed toward them at a run.

"He's just going to have to wait," Chase muttered, shoving open the door to her tower with his foot even as he tightened his hold around her waist. "What the holy hell?"

When Christiana turned her attention to the sight in front of her, she very nearly echoed Chase's exclamation.

"Who are you?" she managed, pushing away from Chase's arms to hurry to the young woman curled up on the floor in front of her fireplace. She was clearly held prisoner, a rope stretching from the iron loop in the fire pit to tie snugly around the woman's ankle.

"Who's done this to you?"

"That would be me, my lady." Halldor stood in the doorway behind Chase. "I'd hoped to warn you before you entered."

"Warn us?" Fury crawled up from the depths of Christiana's emotions. "I'd say you've a much greater need for explanation than warning."

"Bridget belongs to me," Halldor answered simply.

"*Belongs* to you?" Christiana dropped to her knees to fumble with the knot snug against the obviously frightened woman's skin. "People do not belong to other people."

"That one does." Artur had joined the men at the doorway. "Our lord himself gave that one to O'Donar as punishment for her attempt at sticking a knife into our good laird."

"What?" Christiana's hands stilled as she looked from the woman to Halldor. "Is this true?"

"I've not the time for explanations now. Our laird himself awaits me. And you, little brother"—he slapped Chase on the back— "are exactly the one I'd have accompany me."

"But what about this—"

"Leave her as she is. She knows what will happen if she tries to escape. Best she tells you about that while we're gone. Come along, little brother."

Chase followed as Halldor stepped out the open door, but quickly returned carrying the clay jar Christiana had protected all the way from Orabilis's cottage.

"Artur's men are unloading your bags into the storage room. Do as I said and get off that foot. And don't worry. I'll find out what's going on and I'll get back to you."

Christiana nodded, accepting the jar containing her precious elixir before the men filed out of her tower, leaving her alone with her unusual guest.

"Well," she said at last. "Bridget, is it? Let me put this away and I'll find a blade to free you up from that binding."

Surprisingly, the woman laughed. "Dinna be daft, Mistress Christiana. I could remove this at any time I chose. Were you no listening to O'Donar? It's no the binding about my ankle keeping me here, but fear over the alternative."

"The alternative?" Christiana echoed, not at all understanding what was happening.

"Aye," the other woman replied. "The wrath of the beast that O'Donar goes even now to see. The beast you call a brother."

"WHAT THE HELL is going on around here?" Chase caught up with Hall, matching his steps to the big man's. "Who is that woman? Where'd she come from?"

He had a million other questions, like, what had happened to Hall's face? But the ones he'd asked would suffice to start.

"She's one of Malcolm's people. From Castle MacGahan. An innocent, seeking revenge for her father's murder."

"And let me guess. . . . Torquil had a hand in that." Even more confirmation he'd picked the wrong side on which to fight.

"So it would seem. Bridget's father was one of the guards accompanying Malcolm's wife when she brought ransom to gain his freedom a few months back. On Torquil's order, all the men who accompanied her rode the horse of the hanged."

"Rode the . . ." Chase struggled to hide his irritation at his own inability to understand what Hall was telling him. "You mean he had them killed?"

"On his order they were put to the gallows, their only crime serving the wrong master."

"Is it possible there's more to it than that? Something we don't know. Maybe there were circumstances that—" Chase pressed his lips together, remembering all that Christiana had told him about Torquil. What he already knew to be true about Torquil pushed aside any possibility of the laird's innocence.

"There's aplenty we don't know, that's sure enough," Hall agreed. "For instance, were you aware that our little healer travels the Vision world?"

Chase nodded slowly, wondering how Hall had learned of it.

"Were you also aware that you somehow figure into those visions? That Torquil hopes through his sister's visions to determine which of the two of us is meant to suit some purpose of his?"

That, he had not known.

"I thought as much." Hall ran a hand through his hair, blanking the expression of worry from his features. "The web is already woven, little brother. We can but pick our way through, hoping we choose the best paths."

They'd reached the main hall of the keep. As they drew to a stop, Hall knocked upon the door of Torquil's solar.

Chase watched as the familiar, carefree grin returned to Hall's face just before Torquil opened the door. It was a skill he could only hope to copy.

"What's this?" Torquil asked, looking directly at him as a wide smile spread over his face. "You've returned. Excellent. Saves me the trouble of repeating myself."

They were hardly inside the door when another knock sounded and Artur and Ulfr joined them.

"I thought you were unloading the wagon?" Chase knew for a fact Ulfr had intended to do exactly that. Perhaps he'd learned of this meeting from Artur.

"There were others for that sort of work," Ulfr said.

"Very well," Torquil began, seating himself behind the big table at the side of the room. "Since everyone is here now, I want you all to be aware that I'll be sending you as a delegation to call upon the old Sinclair, announcing my desire to bring together the northern clans to counsel on what challenges we could well face in the near future if, as is rumored, the English march against us."

Chase wondered how great a part Christiana's visions played in Torquil's preparation for these challenges.

"Only to Clan Sinclair?" Hall asked.

"Of course no only to the Sinclair. I've already dispatched riders to the other houses in each direction within a three-day ride. I've but a few preparations left before I send you on yer way. Ulfr, see to it the Tinklers break camp and move on before our guests begin to arrive."

"We stand ready to do yer bidding, my lord," Artur offered, earning himself a glare from Ulfr as they all filed out of the solar.

Hall scratched his beard thoughtfully, visibly wincing as his finger passed over the recent wound.

Artur, unwisely, could not let the movement pass unnoticed.

"It's yer whore what's done that to you?" he asked, an idiot-like grin breaking over his face.

Hall didn't answer, but widened his stance, arms loose at his sides.

Chase backed away from the two of them, having seen such a move often enough. You didn't need to be a body language expert to recognize someone preparing for a fight.

"She's highly spirited, that one," Hall said at last.

A normal man would have let it go at that, but Artur didn't seem to notice the threat he faced. Instead, he pushed forward with another foolish question.

"Perhaps you'd care to share her with some of us, now that you've had yer fill of her, aye?"

"And perhaps you'd care to impale your skinny arse on the pointy end of my sword."

In a flash of polished metal, Hall drew his weapon, the ring of steel loud in the stone entryway. He pointed the blade toward Artur, its tip mere inches from the man's throat.

"You'd do well, little man, to mind what business is yours. I've not yet had my fill of what she has to offer. And as I told our good laird last night, I'm not a man to share what is mine. Best you remember that and keep your distance, aye? I won't take it well if I find you sniffing around Mistress Christiana's tower as long as the woman is there. Do I make myself clear?"

Artur nodded frantically, turning and running the instant Hall lowered his sword.

"I'd be watching my back if I were you," Ulfr warned, his gaze following after the departing soldier. "He's no likely to forget this incident."

"Neither will I, good captain." Hall's smile had returned to his face. "Neither will I. Come along, little brother. We've much to do to prepare ourselves."

What Chase wanted to do was to go check on Christiana. Unfortunately, there didn't seem to be a way for him to do that without drawing attention to both the women staying in her tower.

"I've a suspicion about our good laird." Hall clasped his hands behind his back, increasing the speed of his stride.

"Only one?" For his own part, Chase had many. "I'm pretty sure we aren't working for the good guy, Hall."

The big man answered with a snorting noise. "Of that I have no doubt. At the moment, my concern is more centered on the possibility that Torquil attempts to deceive us."

Them and everyone else on the planet, would be Chase's guess. "What exactly makes you think—"

"The man lied to us in there. No riders have left Tordenet. Not a single one. I know the faces and none are missing. If he can't be honest regarding something that seems so small, chances are good that it's not small. The time has come to be tying up our loose ends and making preparations to leave this place. And that's exactly what we go to do now."

Chase agreed wholeheartedly. Nothing around here felt right, except Christiana. She was one loose end he definitely intended to tie up.

"Where are we headed?"

"To have ourselves a chat with the Tinklers," Hall answered, wearing the first real smile since Chase had returned to Tordenet. "To seek out the assistance of your people."

Twenty-seven

"Is there anything else you need?" Christiana watched doubtfully as her guest drew a stitch through her ripped chemise.

"No," the other woman replied, head bent to the task at hand.

Christiana had found an old overdress, but it was much too short for Bridget, making it all the more important that they repair the rent in her chemise so that she would have something to cover her legs from her shins down.

"In that case, I'll retire to my bedchamber. Don't hesitate to call me if you need anything."

Though she was exhausted, it wasn't sleep on her mind as she picked up the clay pot holding the elixir Orabilis had prepared for her. There was much she needed to know, and a visit to Skuld's world was the only place she could find her answers.

She began the slow trek up her winding stairs. Her ankle was healing but stairs, she'd quickly found, aggravated the injury.

After shutting the door to the room at the top

of her tower, she dragged the heavy wooden bar over and fought it into place to ensure she wouldn't be interrupted. Had she not been tired before she began, that effort alone would have seen to it.

But tired or not, she had to do this now. Torquil had twice sent word for her to hasten to his tower that he might be present while she traveled the Visions, and twice she had sent her excuses.

Her half brother was not a patient man. He would not take no for an answer the next time, and she desperately needed to know what she would confront before she was forced to share that information with him.

She removed the stopper from the clay jug and lifted it to her lips. Flavors of the infused herbs flowed over her tongue, coating her mouth in a burst of familiar sensation.

A sigh of relief heaved up from deep in her chest. At last, she was within reach of that which she needed most—foreknowledge.

She stretched out on her little bed, closing her eyes and clearing her inner senses. Within seconds a tiny speck appeared in her mind's eye, growing into the brilliant doorway she sought.

Stepping through the opening, she filled her lungs with the warm, moist air permeating the center of the Nine Worlds, then slowly made her way toward the figures sitting under the sheltering arms of the great ash tree.

They ignored her completely, their hands flying

over the colorful threads forming the tapestry on which they worked. All was as it had been before, reassuring her that her last encounter with the goddesses had been nothing more than a bad dream seated in the depths of her own imagination.

She paused at the Well of Fate, dipping her hand into the icy depths of a freshly drawn bucket and lifting the magical water to her lips. The liquid rolled down her throat, sparking a tingling sensation in every part of her body and lifting her from the ground upon which she walked, allowing her to float high over the gates guarding Past, Present, and Future.

"Wait," she whispered, and her body hung motionless in the air.

Though her time here was always limited and she had much to discover, she shifted her weight to veer off toward Urd's world of the past. She'd done this only once before, to confirm her suspicion as to what had caused her father's sudden "illness." Since finding that proof, she'd avoided this area, finding it more unsettling than that which was yet to come.

But this time something from the past called to her, demanded that she see it. Filling her thoughts with an image of Chase, she pushed forward.

Below her, a sparkle of light drew her attention. A flash of brilliant green burst open like the petals of some gigantic flower and just as quickly, it disappeared, leaving in its wake the body of a man lying on the ground. Chase's arrival in her world.

She watched events of his past play out in a fast-forward movement of time as he was cocooned in the warmth of a sturdy plaid, and as men from Tordenet approached and rode away. She watched as he walked the trails beside a riderless horse, dressed as he had been when she'd first seen him. She watched until he entered the gates of Tordenet and arrived at the door to her very own tower.

Then, as if an unseen hand plucked her from her perch, her body floated upward and she found herself just inside the gates of Skuld's world. Not that she had truly expected anything else. She had never been allowed to see herself as she traveled the Visions. Apparently that prohibition applied to the past as well as to the future.

Far, far off in the distance, she spotted a dark hole in the tapestry of the future. A shining circle of bright green light outlined the spot as if to draw attention to the flaw. A pang of guilt washed over her as she realized that was likely the spot from which Chase had been plucked. She, with the aid of the Elf, was responsible for such damage to the tapestry of time.

What was done was done. That moment belonged to Urd's world now.

Curiosity urged her toward that spot, but she resisted. In prior Visions she'd seen awe-inspiring bits and pieces of Chase's world. It was those bits and pieces that led her to fear his reaction when the day came that he learned of her part in taking him away from all that. Without giving him any choice, she and the Elf had separated him from those wonders and perhaps even from those he loved. She wasn't sure she wanted knowledge of all that he'd left behind.

Besides, it was his path from this point forward that concerned her now. The path he needed to travel to avoid an encounter with death before his appointed time.

As always, the trails closest to her were clear and easy to observe. It was only as they branched off, like roots of some massive tree, that the pathways became obscured with the Mysts of Choice.

Choice obscured what would be, because Choice altered what would be.

She dipped lower, floating over the course Chase currently followed, watching as he and many other men mounted up and passed through the gates of Tordenet, their animals carrying them north at a full gallop. Into the obscuring Mysts.

That was where she must go. It was on that pathway where she'd find the dangers awaiting Chase. The muddied colors snaking through the Mysts were sure proof that evil and death awaited the unwary.

Winds, strong and steady, whipped at her hair and clothing, holding her back, pushing her slowly back out of Skuld's world.

"No," she insisted as she found herself once again standing by the Well of Fate.

The bucket that had been drawn to welcome her had disappeared, a clear message that her visit was at an end. She backed away, head bent, sending her silent thanks to the goddesses as she passed where they sat. It wasn't their fault she'd wasted precious time here, satisfying her curiosity. Still, it was beyond frustrating to have learned so little. She prayed Skuld would once again allow her to visit, to seek the truths she so desperately needed.

As if in answer, a voice rang out from the circle under the spreading branches of the great tree, Yggdrasil.

"Only as you accept the truths we share will we continue to share them, daughter of Odin."

They spoke, just as they had in what she'd assumed had been only a dream! It had been real then, not her imagination.

"I dinna ken yer meaning," she called out, struggling against the winds that pressed her inexorably toward the gaping door ahead. She always accepted the truths of what they allowed her to see.

"But only after they've wrestled you to the ground in your attempt to deny them, aye?"

That wasn't true. She never denied what she learned in her Vision travels.

"Oh, truly? Did you not deny the truth of your feelings for the one you seek to save? As you accepted that, so you must accept what you have seen today. Only then will I allow you to travel my world again."

As if shoved by a giant hand, Christiana fell backward through the shining doorway, into the enormous void that would lead her to her own world.

When her eyes opened, she once again lay in her bed. She had no idea how long she had been gone, only that the sun shining through the window high on her stone wall was gone, replaced with a shaft of moonlight.

Realization hit her like a slap to the face as she rose from where she lay.

Skuld had indeed shared with her something of great importance. And though she had no idea what the things she'd seen meant, she knew she had to find Chase as soon as possible to share what she'd learned. She had to convince him not to take any chances before she again traveled Skuld's world, even if that meant confessing her own responsibility for his being here.

Twenty-eight

"THAT WENT WELL enough." Chase glanced over his shoulder to where the Tinklers scurried around like busy ants, packing their wagons in preparation to move on at first light.

"We've their agreement to help, if that's what you mean, however reluctantly it might have been given. Your people are ever difficult to pin down."

His people. Hall might be more than a little surprised to learn who his people really were. One day, when he had time to kick back and pick Hall's brain, he'd have to find out what it was about him that made his friend so sure he was related to the Tinklers.

"Tinklers have long been the favored peoples of the Fae. Surely you know that."

That hit a little too close to home for comfort, forcing Chase to seek a way to deflect the conversation.

"Except that it wasn't me that convinced them. It was you. I could almost believe that you came straight here from kissing the Blarney Stone. You've got the gift of gab, Hall."

"I've not heard of this blarney stone of yours, but I do not harbor any doubt that those people agreed to my request only because you were there. They would have rejected me."

Chase found that hard to believe, though the leader's wife, Editha, had acted pretty strange around him.

"And now that you've brought up the subject of gifts"—Halldor grinned at him—"there's something of great importance that I've meant to discuss with you since the day of Mistress Christiana's accident. It's the naming you did. I'm owed a ceremony, little brother, and a gift to make the naming official."

"Naming? What are you talking about?"

His companion snorted as if he doubted Chase's seriousness. "You bestowed the name of Hall upon me as we faced the challenge of saving your lady. Where I come from, this practice requires a ceremony and the presentation of a naming gift."

Chase slowed to a stop as they entered the inner bailey, searching his friend's face for any sign the big man was joking.

He found none.

"You're serious about this, aren't you?"

"I am. My people take the gifting of names quite seriously. A child is not part of the family until he is name-gifted and presented for Thor's blessing."

"Okay." Thor. At least the accent made more sense. "If that's what you want."

"It is. The tradition is important to seal our relationship. We've not the time for a formal ceremony, but there must be a name gift given."

"In that case, you absolutely get a naming gift. In fact, here." Chase pulled the carving of the goat he'd been given by Orabilis from under his shirt. Lifting the twine over his head, he handed it to Hall. It felt almost a relief to get the weight of the thing off his neck.

Hall turned it over in his hands, inspecting it from all sides.

"It's a goat. How did you know of my fondness for goats? And carved from the flesh of a rowan tree, favored among all the woods," the big man said thoughtfully. "A fine gift indeed, fit for the likes of Thor himself. The name change is official, little brother. I am well pleased with your gift."

"Good. Now maybe we can—"

"Your woman approaches," Hall interrupted, dipping his head in the direction of a cloaked figure hurrying toward them.

Definitely female, but with her face hidden in the great hood of her cloak, Chase had no way of knowing who it was until she drew close enough for him to see her face.

"I must speak with you." Christiana glanced to Hall before dipping her eyes to the ground in front of her. "Alone, if you please."

Hall slapped Chase on the back before he turned away. "No worries, little brother. For my own part, I'd best go to share word of our arrangements with the hellion occupying your lady's tower."

Chase moved closer to Christiana. "We do need to talk." He wanted to tell her that Torquil would be sending him to the Sinclairs' so that she wouldn't worry when she found him gone. "But not here in the middle of the bailey. I don't suppose you know of someplace more private where we can have this conversation?"

"As a matter of fact"—she looked up at him, a smile curving her beautiful lips—"I do at that."

She hurried ahead of him, all but disappearing in patches of night where the moon's light didn't reach.

"Here!"

Her whisper drew him deeper into the dark. She reached for his hand, her fingers lacing with his, and she led him forward. He knew they'd passed through an entry of some sort; the dark was thicker here, but devoid of the biting winter wind.

"Mind you make no noise," she cautioned in a whisper as she stepped closer to him. "And dinna let go my hand, lest I lose you in the maze."

As if he had any desire to let go. Nothing suited him better than an excuse to hold her hand.

The floor rose and fell as they hurried through the confines of pitch black. Holding out his free hand, he was assured that the passage they traveled was barely larger than the width of his shoulders, as if it had been built for miniature people. Or at the very least, people who didn't have his problem with tight, dark, confined spaces.

He lost count of the right and left turns they took,

leaving him no doubt that Christiana had been absolutely correct in calling this place a maze.

He tightened his grip around her hand. No way was he taking a chance on getting lost in the bowels of this damn castle.

"I need my hand for this part," she whispered at last, pulling her fingers from his.

A strange grinding noise sounded a few feet away, and a small sliver of light appeared.

He headed toward it, realizing as it grew larger that it wasn't so much that it was light as that it was simply not the same level of soul-sucking dark.

His forehead smacked to a sudden stop, the collision hard enough to set off little flashes of light behind his eyes.

"Mind yer head," she cautioned from somewhere in front of him.

"Too late," he answered, stooping as low as possible before starting forward again.

Two more steps and, just like magic, he was free, stepping into a room where moonlight spilled in through cracks in the shuttered windows set high on the wall.

Chase thought his eyes must be playing tricks on him when it appeared the fireplace moved; then he realized that must have been where they entered. Christiana crouched near the floor, and a little flash of light sparked from the flint in her hand. Within moments, she'd coaxed the tinder into dancing flames.

"Come close to the fire," she invited as she knelt by the flames. "Sit by me and let me see what you've done to yerself."

Dropping down to her side, he leaned forward, allowing her fingers to delicately trace his forehead. Her touch alone was worth the pain of the injury.

"There's no sign of blood, though I do feel quite the bump here," she murmured. "I warned you, did I no? I told you to mind yer head."

He reached up to capture her hand between his own two. "Next time, you might want to offer your warning just a minute or two earlier."

The reflection of flames from the fireplace lent her eyes a look of sorrow. "An ongoing fault, it would seem, that I dinna think a thing through before I act upon it. My apologies, Chase, for bringing you to a place you dinna belong."

"It's no big deal. Trust me, I've had much worse." He brushed her fingertips to his lips before breaking the contact. "So where are we right now? This place where I don't belong."

He smiled at her, hoping to lift the look of distress from her face, but she appeared even more unhappy.

"This place," she said, her voice barely above a whisper. "Of course. These were my mother's rooms during her lifetime. Afterward, they were mine. This wing is of little use now, other than to house the rare visitor."

"In that case, I guess it'll be getting a workout soon. Torquil plans to bring together a council of families from all around here. He says he's already sent riders to most of them, though Hall and I have reason to doubt that. I'm due to leave for the Sinclairs' any time now to invite them to Tordenet."

Her eyes widened. "Artur and Ulfr will accompany you, yes? And many others. Far too many men for the simple purpose of delivering an invitation."

"How do you know that?" Artur and Ulfr were to go along with them, though Torquil had said nothing of others.

"I spent the daylight hours traveling the pathways of Skuld's world. I saw you, a riderless horse at your side, along with Artur and Ulfr and a company of my brother's men, riding hard to the north, into the Mysts of Choice." She put a hand on his forearm, her fingers warm through the linen of his sleeve, and leaned closer. "This is the first of what I need to warn you about. What I saw was a series of pathways branching off from the road you traveled. I was unable to remain in Skuld's world long enough to see which pathway you should choose, but I do ken that some will lead to good and some will lead to ill. You must promise me that you'll no set out on this journey until I am able to see what it is you must do."

"A riderless horse?" he questioned. Her visions were as full of riddles as carrying on a conversation with a Faerie. "Hall's supposed to ride out with me. Is a riderless horse supposed to mean that he's in danger? That something is going to happen to him?"

Not an hour ago he'd given the big guy a wooden goat that made them officially family, and considering his decided lack of family in this world, he didn't like the idea of anything that risked what he had.

"I canna say." Her fingers curled into the muscle of his arm, sending little tingles through his thoughts. "I've seen naught of yer brother in any of my Vision travels, no even when I ventured back to watch yer arrival in—"

Her words cut off in a sharp gasp, her fingers darting from his arm to cover her lips.

"But that would be looking into the past, wouldn't it? Not the future." And if she looked far enough back, she wouldn't be finding him there, either. And *that* particular mystery was something he wasn't sure he was completely ready to try to explain to her.

"Aye," she answered, her voice back to a whisper. "I selfishly wasted the better part of my time in the Norns' world traveling the pathways of the past."

"When you say you didn't see Hall there when I arrived . . ." He paused, searching for a way to ask what he needed to know without saying something stupid enough to spark her curiosity. "Let me ask this. . . . How is that possible? We both know he was at my side when we knocked on your door that first day."

She let out a long, shaky breath as she clasped

her hands together in her lap. "I was no talking about yer arrival at my door. I followed you only to the gates of Tordenet."

"Followed me from where?"

The sinking feeling in the pit of his stomach seemed to be telling him he just might be facing an explanation, whether or not he was ready to give it.

Another long, shaky exhale.

"From yer arrival in this world," she answered, her eyes darting to his and away again. "In this time."

She knew!

"Let me try to explain," he started, knowing it would be worse than silence if he were to attempt to lie his way out of this. She was too important to him to tell her anything but the truth.

"You've no a need for explanation, Chase. Certainly no to me, seeing as it's me what did this to you."

"You? I don't think so." He'd been wishing to be where he belonged since he was just a boy.

"I am responsible for bringing you here and placing yer life in danger. I saw you in my Visions. I saw that you were the only chance I had at freedom and, selfishly, I valued my own freedom more highly than yers. It's me what bade the Elf to rip you from yer own life and bring you through time."

"What Elf?"

"Malcolm's mother-in-law, the one who accompanied his wife when she came to ransom his freedom from Torquil. I insisted she give her word to bring you to this world, for me."

"Malcolm's mother-in-law is an Elf," he said slowly. And Christiana was descended from Odin, and the Tinklers were tools of the Fae, and he himself was . . .

"Elesyria is her name. Though in truth, she calls herself a Faerie, no an Elf, and she dinna take at all kindly to my using the wrong appellation." Christiana shrugged, wiping her hands at the corners of both eyes. "I'm so sorry for what I've done to you. So very sorry."

As if the final piece of a puzzle he'd struggled with his entire life fell into place, Chase began to laugh. A small release of air at first, bubbling up from deep inside his chest until it formed great, silent heaving bursts of laughter that left him weak.

All this time, Christiana had struggled with the guilt of forcing him here against his will. All this time, and neither of them had been brave enough or just plain smart enough to open up to the other.

"Oh, Christy, don't cry." He enfolded her in his arms, holding her close to his heart. "You don't have anything to be sorry for. This Elesyria of yours was only the tool that brought me here. I've been waiting for her, or someone just like her, my whole life to do exactly what you asked her to do."

She pushed away from his chest, looking up into his face, her big wet eyes filled with suspicion. "How can it be the truth you speak? What sort of a man would wait for the Fae to rip them from the tapestry of their lives and toss them through time to a place they dinna belong?"

"An unhappy man," he answered honestly, stroking his thumbs down the sides of her cheeks in a vain attempt to dry the still flowing tears. "A man who's spent his life searching for the purpose he was to fulfill, waiting for one particular Faerie to send him where he belongs."

"You believe this is where you belong? In truth?"

Looking down at her face, so filled with trust and hope, he'd never been more sure of anything before. Being here in this time, with her, it was as if he'd been reborn into the place he was always meant to be.

He pulled her to him, covering her mouth with his.

She molded herself to him as he played his tongue across her soft lips, dipping inside to trace the contours of her mouth when those lips parted. She tasted of herbs, of mint and balm and a thousand other flavors, like an exotic dish, fresh and steaming from the oven, prepared to his exact specifications.

Her hands skated over his chest and up to his neck, her fingers tangling in his hair, pulling him closer as if they might melt into one another.

There was only one way he could think of to get any closer.

He lifted her in his arms and carried her to the bed, shoving the heavy curtains open before lowering her onto her back.

She extended a hand, catching his fingers and pulling him down on top of her.

Balancing his weight on his forearms, he dipped his head to capture her soft, willing lips.

He wanted her so badly he could taste it, but he was determined to take it slow. This moment he had waited for all his life was too important to rush through.

Her hands slid under the tail of his plaid to follow the length of his leg, stopping only when one petal-soft finger stroked against the heat of his inner thigh. He sent a silent thanks to every supernatural being he could think of for the invention of the plaid. Had he only known, he would have been wearing them his whole life.

Slow and easy, he reminded himself, kissing a trail down the side of her neck, nuzzling aside the neckline of her dress to trace his tongue over the soft skin of her shoulder. His good intentions almost deserted him when her finger moved again, forging a path around his leg to brush against his swollen manhood.

A quick count of ten, backward, and he pulled at the neck of her dress, almost frantic in his efforts until her own movements allowed the cloth to slip down, revealing one perfect breast.

His mouth settled on the exposed treasure and he circled his tongue around the hardened nipple, his breath catching as she moaned and lifted her body against his.

It must have been a woman who designed these dresses. A man would have invented a snap-front micromini rather than the yards and yards of frustrating fabric that encased Christiana's body.

"Wait," she demanded, her warm fingers deserting the heat of his body.

He froze, one hand wrapped in what felt like fifty yards of linen separating him from where he wanted to be. Disappointment raged with the need to ignore her, but his better angels prevailed.

She wiggled enticingly beneath him and he counted again, backward from twenty this time.

"Better now," she whispered, pressing herself to him, her gloriously naked skin burning into his.

His better angels, thoroughly rewarded for their honorable behavior, took flight, giving way to pure need.

THE FIRE IN her belly raged out of control, turning all rational thought to instant cinders. Nothing mattered as much as extinguishing that fire.

Orabilis had told her there was only one way to accomplish that.

She knew the mechanics involved, even though she'd not experienced it herself. She'd seen animals mating. And she wasn't completely without knowledge of what passed between men and women.

When she was younger, she'd overheard her father's soldiers discuss their prowess at swiving, bragging about the tarse that hung between their legs, and the pleasure they'd brought some maiden in bending her over a table to shove that member into her womb while pulsing out the seed that might create new life.

None of that had sounded particularly pleasurable to her then, so what she'd expected was nothing like the immense pleasure she felt with Chase's hot, wet mouth fastened to her breast. His tongue moved in rapid little flickers across her nipple, creating the most wondrous sensations that rippled through her whole body.

The soldiers must not have known how to do this correctly, because Chase's every touch only seemed to set the fire in her belly burning brighter.

Chase's hand slowly smoothed a path down her side, leaving a trail of chill bumps rising in its wake and creating a sensation in her loins that threatened her sanity.

Once again she slid her hand down to Chase's tarse, trailing one finger from its base to its tip. It was large and stiff and velvety smooth, not at all like she'd imagined. She closed her fingers around it and slid her hand upward. As she stroked it, it twitched as if it had a life all its own.

Chase groaned at her touch, his breath hot against her breast until he lifted his head and cold air covered the spot where his mouth had been.

She waited, every fiber of her body so sensitive even the breeze created when he pulled his shirt over his head felt like a caress.

When he lay back down next to her, her heart pounded in her chest. This was it.

Wasn't it?

Again he bent his head to her breast, his tongue forging a path from her throbbing nipples down the center of her stomach as his hands caressed her waist before sliding down to grasp her hips.

He spread her legs apart and fit himself on the top of her, the heavy heat of his manhood pressing against her delicate warmth.

As if her body had a mind of its own, her legs tensed, fighting to bring her knees together.

"Relax," he whispered as his hands gently smoothed their way from her hips around her thighs to the spot where his tarse pressed against her. "Trust me," he urged. "Let go."

"Let go." She repeated his words breathlessly, willing her muscles to release, allowing him to do as he would.

He nudged her legs around him and she locked her ankles together behind his back. His hands clasped around her waist, pulling her hips toward him as he rocked against her.

Hundreds of new sensations assailed her body and she lifted her hips, fighting to meet the movement of his next push.

"Take it slow," he murmured, his lips tracing a path down her neck. "We've got all night."

"All night," she echoed him again, her mind

unable to think of any words of its own, consumed as she was with the pleasure of his touch.

With each thrust of his hips, she rocked against him, until, at last, he was inside her, filling her.

And still it was not enough to satisfy the heavy need bearing down upon her.

His hot breath fanned over her sensitive skin as he dipped his head to kiss her again. So gentle, so enticing, his tongue flickered over her lips and into her open mouth. With each thrust, slow and deep, an unfamiliar tension built, pulsing and throbbing until, at last, it felt as if her world stopped. She tightened her fingers into his shoulders as a pleasure such as she'd never known gripped her body. It robbed her of her breath, immobilized her except for the intense, rhythmic contractions where their bodies joined.

Her ears thrummed with the sound of her own heartbeat and she gasped for air as Chase stilled over her.

"You are so beautiful," he murmured into her ear as he withdrew and filled her once again. "My own Christiana."

Tiny pinpoints of light sparkled behind her eyes when he stilled over her again, his head thrown back, his body pulsing against hers.

They lay still, bound together as one, gasping for air, their hearts beating in unison so that she couldn't be sure which beat was his and which was hers.

This was not at all what she had expected. This was so much better than anything she'd ever imagined.

You'll know.

Orabilis's promise rang in her ears, keeping time with the pulse of her blood.

There was no longer any sliver of doubt.

"You okay?" he asked, as if he needed reassurance that what had passed between them was as it should be.

"That was . . ." She paused, searching for the words to express what she felt, but failing to find them. "That was more than I had imagined it would be."

"And that's a good thing?" he asked.

"It is," she confirmed. "Perhaps you can help me to learn to give you the same measure of pleasure that you brought to me. If we're to do this again, that is."

"Oh, Christy, my love, we are definitely doing this again." He rolled her into his arms, dragging the heavy woolen blanket that covered the bed over their naked bodies. "Absolutely, most definitely, doing this again."

As if by magic, even his words pleasured her now.

Twenty-nine

CHASE TIGHTENED HIS arms around the warm body curved against his. This was the way he wanted to start every morning for the rest of his life.

Morning? His eyes popped open to confirm what his brain already knew. The beginnings of a new day edged the shutters in hazy purple.

"Shit," he grumbled, sliding his arm out from underneath his sleeping beauty.

Arm retrieved, he bent his head to nibble on her earlobe, instantly realizing the error of his ways as his body jumped to life. There were so many things he wanted to do at this moment.

One, really. One thing he wanted to do at this moment. But time was not his ally today.

"Wake up, Christy. We have to get out of here. We have a big day ahead of us."

A very big day, though between all the sharing and . . . well, *sharing* they'd done last night, he still hadn't broken the really important news to her this morning.

"Come on, sleepyhead," he encouraged, sweeping the curtain of dark hair from her face. "We've got to get you back to your tower before the Tinklers get there."

"What?" Christiana rolled to her back, her eyes tightly shut. "My mind is too heavy with the need for sleep. I canna . . ."

He jostled her shoulder as her words trailed off. "Up. Now. I know you're exhausted, but we have to get out of here."

"Out of here?" She focused on him through narrowly squinted eyes, blinking as her wits came to her. "We're in the keep? Oh, fie, how did we let this happen?"

"I think we both have a pretty good idea of how it happened." He dropped a quick kiss on her forehead as he rolled over her and hit the cold stone floor with his feet.

"What did you say about Tinklers?" She'd pushed up on one elbow, clutching the blanket to her breasts.

He spared a thought to forgetting everything in favor of returning to her bed, but good sense prevailed. It was his only choice if he wanted to make sure waking up with her in his arms was to be more than a onetime thing.

And that was exactly what he wanted.

"Hall and I made arrangements with them to get Bridget away from Tordenet. When they come for her, you're going with them."

"I've no seen that on any of Skuld's paths."

"Then Skuld needs to get herself some new paths,

because this is the way we're handling it. My mind's made up. You're leaving this place this very morning. With the Tinklers. It'll be a twofer when they deliver Bridget back to Malcolm's protection."

"I dinna think what you plan is possible, Chase. That's no the way of it." She tipped her head to the side, reminding him of a teacher lecturing a disappointing student. "The Norns weave the tapestry of our lives. Skuld may well offer choices, but only those she's already woven for us, no the ones we make up for ourselves."

"Is that so?" he asked, pulling open the curtains on all sides of the bed to allow the morning's light to reach her. He didn't have time for the luxury of this debate. The purple haze peeking around the shutters had already lightened to a battleship gray. "Then that must be one crazy-ass tapestry your Norns are weaving, what with your Faerie friend popping me out of the twenty-first century to drop me here."

She chewed on her bottom lip for a moment, obviously struggling with some internal debate.

"No," she said at last. "It is what it is. We've none of us a way around it. Neither god nor Mortal is exempt from the work of the Norns."

"Okay then, no problem. Since we're neither god nor Mortal, but Faerie." He reached for her hand and pulled her from the bed, not letting go until her feet were on the floor. "Let me ask you a question. Did you see this happening between us in any of your visions?"

"No," she said quietly.

"Well, I saw it. From the moment I met you, I knew we would be together. It's *my* path. Now quit arguing with me and get dressed. The way I see it, it's probably best if we aren't spotted coming out of the garden together. So you can go back the way we came, and I'll go out the regular way, through the door."

Confined spaces were not his preference. Not when they could be avoided.

"The garden's no the place for me, either, this time of morning. I'll use a different exit from the passageways. Through the kitchen's storage rooms would likely be best, once the cooks have had time to finish collecting what they need to prepare for their day."

"As long as you hurry. We don't want you missing your ride. You be careful, okay?"

He grinned at her and started for the door, turning back after only a few steps to take her in his arms for a proper parting kiss. She molded to him, her lips every bit as wonderful this morning as they had been the night before.

At last he pulled away from her to say good-bye. The words that popped out of his mouth surprised even him.

"I love you."

Leaving her standing there, the blanket all that separated him from those enticing curves, was harder than almost anything he'd done before.

"Won't be long," he promised himself under his breath as he stepped into the hallway.

He loved her. Not just her body or having sex with her; he actually loved *her*. Where that knowledge had come from or when it had penetrated his thick head, he had no idea. But it was the absolute truth. He'd never been one to say a thing he didn't mean, and to his core he knew that he'd never meant anything more than those words he'd just uttered.

He loved her. And thanks to the Faeries, he would get to spend the rest of his life with her.

Visions of her popping into the kitchen out of some mystery hole in a storage closet filled his thoughts as he made his way through the back halls and down the stairs, until he stood on the bottom step in the main entry hall of Tordenet.

"Here, now! Where do you think yer going?" Cook stood in the entryway to the great hall, a cloth-covered basket on her hip. "What are you doing here at this hour?"

"Kitchen," Chase blurted out, the first word that came into his mind upon seeing the cook. "I'm starving this morning." Not too far off the mark, come to think of it.

"Get back to yer kitchens, Cook. I'll see to him." Ulfr descended the staircase at the back of the hallway, his arm around a smaller figure whose features remained hidden in the recesses of a heavy cloak. "And as for you, Noble, you'll wait for the morning meal like everyone else. Or in yer case, you'll eat what's in yer pack as you ride."

Chase dipped his head respectfully, grateful he'd made it this far unnoticed, considering how many people apparently wandered the halls at this hour.

"Whatever you say, Captain. But it's a damn shame a man can't find some bread or fruit or something fit to put in his belly around here."

His stomach chose that moment to rumble loudly. He really was hungry, having missed his evening meal in favor of something much more appealing.

"It's yer arse, no yer belly, what will get the workout this day. Even now Artur assembles the men to accompany us to the Sinclair. So be off with you. It's time you were readying yer mount for the ride. We leave as soon as I see this one home." Ulfr growled the last, shoving his companion ahead of him.

The woman gasped as a cold burst of wind buffeted her at the open doorway, tossing the hood of her cloak back.

Chase recognized her as one of the servers he'd seen in the great hall at mealtime, a small, dark-haired woman who, from the back, he'd more than once confused with Christiana.

No confusing her now, not with her eyes swollen shut and blood oozing from the cuts to her lower lip.

"What happened to you?"

"Best you move along and forget what you've seen here," Ulfr warned quietly, pulling the hood back up over the woman's head. "This concerns none but our laird."

Torquil had done that to her?

Walking back to the barracks, Chase sent a silent thanks to the Fae that he'd soon have Christiana out of this place, even as his mind scrambled to figure out some way to make the beast who ruled this castle pay for what he'd done to that poor woman.

HE'D SAID HE loved her.

Christiana bent to the floor to retrieve her chemise and dropped it over her head.

I love you. He'd said those very words not five minutes past.

Neither her physical exhaustion nor her concern over Chase's obvious lack of belief in the power of the Norns could steal this joy from her. She wouldn't allow it.

Instead, she'd consider how to keep him safe in spite of his erroneous belief that he could control what was to come. The future was woven and could not be undone. She was confident in that knowledge, though the memory of the gaping hole she'd seen in the distance did trouble her a little.

What if, as Chase claimed, the Faerie's interference had changed everything?

"No," she whispered aloud, crossing the room to pick up her overdress.

She couldn't lose faith now. It was much more

likely that the alternative Chase had devised was waiting there in Skuld's world, a path already woven, simply obscured by the Mysts.

With a sharp snap of the cloth, she shook the overdress in an effort to eliminate a few of the wrinkles caused by the garment's lying in a crumpled heap upon the floor.

"Worth every wrinkle," she murmured, a smile returning to her lips.

She would not waste her energy on this worry. It could all be resolved easily enough when next she traveled to Skuld's world.

A glance at the deep gray light around the shutters assured her the morning's sun hadn't yet pushed its way above the horizon. Even now the cook's helpers would be buzzing about the storage rooms, like bees at a hive, gathering all the ingredients for the morning meal. She had a good half hour or more before she could slip unseen through that exit.

Plenty of time to spread the blanket back over the bed so it wouldn't be obvious anyone had been here. Plenty of time to lie down for a moment or two, just to rest her eyes while she held to her breast the pillow that still carried Chase's scent.

Thirty

Standing at the window, high in his tower, Torquil surveyed the activity below. As the sun spread its rays, more and more of his people emerged from their hovels to scurry about their day's work, indistinguishable from this height.

Pathetic, interchangeable little beings, all of them, with no better purpose for their existence than to serve him as docile cattle.

Not all of them interchangeable, he amended his thoughts. And not all so docile. Though the little whore who'd spent the better part of her night begging for her life would think twice before she questioned his demands again.

Her and her ugly, muddy eyes.

He should have given her to the beast stirring within him. Next time, he just might.

He leaned his arms on the windowsill, drawing the crisp, fresh air into his lungs in an attempt to forestall his need for sleep. The whole of yesterday had been given over to the pursuit of the scroll's spell.

He was so close in his efforts, he'd actually felt

his body turning to mist on his last attempt. But then his cluttered, mortal-contaminated mind had betrayed him and the moment had slipped from his grasp.

Today, if he could but push beyond the limitations of his body, if he could but ignore his need for food and sleep, today could well be the day he succeeded.

The air he drew deeply into his lungs burned, the acrid stench of peat searing a path up his nostrils.

Peat? Impossible! He'd forbidden its use at Tordenet. He detested the smell. Wood or nothing, they'd all been warned; but someone down there had chosen to ignore that warning. Someone who would pay for such defiance.

Torquil leaned out the window, searching for any sign of who had dared disobey his order. Smoke curled from every building within sight, including several stacks on his own keep. The smoke coming from the chimneys all looked the same whether it was from the soldiers' barracks or the east wing of the building in which he stood.

Irritation tightened his chest as he pulled his head back inside. It was as if they knew he didn't yet dare take to wing in the light of day. As if they intentionally sought to highlight his failure.

But that wouldn't save whoever did this. He'd send a party of men to check each of the structures on the castle grounds, one by one. A sound plan, that. They would be found there, not within the keep itself. Though even if he were to search the keep, it wasn't as if he needed to check every wing. There would be no fires at all in the east wing of the keep. That had been shut down since . . .

He lunged back to the window, straining to peer out to his right.

There *should* be no fires in the east wing. None of those rooms had been occupied in the months since Malcolm's wife and her companion had been housed there. Yet, like a mystery waiting to be solved, smoke curled up from the chimney.

And solve it he would.

Artur. Ulfr. Come to me.

He stepped back from the window, panting as if he'd run a long distance, more exhausted than usual from the effort required by the Magic. His night without sleep had clearly taken its toll.

Crossing the room, he stopped in front of the fireplace, adjusting the stones under the mantel until one gave way, revealing the resting place of his treasures. He would need the scroll this day. It was his intent to master the spell of transport before he allowed himself to rest again.

He carried the polished wooden box to the great table and placed it reverently in the center before lifting the lid. Freed of their confinement, it was as if the scrolls spoke to him in a melodic murmuring he could not yet fully understand.

A murmuring that soothed his soul even as it soothed the sleeping beast within.

He braced his arms on the tabletop, resting in the comfort of the sound only he could hear, while he waited for the men he'd summoned. They had no choice but to obey. It was one of the more useful spells he'd mastered from the scrolls.

When they did arrive, two grown men doing their best to mask the confusion they felt at the compulsion of his call, he was ready.

"Follow me," he instructed, leading them from his tower to the stairs in the east wing. "Swords at the ready, men. It would appear we've an intruder."

That the security of his keep had been breached was of great concern to him. It was for that reason alone he'd called these two men to accompany him, delaying the start of their journey to capture the Sinclair heir.

Only one set of rooms in this wing housed a fireplace large enough to have the chimney he'd spotted from his window. The rooms his father had built for his Tinkler whore. Deandrea's chambers.

Though he'd expected resistance, the door opened easily to his touch and he stepped inside the room. Through the parted curtains surrounding the bed, he spotted his prey. One lone body curled upon the bed.

A body he recognized instantly, pushing all security concerns from his consideration.

"I can handle this from here. The two of you have men waiting their departure for you to join them, do you no? Go, without delay."

He closed the door behind him and surveyed the room before silently making his way to the bed.

Clad in nothing more than her chemise, Christiana slept on her side, one slender arm curled around a pillow she clutched to her breast, one shapely leg stretched out, freed from the confines of the garment that twisted around her body.

He reached out a trembling hand to trace a finger along the soft white limb, from her ankle to the back of her knee and beyond, onto the smooth, warm skin of her thigh.

She moaned in response to his touch, the sound flushing his body with heat. In that heat, the beast within began to stir.

Stilling his hand, he leaned down over her, to whisper into her ear.

"Wake up, little sister. I have need of you."

Her eyelids fluttered open to reveal the brilliant blue of their shared ancestors, the haze of sleep giving way first to surprise and then to fear.

"Torquil." Her voice shook with the latter emotion and her leg twitched under his touch. "What are you doing here?"

Fed by Christiana's fear, the beast fully awakened, requiring his attention to maintain control. He breathed through the moment, lifting his hand from the heat he desired to explore.

"No, Christiana, the better question is, what are *you* doing here?"

She pulled the pillow closer to her breast as if it were a shield. "The woman, Halldor's prisoner, is in my tower."

He'd almost forgotten the wench, though the beast within roared its need for revenge at mention of her. He'd certainly forgotten that she dwelt in Christiana's tower. No doubt Halldor's use of the woman was troubling to his sister.

"And so you sought refuge here, in your mother's chambers." In the rooms his father would have visited regularly.

"These were my chambers for many years."

"So they were," he murmured holding her gaze with his own.

They had indeed been her quarters, the rooms where she spent her nights. Until his father's demise. Until the time when he could no longer resist the temptations of flesh she presented, and he'd banished her to the tower across the courtyard.

He reached for her hand, tightening his fingers around hers when she would have pulled away. "I grow weary of waiting for you. I'd have you travel to Skuld's world for me now."

"But I canna," she began as he pulled her from the bed. "The herbs I need are in my tower. You ken I've no the ability to direct the Vision without—"

"Then we go to yer tower."

He was having no more of her excuses or delays this time.

She dawdled with her overdress, running her

hands over the cloth until he ripped it from her grasp and threw it to the floor.

"Now!" he insisted, capturing her wrist to drag her forward, slowing only to scoop up her cloak from the floor.

Not that he really cared if she suffered the indignity of crossing the courtyard in nothing but her chemise. It was only that neither he nor the beast felt particularly open to other eyes feasting upon what belonged to them.

He all but dragged her behind him, down the stairs and out the entrance, ignoring the servants' openmouthed stares.

Christiana wisely held her tongue, as if she recognized the force within him driving him forward.

Inside her tower, he tore the cloak from her shoulders and tossed it at their feet.

"Where is the elixir?"

"In my bedchamber," she whispered, keeping her eyes averted from his. "I'll go get it."

"No!" he roared.

Or perhaps it was the beast who roared; he couldn't be sure as he wrapped one arm around her waist, guiding her up the narrow winding stairs ahead of him. Up to the room at the very top of the tower.

"Now," he said, his voice once again his own as he forced himself to release his hold on her.

Christiana stumbled toward the fireplace, where she pulled a clay jar from the mantel and removed its stopper before lifting it to her lips to drink.

He waited in the doorway as she stretched out on her bed and closed her eyes as he'd seen her do so many times on the pillows in his tower. Within minutes, her breathing slowed and she traveled the pathways of Skuld's world.

It took longer for him to regain control. Longer to shove the beast back down into the depths where it belonged. Once he'd managed that, he moved toward the bed, his eyes fixed on the gentle rise and fall of the chemise covering her chest.

An odd lump in her form caught his attention and he reached for it, dipping his fingers inside the neckline of her gown to discover what she thought to hide from him.

A small pouch hung from a cord around her throat and, inside, two small carvings.

Runes. He recognized them immediately, though the ability to read the future from the tiny bits of wood was her gift, not his. Two of them, Tiwaz and Berkana, the warrior and the birch tree, special enough she wore them about her neck. One to represent each of her parents, perhaps? There was no way for him to know at the moment. And certainly not important enough to disturb her travels in Skuld's world.

He returned the little carvings to their pouch, enclosing it in his fist, delaying its return to its original resting spot between her breasts.

His eyes fixed again on the rise and fall of the cloth, on the way it molded to her breasts with each exhale. Frustration held him prisoner, his fisted hand motionless only inches from that which he wanted.

It was unfair that even now he must deny himself the one pleasure of the flesh he wanted most lest the beast within break free and tear her tender body to pieces, depriving him of her foreknowledge.

For now, willpower alone was his ally. One day, when he'd mastered the Magic and no longer needed word of Skuld's world to guide his steps, he would reward himself with that which he wanted. On that day when he no longer needed to fear the actions of the beast, he would have her and satisfy all those craven Mortal desires.

His breath caught in his throat when he at last slipped the pouch into her neckline, his unnatural need for her battering at his senses once again.

Not unnatural at all.

"Who said that? Who's there?" he demanded, scanning the small empty room for some unseen enemy.

Our need for her is reasonable.

The words rang not in his ears, but within his mind.

The beast spoke to him? It was not possible. He alone conjured the beast, and he alone controlled it.

Not unnatural but sensible, the Beast assured him.

"The need is totally without reason. She is but the spawn of a Tinkler," he countered. "And fruit of my father's loins even as I am." It took more from him than he'd anticipated to admit aloud that last bit of degradation.

Nonsense. Tinklers are the favored of Faeries, and what are Faeries but the counterpart of Elves? Elves, who are the favored of the Vanir.

The words pounded inside his head, chipping away at the wall of guilt and denial he'd built up over the years.

It's not our fault. The desire runs in our blood.

He had never considered these things on his own. A bubble of laughter grew in his chest, working its way up to burst into the silence of the tower bedchamber.

It was in his blood. Though he carried Odin's bloodline through his father, from his mother he claimed ancestry with the Vanir, her line rumored to descend from the goddess Freya. It was the reason she had been pledged to his father long before Alfor had left their home shores in the Viking longboat that carried him to this land.

Do not fight that which we feel for her. She is the vessel to ensure the purity of our bloodline.

Could it be true? Torquil paced the small room, sweat beading on his forehead and rolling down his face in great salty drops. Or could it be simply a new ploy by the beast, growing ever stronger each day, seeking to control them both?

I could help us.

Perhaps. Or perhaps it could destroy them both. He couldn't decide which at the moment. Couldn't concentrate well enough to keep all the barriers in place. Couldn't stay here any longer, allowing Christiana and the beast to fragment his mind and his energy.

There was no need for him to remain, in any case. She would be gone for hours, and once she returned to her body it would take time and energy to tease out the truths he needed. Energy he simply didn't have.

Down the stairs he ran, one hand sliding along the contours of the wall for balance. Not until he stepped into the light of day was he able to regain some semblance of himself.

With a dignity befitting Odin, he lifted his head and made his way back to the keep, heading for his bedchamber. An hour or so of sleep and he would be strong enough to cope. Then he would return to his tower to attempt the scrolls again.

But not now. Not with the beast curled in his chest, waiting to take advantage of him. And certainly not with the beast's seductive promises ringing in his ears.

Thirty-one

CHASE CONCENTRATED ON the trail ahead, ducking the occasional low-hanging branch. He did his best to ignore the warning tingle running up the back of his neck, and kept a sharp eye out. Something didn't feel right.

His thoughts continued to wander back to the castle they had departed early this morning, to the woman whose safety was his biggest concern.

Halldor had assured him the tower had been completely empty when he'd slipped over to check on the success of their plan. That surely meant Christiana had gone with the Tinklers when they spirited Bridget off the castle grounds. And he knew for himself that the Tinklers' wagons were gone when they'd headed out the gates of Tordenet.

It was good. It was all good.

Now if he could just convince himself of that.

Ahead of him, Ulfr held up a hand as he reined his mount to a walk.

"We'll rest the horses here for a few minutes and let them have their fill from the stream."

It was as they'd done all day. Push the animals, slow them to walk, push the animals, give them a short rest. He climbed off his mount, suspecting the repetitive schedule was as much for the endurance of the riders as it was for the horses.

He shouldered between two of those riders to lead his horse to the fast-moving waters, wondering once more at their number.

"There are twelve of us. Seriously, does it take twelve heavily armed men for a two days' ride to deliver an invitation?"

"Are you daft, man?" the soldier nearest him asked. "You ken it's no the invitation, but the refusal of it that requires our number."

"And our arms," the one on the other side of him added.

A few feet behind him, Ulfr spoke up.

"Had you been present for the briefing rather than trying to raid the kitchens to satisfy yer empty belly, you'd have heard our orders along with the others. We're to return with the Sinclair heir, whether or no he wants to accompany us."

So now he was to become a kidnapper. Great.

He glanced toward Hall, recognizing his own feelings reflected in his friend's solemn expression.

"Have the Sinclairs done something to us to warrant this?" Perhaps he was jumping to conclusions. After all, once he lost trust in Torquil, following the laird's orders had become much harder.

Ulfr shrugged, pushing by him to lead his mount

to the water. "Our lord simply wishes to ensure the support of the Sinclair laird come spring, when we march against Castle MacGahan."

Kidnapping and conscription. Thank God he'd managed to get Christiana away from this. All he needed now was to find the perfect opportunity to make his own exit.

"Seems kind of harsh to me," he said as he backed his mount away from the stream.

"No half as harsh as he is to the maids he takes to his bed," the man beside him muttered.

"What?" Could it be that the woman he'd seen this morning wasn't an isolated case?

"It's no his fault they can none of them satisfy him, Fergus." Artur led his own mount forward. "No matter how much they may look like her, none of them will actually be her, so he'll no ever be pleased no matter how good they are between the sheets."

"Look like who?" Chase asked, his stomach knotting with suspicion. He knew all too well who this morning's victim had looked like.

Several of the men around him chuckled as if he asked what was plainly known to all.

"Yer still new to Tordenet," Artur observed, moving to stand beside him. "It's well known among those of us who've lived our lives under the Mac-Dowylt that our lord has always had an unnatural desire for his sister. I've heard tales that say the auld laird himself had seen it, and it was that as much a anything what caused the bad blood between father and son."

"That's enough of yer blether," Ulfr cautioned as he climbed back into his saddle. "Yer little better than the old crones in the kitchens, the way you run yer mouth. Mount up, all of you. We've a long way to travel before we lose the sun's light."

"It would appear you made the right decision," Hall murmured from beside him.

Absolutely. Getting Christiana away from that monster was the smartest thing he'd ever done.

Ulfr moved ahead, putting distance between them by the time Chase climbed into his saddle.

"Say what you will." Fergus drew even, speaking over his shoulder to Artur. "I figure one day our laird will stop asking for those maids and he'll satisfy himself with that which he really desires."

"In truth," Artur replied. "Wouldna surprise me to find he did that exact thing after we found her sleeping in the old chambers this morning. He sent Ulfr and me away quick enough once he saw it was her, he did, and shut himself inside the room with her."

They found Christiana in the keep? Chase jerked on his reins, pulling his horse to a stop, his stomach knotting in fear. She hadn't escaped with the Tinklers. She'd never left the keep.

"Keep moving," Hall hissed close at his side.

"Didn't you hear what—" Chase could hardly force the words from his mouth. Torquil had found her because *he* had left her there alone. It was his fault. He should have insisted that she leave when he did. He should have followed her and made sure she got out of the keep.

"I heard well enough." Hall cut into his recriminations, jerking the reins from his hands. "We've less than an hour before sunset. When we've the cover of dark, we'll make our move. If we ride through the night, we'll be back at Tordenet before the sun fully warms the day. Patience, little brother."

Hall was right. Another hour wouldn't change what had already happened and risking a fight, outnumbered as they were, would be foolish.

He needed to get back to Tordenet in one piece.

One pissed-off, ass-kicking piece.

Thirty-two

CHRISTIANA STOOD BY the well, a soft wind blowing through her hair, an overwhelming relief filling her heart.

"Thank you," she whispered, choking back her emotion to lift her voice. "My thanks to each of you for allowing me to escape to your world."

None of the three figures sitting under the great tree so much as glanced in her direction.

"You cannot remain here. We are not meant as your refuge. Drink the water and be about your business."

She touched the cold, crisp liquid to her lips and lifted immediately from her feet to float above the land. This time her focus was homed solely on what was yet to be.

Below her, the Mysts thickened at the edge of Now and she dipped lower, batting at the puffy discolored clouds to dislodge them that she might see what they hid. So many paths, but only one held interest for her now. The one leading to the Sinclair's keep, where Torquil had indicated he would send Chase and Halldor.

Eleven men rode toward the Myst. Eleven men but twelve horses. From this height she recognized them all, even the empty saddle keeping pace next to Chase. The empty saddle belonged to none other than Halldor O'Donar.

Hovering above them, a shock of realization swept over Christiana as she accepted what she was seeing. She knew Halldor existed in that scene. If she dipped lower and concentrated on the spot where he should be, it was almost possible to decipher his form. Yet, for reasons she couldn't understand, the sight of him was masked from her.

Second, and possibly more confusing than her not being able to see him, was the realization that Halldor could not possibly be Chase's brother. She should have recognized that long before now. Unlike Chase, Halldor existed in *this* time, whether or not he was visible to her in the Visions.

Like so many other enticing strands, these would be paths of knowledge for her to pursue at another time. Though she had no doubt of their importance, they were not her purpose for being here today.

Pulling back to regain her perspective only increased her frustration. So many paths branching out from each of the men below presented a tangled maze for her to sort, requiring her to carefully pick and choose a single thread to follow. Her focus sharpened on Chase, as it must if she were to have any hope of finding what was to come if he traveled these paths.

She'd seen this part before. She'd watched as their horses entered the Mysts bound for Sinclair Keep. It was what lay beyond this that she must find now.

Once again she dipped lower, plunging into the heavy Myst to find a point in the future where the horses followed a return path to Tordenet. There were only six animals along this particular strand of the future, galloping hard, their sides bellowing in and out. Two were riderless, one of them belonging to Chase.

Not that path!

She backtracked, blinking at the burn in her eyes and the acrid taste in her mouth as she plunged again down through the Myst. Each of the paths she followed from Sinclair Keep led to the same result. Chase would not survive.

The realization buffeted her, rolling her feet-over-head and tossing her like a leaf high into the air. By the time she recovered her stability, she was so far above them, what little she could see appeared as no more than insects.

The wind of return began its insistent pull even as she struggled to continue forward. There *had* to be another path. One she'd somehow missed that would lead Chase safely back to her.

Instead, ahead in the distance, a patch in the Myst revealed Tordenet, her tower in flames.

Screams drifted to her ears, screams she knew to be her own.

But which path did this lie upon? She could not decipher where or how it connected beneath the Myst-covered maze any more than she could resist the force pulling her away from the knowledge she sought.

Her eyes lifted to seek the glowing rip in the tapestry of the future, the hole where Chase's life thread had been altered. It seemed to lie in a different direction than it had before. It and another very much like it. And yet another.

The sprinkling of dark holes across the web of time could mean only one thing: his was not the only life thread that had been altered in the vast landscape of the tapestry!

Her feet touched the ground and the door between her world and this one shimmered. With so much to consider, she did not resist when the force pushed her gently toward the opening.

What could they mean, those shiny, tattered holes in the tapestry of the future? Was it possible that Chase had been right? Perhaps the choices woven by the Norns were not the only pathways into the future after all.

Thirty-three

I 've a bad feeling about this place, Hugo. We should go now, while we still can." Mathew MacFalny pulled his cloak tight around him in a useless attempt to ward off the shiver that wracked his body.

"You've made yer feelings clear. As you did yer desire to remain with the Tinklers. But as I told you then, when the MacDowylt learns what news we bring to him, the Tinklers' wagon will be precious little haven."

Yet Hugo hadn't hesitated to leave their cousin Eleyne behind to face the wrath of the powerful MacDowylt right along with the Tinklers who'd been so kind to them.

"I dinna like that we abandoned our instruments." Mathew debated risking his brother's anger yet again. "Or Eleyne."

"Once we finish with the MacDowylt, we'll have no need for either instruments or a lamed dancer." Hugo turned on him, wearing the look that so often crossed his face before he meted out a beating. "I'd think you'd be fawning all over yerself to show some gratitude for my bringing you along, you witless cur. We'll be men of wealth when we leave this place, you mark my words. Now go. Leave me to deal with Tordenet's laird."

With one last look over his shoulder, Mathew stepped into the early-morning shadows of the hall and made his way into the back passageway.

The night of their performance, a young maid, drunk on ale and the charms of his music, had told him this way led to the laird's private rooms.

Something in Mathew's gut warned him Hugo's plan would not go well. And without his pipes to provide him a living, he hoped to find something of value to carry away from this awful place.

He sent up one prayer for Eleyne's safety, followed by a second prayer that his instincts would prove wrong for once. But things that he sensed too frequently came to pass, so he forged ahead to locate the stairs that had been described to him and disappeared into their lightless gloom, knowing the time might have come when he'd need to fend for himself.

"Laird MacDowylt! Please!"

Torquil rolled from his bed, confused as to where he was until his bare feet hit the cold stone floor. His own bedchamber, with the voices of all those women tormenting his dreams.

"Laird MacDowylt?"

That voice was certainly no dream.

He rose to his feet, his body stiff and cold. A glance around the room confirmed that the fire had long ago burned out, leaving not so much as a single live ember behind.

How long had he slept?

"Laird MacDowylt!"

"Quiet yer damned pounding," he yelled in response, his wits fully returned at last.

From the location of the sun and the condition of his fireplace, not to mention the stiffness of his body, he'd say he'd likely slept through the whole of yesterday and the night as well.

And though the beast felt calm, his own mood was foul enough for both of them.

"For what reason do you dare disturb my peace, woman?" he demanded, throwing open the door.

The servant shrank back, dipping her head as she scooted away. "Begging yer pardon, but there's a man belowstairs, my lord. A man insisting he must speak with you immediately."

"What man?" he snarled, beyond annoyed to be disturbed when he'd actually managed more than an hour or two of sleep for the first time in months.

"He gave his name as Hugo MacFalny, sir. I believe him to be one of the minstrels. He claims to have urgent information for yer ears only."

He'd recognized the minstrel for a greedy fool at their first meeting, but, obviously, he'd underestimated how great a fool. That he'd allowed any of them to leave with their lives, after what their dancer had tried, should have been enough to guarantee many miles' distance between him and this man.

However, if the idiot thought to tempt fate by returning to Tordenet, it was just possible that he did indeed carry important information.

"Have him wait in my solar. I'll join him shortly."

The servant ran the length of the hallway and disappeared down the stairs.

After so many hours spent sleeping in his clothes, Torquil felt the need to change. He tossed his shirt off over his head and drew on a fresh one, regretting having sent the little maid away before having her lay a new fire for him.

Even after refreshing himself, he still felt oddly out of sorts.

"A perfect way to approach a guest such as awaits me," he murmured, setting off down the hallway to the stairs. Though definitely not perfect for the guest.

"Why have you come back, MacFalny?"

The man jumped as Torquil entered the room, his nerves apparently on edge with waiting.

"My laird MacDowylt!" He started forward, his hand extended. "How good it is to see you again."

Torquil kept his hands at his sides, staring the interloper into submission. "I ask again. Why have you returned, when you were clearly told you'd not be welcome here again?"

The oily smile Torquil found so distasteful covered the man's visage as he opened his mouth to speak.

"Such an unfortunate incident colored our last meeting, my good laird. It brought sorrow and shame upon my family, indeed. So it was only natural that when I came upon a situation which I felt merited yer attention, I could think of nothing but how I might be of assistance to you."

"Indeed. And what is this situation which you wish to bring to my attention?"

"Ah well, you must understand, I find myself in a bit of a pinch. By thinking of yer needs first, it would appear I've lost my place with the Tinklers, along with all the belongings I was forced to leave behind in my haste to return to you with this news. I felt sure, however, that you would be willing to compensate me well for the news I bring."

The man wanted the silver he had been denied after the attempt on Torquil's life. Deep within, the beast stirred.

Foolish, foolish man.

Torquil agreed. The fool should have been satisfied to have escaped with his life the first time.

"So you come to me with the gift of information. A gift for which you expect me to hand over a few coins to grease yer palm. Do I understand you correctly?"

"More than a few." Hugo chuckled as he leaned against the wall, a newfound confidence in his eyes. "The information I have for you is quite valuable."

He would withhold the knowledge he claims we need. There is no loyalty in such an act.

No loyalty at all, from one such as this. But a greedy man could often be a useful tool.

"Why should I trust you, MacFalny? It was yer own woman who attempted to take my life. Would it not be more likely that, failing to murder me, you're thinking to steal from me now?"

Deep within, the beast growled.

"You wound me, MacDowylt. You've no reason not to trust me. Why would I risk my life to come here and tell you falsehoods?"

The reason was clear enough. A reason that would jingle in the man's pockets.

"I would hazard to guess it's yer desire to reclaim the silver I refused in payment after your she-devil made her attempt on my life that brings you back."

"She's not one of mine," the minstrel answered contemptuously. "She's a runaway from a castle we visited far south of here. We only agreed to allow her to accompany us to replace our dancer, who she herself injured when she was discovered hiding in the wagons. I warned the Tinkler then and there she'd be nothing but trouble, but he listened instead to his woman, and foolishly gave his permission for her to travel with us."

The Tinklers always listened to their women. It

was the failing of their sponsors, the Fae, who had foolishly separated from his people eons ago. The Celts and the Fae and their ridiculous adherence to the superiority of their goddess over his own gods had long been a source of irritation.

"In that case, I'd have you tell me this news of such great import that you have brought to me."

MacFalny shrugged, lifting his hands in a gesture of helplessness. "But my laird, once I have given all that I have of value, how am I to know that I will receive payment?"

"Trust, of course," Torquil answered, struggling to hold back the beast that raged at the insult. "I would have you exhibit the same trust you ask from me."

"I will require enough coin to finance my travels from here to Inverness. And a horse, as well."

He insults us, setting terms as if we are some common trader!

"You have my word, minstrel. The word of Torquil of Katanes, laird of the MacDowylt, chosen son of Odin. My bond that you will be paid all you deserve. And more if the information warrants. Surely that is good enough to earn yer trust."

Deep within the beast roared his agreement, clawing at Torquil's innards, demanding his release.

MacFalny rubbed his hands together, greedily. "The woman who attempted to take yer life has escaped."

Impossible!

"If this is true, how did you come by such knowledge? Where is she now?"

"It is true, I swear it. I saw her with my own two eyes. The Tinklers agreed to assist in her escape. They returned to the camp with her early this morning. Even as we speak, they carry her south to return her to the safety of her home."

She was supposed to be ours!

"Well?" Hugo continued to grin as if he'd somehow gained the upper hand. "Is this news no every bit as valuable as I said it would be? Am I no deserving of a proper payment?"

"Deserving indeed."

The Beast spoke in unison with him, the words echoing off the stone walls, vibrating within his chest and in the sensitive tissues deep inside his ears.

Hugo's eyes widened, the man only now beginning to suspect the danger he faced.

"Too late."

Too late, indeed. The Beast would no longer be silenced. With a strength beyond Torquil's power to contain, it traveled from the Deep Within, past his belly, up past his chest to fill his mind and burst forth.

Torquil gave himself over to the beast as he moved to block the door with a fluid lengthening of his gait. His arms, his legs, every part of him expanded to accommodate the beast within.

A joy previously unknown to him flooded his mind. Why had he ever feared this? The Beast did not seek to replace him. It did not in any way diminish him. It completed him. They were one.

"You . . . you owe me nothing," Hugo babbled, his head turning from side to side, in search of some way out of the room. "Consider the information my gift to you. To seal our bond of friendship."

Fear rolled off the little man in great heaving waves, tinged a bright orange with panic.

"Here now, MacDowylt. I demand you step aside." Hugo moved hesitantly toward him, toward the only door in the room. "Our business is finished."

"Not yet finished."

Torquil marveled at the size of his own hand reaching out to close around the minstrel's neck. Marveled at his own strength as he lifted the struggling man from his feet. Marveled at the pleasure of the thick, warm liquid filling his mouth, slaking a hunger such as he'd never before experienced.

When he hungered no more, he tossed the pieces of the body to the floor and filled his lungs with the essence of fear lingering in the room.

As quickly as the beast had joined with him, it now departed, slinking back into the deep recesses of his soul.

He leaned back against the door, feeling the loss as if it were a physical blow. A search within left him weak with relief when he at last discovered the beast, tightly encased behind the Magic as it had been before the first time he'd called upon its power. Not gone, only resting, at peace for the first time since he'd discovered it in the scrolls.

So many new sensations bubbled inside him, so many raging emotions. It was as if in joining with the beast he had opened up a whole new piece of himself. A piece filled with a reservoir of Magic he had only dared to imagine in the past. He could feel it coursing through his veins. With this power, he had no doubt he could conquer the spells on the ancient scroll that waited for him in his tower.

As he reached for the door, a wave of nausea and dizziness washed over him, reminding him of his body's need for food. How long had it been since he'd last eaten? One day? Two?

The scroll warned of such a hazard. Even as he nurtured what grew within him, so too must he care for the Mortal shell that housed it all.

He stepped from his solar and closed the door behind him, his mind whirling with half-formed thoughts and emotions, the mass of them disconnected from one another.

The hunger was draining his strength. A trip down to the kitchens would allow him to center his thoughts and rid himself of the vague worry riding his shoulders like an annoying winged creature refusing to take flight, marring his otherwise perfect morning. An annoyance, really, a small nagging disquiet, as if he'd failed to recognize something important.

Mathew slipped from the shadows as soon as the Mac-Dowylt laird disappeared through the doors leading to the great hall. Odd that the laird had come out of his solar without Hugo. Surely his brother wouldn't have left earlier without him.

Even as the thought crossed his mind, the cold finger of reason flicked it away. If the MacDowylt had given Hugo the silver he wanted, his brother would have left him behind without a thought—just as he had abandoned Eleyne to the Tinklers' mercies.

He should have stayed with the Tinklers. Should have kept his pipes and his cousin close.

"Too late for should," he whispered, repeating his aunt's favorite saying.

With one more check of the hallway, he stepped forward, his hand hesitating at the door to the laird's solar.

If he found the room empty, it would mean he had been abandoned, as he feared. He would be well and truly alone.

He had to know. With one more glance in either direction, he gave a push and slipped into the opening.

Carnage such as he'd not seen in the entirety of his sixteen years greeted him, locking up every muscle in his body. Even the scream crawling up his throat refused to come out.

The metallic scent of fresh blood snaked into his nostrils, identical to the smell of men cleaning their kill after a hunt. Across the room a headless body lay crumpled, no doubt the source of the blood splattered everywhere.

He knew whose body it was even before his eyes tracked down to the floor at his feet. Even before he spotted the head staring up at him with its sightless eyes, its mouth hanging grotesquely open as if the jaw had been broken in mid-scream.

Mathew forced himself to take the next breath. And then one more, as fear threatened to overwhelm him.

He stepped back out of the solar. Closing the door behind him, he moved silently to the keep's entrance, lifting the hood of his cloak as he slipped outside. He could only pray that no one would take note of one lone boy making his way across the early-morning courtyard.

He would hide within the storage buildings as he had when he'd arrived. The sun had already begun its ascent into the sky, but once its rays no longer lit the land, he'd make his way outside the gates and travel south. Perhaps to Inverness, where he could sell the treasures he'd gathered in the keep.

And then?

He fought back the panic, exiled it to a little box at the bottom of his heart. He couldn't give up now, or all would be lost. He must have a plan to survive.

Once he'd sold the treasures he would track down the Tinklers to find Eleyne. Together they would return to MacFalny Keep and beg her father to take them back.

All he had to do now was to keep his head attached to his body long enough to escape this evil place. A feat his older brother had not managed.

Thirty-four

"THE HORSES CANNOT long maintain this pace."

Chase recognized the truth of what Hall said, even if he didn't want to acknowledge it. Already his animal's sides puffed in and out like a smithy's bellows. Killing his mount would only slow him down in the long run.

Yielding to better judgment, Chase pulled up on the reins, directing his horse once more to a slow walk.

"Someone follows." Hall's head cocked to the side as he drew up next to Chase, much like a bird eyeing seed on the ground.

Chase tilted his head in a similar fashion, straining to hear whatever it was that had caught his friend's attention. Nothing other than the heavy breathing of their horses and their hooves hitting the trail reached his ear.

Not that he didn't think Hall was telling the truth. It would surprise him more if someone didn't follow. In all likelihood, Ulfr himself led them. With little love lost between them, Ulfr would no doubt relish the opportunity to come after him.

"We must be getting close." Rationalizations were all that kept him from losing it entirely after all the hours he'd put in the saddle. If that son of a bitch had laid one hand on Christiana . . . Chase breathed deeply through his nose and forced the air back out again, directing his thoughts to the here and now. "If we have to slow down, so does whoever is following us."

"They do. Though at some point, we will have to stand and fight." An eerie glow emanated from Hall's eyes in the predawn light. "Whether on open road or after we reach Tordenet, I cannot yet determine."

Again he strained without success to match the other man's hearing.

"You have any guess as to how many of them are coming after us?"

They'd left ten men behind sleeping. Well, nine. The sentry had been awake before they bound and gagged him. The question in Chase's mind was whether Ulfr would bring the full number after them, abandoning the task his lord and master had sent him to perform, or if he would come with just a contingent of one or two.

It didn't matter. Not even all ten men combined could keep him from reaching Christiana.

Thirty-five

"MORE."

The old cook continued slicing meat from the roast, piling it upon the table as Torquil instructed. His stomach growled in ravenous anticipation.

"And the cheese," he directed. "That's no enough."

Not nearly enough. With a desire for food he hadn't felt for years, he snagged a bite from the pile and slipped it into his mouth.

Everything tasted so wonderful. When had he stopped enjoying this simple pleasure?

"It's good to see yer appetite returned, Master Torquil." The old cook flashed a ragged grin. "I've a special bit of sweet prepared and set back for later today. Would you like to try some?"

He nodded and gestured for her to bring it, his mouth too filled with the creamy cheese to speak. With each bite he felt more and more himself, his thoughts less chaotic and fragmented.

"Here you go." The cook placed a sticky bun in

front of him. "I think you'll find it quite enjoyable. Everyone who's tasted it has agreed."

As if the vague disquiet hanging over his shoulder had just grown by half, Torquil stopped chewing. Something the old woman just said had annoyed the worry, like someone poking a sharp stick at a trapped animal.

"What did you say?"

"Only that I hope you'll enjoy it." She wiped her hands nervously down her apron.

"No. What exact words did you say? Repeat them for me."

"I . . . I think you'll find it to yer liking," she stumbled, obviously trying to remember. "Everyone what's had a taste has agreed that I've done a fine job on it."

Not the exact words, but close enough.

"Leave me," he ordered, and she ran from the kitchen.

"'Agreed,'" he muttered aloud. "Why does that word rankle at my memory?"

Agreed, agreed, agreed . . . Surely he'd heard it only a short time ago. A commonly used word. Anyone could have said it. . . .

The minstrel had used the word. He could hear the man's voice in his memory.

The Tinklers agreed to assist in her escape.

But with whom did they agree? Who at Tordenet would care what happened to the stranger who had attempted his murder?

He rose from the bench to pace, his thoughts swirling.

If not the minstrel himself, there was only one other who would have an interest in saving the woman. The one who had interceded to save her the night she'd come at him with a knife.

Halldor O'Donar.

Of course! It was the only option that made sense. And if O'Donar had plotted against him, he could hardly be the champion Christiana had foretold.

At last, no matter how his sister might try to parse her words when she answered his questions, he had the answer for which he'd waited so long. Chase Noble was the champion who would guide him into the future, riding at his side, leading the way to his victories.

Laughter rose in his throat, bursting forth until his sides were aching and his throat parched.

"Ale," he managed to croak, motioning to the cook when her face appeared through the open door.

She scurried forward, her hand shaking as she filled the tankard.

"Perhaps, dear lady, I should decree that everyone should eat in the kitchen before meals are served, rather than wait for them in the great hall." He tried for a gracious smile, feeling magnanimous in his joy. "The food tastes so much better served here. Or perhaps it's only that my hunger does not wait for regular meal service."

"Seems to be a popular problem of late, my lord."

"Indeed? What makes you say that? Has someone else dined in the kitchens recently?"

Again she backed away, as if she feared his wrath at her candor. "One of the new men wanted to. Noble, I believe Ulfr called him. Though he dinna make it all the way to the kitchen. I found him at the bottom of the big staircase, in the entry hall before preparations for the morning meal were hardly even begun. But then Ulfr showed up as well, telling him he'd best be worrying about his arse, no his empty belly." Her eyes rounded and she hurried to add, "Begging yer pardon for my language, my good laird."

What would have brought Noble into the entry hall so early in the morning? If he'd wanted food, why not enter through the kitchen? Again the small animal of disquiet living on his shoulder flapped its wings. "When was this?"

"Yesterday, before the men left, sir."

"Early yesterday," he murmured, the wings flapping in his ears as if an entire flock of birds beat about his head. "Was Ulfr alone when you saw him?"

She shuffled a few steps farther away, darting her eyes to the floor. "There might have been someone with him," she answered hesitantly. "Though I canna say with any accuracy who it could have been wrapped in that heavy cloak."

He knew exactly who Ulfr had removed from his tower at yesterday's dawn. Dawn—not a time for any of his soldiers to make their way down his stairs.

Not unless they had spent the night in the upper chambers. Chambers housing no one except on that particular night when Christiana had chosen to spend the night there.

"You say you found Noble at the base of the stairs. Could he have been coming down those stairs, do you suppose?"

"Now that you mention it, he was stepping off the bottom stair when I first called out to him."

The flapping of wings stilled, and a heavy black haze of anger colored the remaining dregs of suspicion and doubt.

Torquil rose to his feet, knocking over the bench upon which he had sat, and in long, determined strides he made his way from the kitchen through the great hall.

Each conversation he'd had with Christiana, each interaction, played over and over in his mind, from her first foray at encouraging him to seek out new men to swell his ranks.

It was essential that he do so, she had informed him, because her Vision had shown her that there would be one among them who would be essential to the outcome of his efforts. His new champion, she had confirmed. But now that he recalled her exact words, she had never claimed the champion would be *his*, any more than she had claimed that the outcome would be to his liking rather than to her own.

She had deceived him. From the moment she had returned from the glen after Malcolm's escape, right up until yesterday morning when she greeted his waking touch with her moan of pleasure—until she had opened her eyes and recognized it was he standing over her bed. He, Torquil of Katanes—not some vagabond mercenary who sold his skills to the highest bidder.

Even the runes she wore hanging from her neck made sense now. One for her, and one for her warrior lover.

She had fooled him with her clever use of words. Lured him into unknowingly acting on her behalf, in a vain attempt to defeat him.

He paused in his rampage across the courtyard for the moment it took to send his command winging through the ether to Ulfr and Artur. They would deal with Noble and his brother, even as he dealt with Christiana.

His sister would pay dearly for her disloyalty. They all would.

Thirty-six

CHRISTIANA LEANED OVER the fire, inhaling the soothing aroma that drifted up from the heavy iron pot that held her simmering herbs. Once she strained the bits and pieces from her tisane and allowed them to cool, she would use them in a poultice to place over her tired, scratchy eyes.

It would have to do, since she didn't see any restful sleep in her immediate future.

When she'd awoken from her Vision travels yesterday evening, she'd been overwhelmed with relief to find herself alone. She'd sought out Chase to tell him of what she'd seen, but her relief had been short-lived when she learned it was too late to warn him. All that was left was to wait and worry.

While her hands performed the familiar task of straining the herbs, her thoughts drifted to the gates of Sinclair Keep, the stronghold she'd seen along the pathways of her Vision.

A sense of foreboding hung in the air this morning, thick and cloying, hindering each and every breath she took.

Perhaps that was due to the heavy dread in her heart. The images she'd seen haunted her. None of the paths that she had managed to explore had ended well. Not one of them.

Her only slim hope lay in her final fleeting glimpse of the future, in the small scattered shining holes where something—or someone—had been ripped from Skuld's carefully woven tapestry.

The pot shook in her grip as she poured the hot liquid into the straining cloth. Its heat seeped through the pad she'd wrapped around the handle, burning into her skin, and she dropped it to the hearth as soon as she'd filled her cup.

If only she'd managed to warn Chase before he'd left. If only she'd never insisted the Elf interfere. If only she were smart enough to properly interpret what she had seen.

"If only, if only, if only," she muttered, balancing the steaming mug of clear liquid as she sat on the rumpled blankets where she had tried unsuccessfully to sleep.

At some point she would need to dress, to eat, to prepare for the inevitable encounter with her brother. She needed to move all the bags of dried herbs from around the hearth, where Ulfr's men had carelessly tossed them, to the upper tower. One random spark and her treasured herbs would be gone in a bonfire.

So many little tasks awaited her attention, but right now she hadn't the strength of will to ignore the dark clouds of sorrow hanging heavily over her.

Right now, she could only watch in her mind's eye as the steed Chase had ridden galloped wildly from the Sinclair's gates, riderless.

She lifted the cup to her lips, to sip the hot liquid, when the door was flung open, crashing back against the stone wall.

Her cup jostled, splashing hot liquid on her, but Christiana barely noticed. She had eyes only for the angry man filling her doorway.

"I'd have the truth from you," Torquil snarled, his eyes wild with rage.

"I canna speak to you with any words that are not true, brother. Well you ken the limitations—"

"Silence," he roared, kicking the door closed before he moved slowly in her direction, one foot after another like a beast stalking its prey. "The time for yer clever deceptions is past. I'll no be making the errors I have in the past, allowing room for yer words to dance with the truth."

Christiana's thoughts raced, searching for what could possibly have happened to set him off.

"Neither Noble nor O'Donar is here for my benefit, are they? They were never meant to be *my* champions, but yers. It's yer preference for the future they serve, no mine, is that no the way of it? You've betrayed me in my own keep, have you no?"

He knew. Somehow, he'd learned the truth.

She desperately sought a way to divert him

from his questions as she rose to her feet, but the fury on his face did not bode well for her success.

"Dinna bother to search for a clever riddle to put me off. I see the truth in yer silence. And I'll be having no more of yer deceptions. Straight answers to straight questions, Christiana."

"What would you have me say?"

If she could keep him talking, she had a chance. He loved the sound of his own voice. If she could get him to carry on, pontificating, he'd say something that would enable her to answer any question he might ask.

"Did you lie with Chase Noble? Is that why you were abed in my keep?"

Her heart stopped. "Why would you ask me such a—"

"No!" he hissed, grabbing her elbow to jerk her toward him. "No twists upon yer words, sister. Yes or no. Did you sleep with him?"

His breath came in great heaving pants, buffeting her face with each exhale.

"This is no the sort of question—"

"Yes! Or! No!" he yelled, and it felt as if the very walls of her tower shook.

"Yes."

She had no way to restrain herself from speaking the truth. It was the curse of her gift.

"Did he force yer favors or did you give yerself to him freely?" His fingers bit into her skin as he ground out the question, his voice quiet with deadly intent.

"Freely." It mattered not now. All her secrets were revealed. "I offered myself to him freely."

He reached to her neck and fastened his fingers around the cord hanging there to rip the bag from her. The cord sliced into her skin before it gave way and he held it aloft, baring his teeth.

"And these paltry bits of wood? They're to represent the two of you together, are they no?"

"One for each of us, yes."

"Yer but a Tinkler whore." He spat the epithet, and threw the bag to the floor before shoving her to her knees. "After all the years I've denied myself what I wanted, you tainted yer purity by giving yerself to that commoner. Yer no better than yer mother."

She glared up at him, no longer making any attempt to disguise her hatred and loathing. "Given the choice, brother, I'd rather be a Tinkler whore than a wastrel who murdered his own father. I ken what you did to our father. I saw with my own eyes when I traveled the Visions of Urd's world."

She'd seen it all. Seen him prepare the potion and slip it into their father's ale. Seen him wait, watching over Alfor's final moments.

His expression changed as she spoke, as if calm determination had replaced whatever he'd felt before.

"Perhaps you'll beg for Alfor's fate before I've done with you, Christiana." He dropped to his knees in front of her as he spoke, a vile grin curving his lips. "When Ulfr and Artur return with Noble's severed head, I'll present it to you as payment for the gift yer about to give to me."

"What gift?"

"The only one that's fair. The only one I want. The commoner sampled yer pleasures, and now so shall I."

Surely he only sought to frighten her.

"But yer my brother," she denied, attempting to scramble back from his grasp. "My own blood. Even you canna consider such an abomination."

He laughed. "I am Torquil of Katanes, heir to Odin. I can do anything that pleases me. And right now . . ." He grabbed her shoulders and pulled her face to within inches of his. "Right now nothing will please me so much as having you."

She swung her cup at his head but he deflected her attack with his shoulder, shoving her to her back, banging her head to the floor and knocking the wind from her lungs before he crawled on top of her.

His knee pressed down, forcing her legs apart as she struggled to catch her breath.

She wasn't strong enough to fight him like this. She needed a weapon.

The pot! It was small but heavy, and the iron would still hold the heat of the fire.

She stretched out her arm and her fingers closed around the handle, waiting for her chance.

When he lifted his hand from her shoulder, she

swung the iron pot up and around with all her strength.

The pot caught him in the center of his back and he yelled out in pain, arching away from her.

As his weight shifted she kicked for all she was worth, shoving him, the blankets, everything toward the fireplace as she scrambled to her feet and ran for the door.

He roared in anger, recovering much faster than she had hoped.

His hand tangled in her hair, jolting her to a stop and dragging her back to him, slamming her against his chest.

"Nothing worth having is worth having without a fight, is it, little sister?" he panted into her ear as he wrapped one arm around her midsection and slammed her face-first onto the table.

She lifted her arms just in time to shield her face but the table edge caught her across her stomach, forcing the wind from her lungs. Before she could move, Torquil's weight was on top of her, his arms pinning hers above her head, his mouth hot next to her ear.

"You canna escape me, little sister. I'm as willing to take you from behind as from the front." With his free hand, he lifted the skirt of her nightgown to trace his hand up her bare leg. "At least the first time."

"No, no, no!" she screamed, bucking her head back toward his, rejoicing when she hit his face and he grunted in pain.

Her short-lived joy evaporated when he laughed, a humorless, vindictive sound, as he twisted one of her arms up behind her to immobilize her by leaning his weight against it. She gasped for air, feeling as if her arm would rip from her shoulder, and choked as her lungs filled with the acrid taste of smoke.

She couldn't move. She couldn't catch her breath to scream. Her only escape was to plunge headlong into the rage-filled chasm within her mind.

Thirty-seven

"FOUR OF THEM follow us."

Chase nodded in acknowledgment as Halldor pulled up beside him. They'd almost reached the gates of Tordenet.

"Five. Sorry," the big man corrected with an embarrassed grin. "Two of them canter in unison. It's an easy enough mistake."

The guy must have the most sensitive ears of anyone ever born.

"How much time before they get here?"

Chase wasn't concerned about dealing with five men; he and Hall could make a quick enough business of them. But once Ulfr's men arrived, Chase had little doubt they'd put up a call of alarm—and fighting his way through an entire garrison while he hunted for Christiana would slow his efforts considerably.

"Not long. I say we head for the keep once we're through the gates. I'll take the laird's tower. I've an interest there of my own."

"Fine," Chase agreed. "I'll take his solar—and his

bedchamber. And I swear to God, if that's where I find her, there won't be enough left of that son of a bitch to fill a piss pot."

"Best you hold off on confronting Torquil until after I've been to his tower, aye?"

They'd reached the gates, leaving Chase no opportunity to pursue Hall's odd piece of advice.

"Open!" Hall's command boomed up to the guard on the wall walk and the chains rattled in response.

As soon as the metal grate rose high enough, Chase urged his horse forward quickly, Hall at his side matching his pace. They rode straight to the keep, and at the base of the stairs, he leapt from the horse's back, hitting the steps at a run. Hall's feet hammered behind him as he reached the top landing and fastened his hand upon the door.

"Go on," the big man urged. "I'll slow them down for you."

Chase turned and saw five riders galloping toward them, their horses covered in lather.

"Go!" Hall yelled over his shoulder.

With one last scan of the courtyard, Chase pushed on the heavy door and slipped inside. Once the door swung shut, no sound but his racing steps echoed off the stone walls. In the quiet seconds, a tiny spark of discord stirred in the back of his brain, as if he'd seen a picture with something out of place. But no time to worry about that now. Whatever he'd seen out there would have to be Hall's problem to deal with.

He pushed all thought away to concentrate on

his anger as he hit the door to the laird's solar at a full run, drawing his sword as he entered.

He skidded to a stop just inside the room, where the grisliest of blood-spattered horrors greeted him.

Chase had experienced gruesome on multiple levels in his life. He doubted anyone could pull two tours in a war zone and avoid it. But to stumble into a scene this grotesque when he'd expected something so totally different shook his resolve and rattled his momentum.

Or perhaps it was just the fear that if this could happen to whomever that head had belonged to, it could as easily happen to Christiana.

His stomach roiled at the thought and he backed out of the room, tamping down all emotions. What was left in there was somebody else's problem, not his. Christiana's safety was his only consideration now.

She filled every corner of his thoughts as he ran to the stairs and started up them. Scenes of her flitted through his memory like a movie trailer on fast-forward. Her eyes as she lay beneath him in the room upstairs. Her laughter as she sat on the bench in Orabilis's animal shed. Her smile as she stood at the door of her tower.

As if a computer inside his head finally loaded the site it had searched for, the discord eating at the back of his mind blossomed fully, and he stumbled to a stop midway up the great staircase.

The last glimpse of her tower, when he'd quickly

scanned the courtyard, replayed in his mind. He'd spotted smoke wisping out through the ground-level window.

She was in her tower—and in danger. He knew it as if he could hear her calls for help.

He raced down the stairs, leaping from the third step to hit the floor running, and flung open the massive entry door. Hall held his ground on the top stair with his sword, fending off the two men on the steps below him, holding them back as he'd promised.

Chase could either join in the fray, hacking his way through the four men blocking the stairs, slowing his progress to Christiana, or he could find an alternative route.

"Her tower!" Chase called to Hall, sheathing his weapon as he chose to follow the alternative.

Bracing his hands on the wall surrounding the landing, he hefted himself up to balance upon the top ledge, and then, after a quick scan below, he jumped, aiming for a hay-filled wagon off to one side.

The impact of the landing jolted up his legs, but he had to keep moving. Across the courtyard, the dark tendril of smoke curling from Christiana's window had grown.

He rolled from the wagon and ran, drawing his sword once again and losing it just as quickly when Ulfr tackled him from the side, driving him to the ground.

There had been four on the stairs with Hall. He should have remembered to check for the fifth.

"The tower burns," he managed as Ulfr's knee crashed down on his chest.

Above him, Ulfr lifted his arm, drawing back the knife he held with a scream. Grabbing Ulfr's shirt at the shoulders, he jerked the man forward, smashing his head into his opponent's face. Blood spurted from Ulfr's nose and he fell back, but only for a moment.

A moment, as it happened, was all Chase needed to scoop up his sword and have it at the ready as Ulfr attacked, with the single-minded ferocity of a maddened animal. Chase's blade slid into the other man's chest, slicing a path through muscle and organ, and Ulfr dropped to his knees, surprise blanketing his expression. Chase withdrew his weapon, already running toward the tower before Ulfr's body hit the ground.

At the tower he stopped, drawing in a deep breath before kicking the door open to the sound of splintering wood. Smoke billowed out around him as he burst into the room. Flames licked up around a pile of blankets, their unburned ends trailing out onto the hearth.

Torquil held Christiana facedown on the table, where the bastard bent over her with obviously only one thing on his mind.

HALL CUT HIS eyes toward the tower, but only for a second. The blades flashing in his direction required his full attention.

The sight of smoke curling from the tower explained his little brother's leap from the railing.

"Godspeed," he huffed in Chase's direction, though he knew the other was too far on his way to hear it.

He hoped the lad hadn't broken his legs upon landing, just as he hoped Chase would make it to his lady in time. But if Torquil waited in Christiana's tower, no amount of good intentions would enable his fine Faerie friend to destroy that monster unless Hall was successful in his part of their siege.

With a roar that had weakened the knees of far better men than these, he lifted his leg and kicked, his foot landing solidly in the center of the lead man's chest. Like a row of shoddily stacked peat staves, they all toppled backward, each tumbling onto the man behind him as they scrambled to break their fall.

Freed of them, Hall slipped through the door and headed for the back stairs. The object of his search would be found in the laird's tower, behind a stone above the fireplace, if Bridget MacCulloch was to be believed.

A glance into the open door of the solar revealed evidence of his worst fears. Hugo the minstrel had met a fearsome end indeed, his head torn from his body. No man could have done such as that, lending credence to his suspicion that Fenrir himself had joined with Torquil. Which made finding what he now sought that much more imperative.

He hurried on, nearing the narrow staircase

before he was set upon. Artur pounced on him, wrapping one arm around Hall's neck to cling there like a fetid tick upon a dog's ear as he plunged his knife into Hall's right shoulder.

Pain radiated out from the wound, slowing Hall's movements as he took stock of his injury. Nothing vital. No important organs involved, just a clean slicing of meat and sinew.

Then the little bastard withdrew the weapon and, with a madman's scream, plunged it down again.

Like a horse under attack by a bloodsucking fly, Hall flung himself backward, smashing his attacker into the wall behind him, taking them both down in a heap.

The hilt of the knife protruded from Hall's shoulder, twisted at an ugly angle. It was higher than the first wound, making it difficult to reach his sword when Artur came at him a third time with his sword drawn.

"I guess we'll see whose arse ends up on the pointy end of a sword now, won't we?" Artur sneered, slowly moving in for the kill.

Hall pushed himself up the side of the wall to stand, waiting, watching the other man's eyes. When Artur circled his wrist, taunting with the motion of his blade, Hall threw himself forward, knocking aside the smaller man's blade as he jerked the protective token from around his neck with his left hand. He brought it slamming down, feetfirst, into Artur's throat as they fell back.

It took a moment for the man to stop his twitching. A moment that Hall used to catch his breath and gather his strength before pushing up to stand again.

Leaning heavily against the wall, he followed the narrow, curving stairs up to the little guardroom and into the laird's private chamber.

There he found the hiding place under the mantel already open and the box he sought sitting out on the table.

At least he presumed it was the same box, though the jewels Bridget had claimed adorned the lid were gone. Deep scratches marred the wood, as if someone had dug the jewels out of their resting place.

But the loss of the jewels wasn't the worst of it.

The box was empty.

FURY FILLED CHASE so completely, nothing remained but the bright, blistering need to cut Torquil into a million tiny pieces.

He launched himself across the room, but his prey was faster. Torquil danced away, Christiana held in front of him like a shield. A shield whose head lolled to the side while coughs wracked her body.

"You came for this?" Torquil taunted, dragging her head back by a handful of hair, revealing a swollen red welt on the side of her face.

"No," Chase answered, his vision tunneling on the man in front of him. "I came for you."

Torquil laughed and continued to move away, placing the table between the two of them. Chase kept his back to the door, the only means of escape from the tower.

A *pop* and *poof* sounded to his left as the fire leapt to the bags of herbs piled there. Flames shot into the air, reaching the edges of the tapestries covering the walls—but Chase's quarry was more important.

"Think fast, warrior," Torquil shouted, shoving Christiana toward the fire as he lunged for the opening to the stairs leading up to the top of the tower.

Chase dove to grab Christiana, reaching her as the flames licked up the sleeve of her gown. She scrabbled away from him, breathlessly pleading for him to stop, to wait.

There was no time to stop and wait. The whole damn place would be a blazing fire pit in a matter of minutes. He pulled her close and rolled over her to smother the flames eating away at her gown. Then he scooped her up in his arms and ran for the door and fresh air. Let that evil bastard Torquil burn.

"WHERE, WHERE, WHERE are you?" Torquil demanded, his back against the door of Christiana's tower bedchamber.

That the beast should desert him now was simply wrong.

"I would have given you free rein," he railed, rushing to the window to gasp in great gulps of fresh air. "I would have allowed you to destroy them both, as you did the minstrel."

Perhaps that was why the beast slumbered. His thirst for blood already had been well slaked today.

Below his feet, smoke slithered up between the floorboards.

If ever he had needed the Magic to work for him, now was that time. If ever he had needed to marshal every scrap of his concentration, now was that time.

His gaze landed on the clay pot at the end of the mantel. The clay pot holding the elixir that was the means to his sister's Visions.

Perhaps it would work for him as well.

He lifted it from the mantel and tossed the stopper to floor. Tilting back his head, he drained the contents of the bottle and threw it toward the fireplace.

Now was the time.

CHAOS HAD ERUPTED in the courtyard, with people scrambling everywhere to move their possessions as far from the burning tower as possible. The entire company of soldiers busily raced from the well to their barracks, wetting down what they could to prevent the fire's spread.

Chase came to a halt in the middle of that bedlam and allowed Christiana's feet to touch the ground. He held her close as she coughed the smoke from her lungs, murmuring reassurances, but never once taking his eyes from the doorway they'd come out.

Whether her bastard brother met his end on Chase's sword or burned alive, Chase didn't care. All that mattered was that his life ended this day.

He waited, watching, until flames licked up along the wooden supports of the tower's outer walls and shot from the highest window at the top. Waited and watched as the roof gave way and crashed in. Waited and watched, until he was sure nothing and no one could have survived the inferno.

"I see you found your lady in time."

Halldor stood calmly at his side, blood soaking the right side of his shirt.

"What the hell happened to you?"

"Artur and I resolved our feud." He shrugged, wincing at the motion. "While it's on my mind, little brother, I'd thank you again for the amulet of protection you gifted me. Fortuitous, indeed."

Christiana lifted a hand toward Hall, then let it drop to her side. "I've nothing left to help with the healing. All my herbs are gone, but perhaps we can locate some whisky in the kitchens to clean the wound before you seek yer rest."

"There will be no rest for us here, my lady. We must leave this place before we're confronted by Torquil."

Chase shook his head. "No worries there, big brother. Torquil's dead. He isn't going to bother us again."

Hall's look of skepticism wasn't the expression Chase had expected.

"How did he meet his demise, that you can be so sure of his death?"

"The bastard is toast. Literally." Chase inclined

his head toward the still-smoldering ruin. "He was in there with no way to escape but the front door. And I made sure nobody came out the front door."

"He is not dead. He will be back, and it would be wise for us to be long gone before he returns." Hall held up a hand, continuing with his explanation. "I know what you think, Chase Noble, but in this you are wrong. Fire cannot kill him. Only the Sword of the Ancients has the power to end his life now."

"My father spoke of that weapon." Christiana looked hopefully from one of them to the other. "I believe from the things he said, it may be here at Tordenet."

"It was here, my lady, of that I have no doubt. But it is here no longer, and until we have it in our possession, we cannot hope to defeat Torquil and the beast that lives within him."

"Wait. What beast? What are you talking about?" Chase felt as if he'd slipped from the History Channel to Sci-Fi Central. "Are you trying to say that Torquil is possessed?"

"Call it what you will. But whatever you call it, we should be putting distance between us and this place while you do."

"Okay. Fine." It was pretty damn clear to Chase that the Faeries had meant him to be with Christiana, and wherever she was, that was where he needed to be. "Let's find some horses and figure out where to go."

"South to Castle MacGahan, to carry warning to

Malcolm and Patrick. Ella!" Christiana called out to a servant girl running past them. "Find Rauf. Send him here to me."

The girl's eyes were enormous saucers of fright, but she nodded her agreement before running away.

"Castle MacGahan it is," Hall agreed.

Thirty-eight

A SMALL, COLD HAND covered his, drawing Chase's attention from the distance into which he stared.

"Rauf assures me Castle MacGahan lies just over the next rise." Christiana peered out from the depths of her cloak, her nose red from the cold.

Chase captured her hand in his, rubbing it to restore some warmth. A cold front had hit overnight, bringing temperatures too low for traveling safely outside as they did.

"He'd better be right, or we'll need to stop and build a fire before you turn into an ice cube."

"Pfft," she scoffed. "I'm stronger than you credit me." Her chattering teeth belied the confidence of her assertion.

"It's there," Rauf called out, standing in his stirrups to point into the distance. "There upon that hill, do you see?"

"I do," Chase answered, relieved that their journey's end was at last in sight.

Rauf had been their saving grace in their preparations for a hasty exit from Tordenet. He'd gathered food, found a horse for Christiana, and, thankfully, had been to Castle MacGahan before, so that at least one of them knew the way.

He was also totally devoted to Christiana, which had quickly won Chase over to his side, even if he did look like a classic movie bad guy.

"I for one shall be glad of a fire and a hot meal." Hall drew his horse alongside Chase.

Chase nodded. Not to mention the relief of being able to close his eyes at night without worry that some mythological wolf-monster was about to attack them.

Rauf spurred his mount, riding on ahead of them to alert the castle to their arrival. By the time they reached the open gates, a small cluster of people had gathered in front of the main keep.

Family, waiting to welcome a loved one back into the fold. Chase had seen this sort of gathering too many times not to recognize that. The excited, hopeful expressions these people wore were no different than any he'd seen as he'd stepped off an airplane and back onto home soil.

And just like all those times, the familiar oddman-out feeling gripped him, urging him to hang back out of the way while those who belonged gathered together.

"Welcome home, little sister." The dark-haired man at the center of the group held up his arms to assist Christiana when she dismounted. "You canna imagine how often I've pictured this moment in my thoughts."

"As I have, Malcolm," Christiana agreed, her feet finally touching the ground.

As with other family reunions he had witnessed, Chase felt the familiar twinge of envy nipping at his heart as he watched Christiana wrap her arms joyously around the stranger's neck.

"And these men who accompany you, we've them to thank for your liberation, have we no?" Malcolm smiled broadly, opening his arms wide. "Introduce us to yer champions that we might welcome them into our home, as well."

"Halldor O'Donar, a fine champion indeed, and my friend." Christiana beamed up at the man. "These are my brothers, Malcolm and Patrick, and Malcolm's brave and beautiful lady, Danielle, and, this is my friend Elesyria."

"Syrie," the little redhead and Patrick corrected at the same time.

"Syrie," Christiana repeated with a lift of her brows before turning toward Chase. "And this is Chase Noble."

She held out her hand to him and he dismounted to stand at her side. He had no choice. He couldn't resist the sparkle in her eyes when she smiled at him that way.

"I must tell you all, Chase is far more than champion to me." She entwined her fingers with his. "He is the love of my heart."

She gazed up at him and his heart was full. He had no reason to envy anyone. All he needed stood before him, holding his hand.

"As you are mine," he answered quietly.

"In that case"—Malcolm stepped closer, slapping a hand to his back—"looks to me as though we'll soon be welcoming a new brother into the family."

"If he kens what's good for him," Patrick added from his spot near the stairs.

Chase knew what was good for him. He had her hand tightly clasped within his own right now.

"Enough of this lollygagging around out in the cold." Malcolm's wife tightened her cloak around her and started up the stairs. "Let's get you all inside and warmed up, and then you can tell us all about what's happened that allowed you to come home to us."

"And what is yet to come," Hall added as he passed by.

True. Chase pulled Christiana close under the shelter of his arm and started up the stairs behind Hall. Though they'd reached their destination, their journey was far from over.

They followed their hosts into the main level and up a second set of stairs, entering a room that looked more like a living room from his own time than one that belonged here.

Three long cushion-covered benches with backs faced one another in front of a huge fireplace, with a low round table between them.

"Make yerselves comfortable on a so-fa." Malcolm pronounced the word as if it were some foreign object.

From the looks passing between Christiana and Hall, Chase could only surmise it was.

Minutes later, Danielle swept into the room accompanied by a servant, who handed Chase a mug of what turned out to be hot apple cider, just before offering him a tray filled with . . .

"Cookies?" Chase swiveled his head from the tray in front of him to Malcolm's wife.

"Yes, they are," she confirmed. "My very own recipe. And considering all the ingredients I didn't have to work with, I think they turned out pretty great."

"She comes from your time," Syrie offered in a low voice as she sat down next to him. "I am quite relieved to see you here at last. You certainly took your time."

"Little thanks to you." Patrick leaned past her to pick up one of the mugs from the center table.

If this was the woman Christiana had told him about, his presence here was almost *entirely* thanks to her. "You're the Elf, right?"

Christiana's elbow to Chase's ribs coincided perfectly with Patrick choking on his drink.

"Faerie," Syrie corrected, even as she pounded her hand on Patrick's back. "Lift your arms and lean over. You'll catch your breath. Not that you deserve to."

"Has Bridget yet returned?" Hall's question drew attention to where he stood by the fireplace.

"Bridget MacCulloch? The lass has been missing for weeks. You have knowledge of where she is?" Malcolm leaned forward in his seat.

"I wondered when I saw no sign of Tinklers in the courtyard. After her escape from Tordenet, they were to bring her back here." Hall turned to stare into the fire. "They had a day's head start on us."

"But we cut cross-country because Rauf said it would be faster. Chances are they haven't had time to get here yet." At least that was what Chase hoped.

"I can have Eric send some of the men along the road. If they find anything . . ." Patrick shrugged. "Either way, they can get word back to us faster than if we were to simply wait."

"Make it so," Malcolm ordered, sounding every bit the laird of the castle.

"I've no wish to insult your hospitality, but I'd ask to accompany those you send. I've a need to speak with the Tinklers about those who traveled with them." Hall scratched his fingers through his beard, his gaze on the fire. "If you could spare provisions and have all arranged by first light, I'd be grateful."

"You'd be better served by having that shoulder of yers properly looked after, now that we're here." Christiana set her cup on the table. "A day or two of rest will do you good."

Hall turned to acknowledge her concern, a trace

of his former smile back in place. "My wound is of small consequence, my lady, but I shall allow you to properly dress it before I leave. Which I must do with all haste, if I'm to have any hope of tracking the Sword of the Ancients."

"For what reason would you seek a weapon of that reputed power?" Syrie asked.

"Because, my lady Syrie, it is the only weapon that will serve to fell Torquil when he rides against Castle MacGahan in the spring."

Malcolm rubbed a spot between his eyes. "So you believe he will yet bring his men to attack us. I had hoped—"

"No, Malcolm," Syrie interrupted, bouncing to her feet to pace the room. "You don't understand what this man is telling us. Why would you need the Sword of the Ancients to meet Torquil in battle? For that matter, by what reason do you possibly expect to find it?"

Syrie came to a stop in front of Hall, her hands rising to her hips like those of a mother accusing her child of carrying stories. Though the sight of the two of them squaring off should have been funny, the petite redhead's challenge of his enormous friend was anything but amusing.

Chase might have attributed the tension tightening his chest to his imagination, had Christiana not slid her hand into his. One look at her and he knew she felt it, too.

"I believe there is a trail because Torquil had the

Sword in his possession, and now it's gone. But not with him. I suspect one of the minstrels, the surviving minstrel, might have . . ." Hall paused, choosing his words carefully. "He might have liberated the weapon. Along with the Elven Scrolls of Niflheim."

Syrie gasped, her hand flying to cover her mouth as Patrick rose and all but lunged to her side.

"Torquil had access to the dark Magic of the scrolls? That would certainly explain the drain on my powers I experienced at Tordenet. As it would explain your need to find the weapon. Our need." She waved Patrick off and resumed pacing. "He is possessed, I assume. Have you any idea what it is we deal with?"

Hall shrugged. "An heir to Odin? Fenrir would be my best guess. Especially after seeing the condition in which he left one of the minstrels."

That memory was all too fresh in Chase's mind, as well.

"I would appreciate an explanation," Malcolm said, looking to his sister. "Christiana?"

Her fingers tightened in Chase's grip. "I canna give one to you. I have seen no hint of this in my Vision travels. But I believe it. What I saw staring out of Torquil's eyes was not our brother."

"Little wonder you were unable to see such as this from the Norn's world, Mistress Christiana. A *seid* as black and as ancient as the Elven scrolls hold would be beyond the power of the Norns' accounting."

"What is this Fenrir?" Chase looked to Hall. "You've mentioned that name before."

"A monstrous wolf-creature of legend, enemy to Odin."

"Oh my God, Malcolm." Danielle dropped to her husband's side, wrapping her hand around his arm. "That's exactly what we saw in the clearing. That enormous wolf that tried to kill you in the woods. The thing that turned into your brother after I stabbed him."

"With the stake of rowan wood," Christiana added.

"A fork, actually," Danielle murmured, sinking back against Malcolm.

"I'm guessing we need to find these scrolls and make sure they're locked away somewhere, too." Chase again looked to his friend for confirmation. "And I'm also guessing we won't be the only ones looking for this stuff. Am I right?"

"You are correct, little brother. All the more reason why I must be off at first light."

Thirty-nine

MEET ME OUTSIDE the entry doors. I'll wait for you."

Christiana paused to make sure Chase had heard her whispered request over the noise and clamor of the great hall. Though she appreciated the celebration in honor of her arrival, she'd not been allowed one single minute alone with him since they'd arrived.

She casually made her way down the long aisle separating the two halves of the great hall, stopping to acknowledge the greetings and good tidings from the people she hoped she would one day think of as friends and family.

Once through the entry, she moved behind the door to wait. Chase arrived only minutes after her, his face breaking into the smile that set off the fire in her belly each time she saw it.

"Come with me," she invited, holding out her hand to lead him down the hallway to her brother's solar. It was only used for formal meetings, Syrie had informed her, since Malcolm preferred conducting his business from the sitting room upstairs.

She lifted a small torch from the wall as she opened the door to the dark room, and they quickly slipped inside.

Almost before the door shut, he closed his arms around her, turning the smolder in her belly to flames as his lips covered hers.

"I was beginning to wonder if I'd ever get you to myself again," he murmured after he broke the kiss. "It feels as if someone has been hanging over my shoulder every minute since we left Tordenet."

She felt the same, and it had only gotten worse since they'd arrived at Castle MacGahan.

"I suspect my brothers fear for my virtue, now that they ken how I feel about you. I also suspect they will go out of their way to keep us apart until . . ."

Her tongue suddenly tripped and her face heated with embarrassment. Though Chase had declared his love for her, he'd not indicated any desire to wed her. And even if he did harbor such a desire, she wasn't at all sure it was the fate the gods had in store for them.

"Until?" he asked. "Until what?"

She had no intention of pursuing that question just yet. Besides, she had another reason for wanting to speak to him alone.

"I've something I need to show you."

From her pocket she pulled the little bag of runes,

its cloth now charred and almost too fragile to withstand being opened. She emptied the contents into her hand, clutching the little treasure tightly before extending her fingers to display the dark lump resting on the flat of her palm.

"What is it?"

"When you first came to me, I called upon the gods to share with me what the path of our future might hold. I drew from my bag of runes to seek their answer. This"—she rolled the lump on her palm—"was their answer. I managed to save it from the fire before you pulled me out of the tower."

"This little lump of charcoal is why you fought me off when I was trying to get you out of there?" Chase brushed a strand of hair from her face, his fingers lingering on her cheek. "I thought you'd lost your mind. So this was your answer from the gods. What did they tell you that was important enough for you to crawl through fire to try to save?"

Again she lifted her hand toward him. "The runes I drew represent us. One for you and one for me. *Tiwaz*, the warrior, and *Berkana*, the birch tree. The first advises courage and strength of conviction, while the second is a harbinger of new beginnings, of rebirth."

"And yet, I only see one thing in your hand."

"It is as if they are melted together—something I've never seen wood do before, though, in truth, they were very old." She forced a smile to her lips though she felt only sorrow over the loss. "Where there were two, now there is only one."

Chase picked up the wooden treasure between his thumb and forefinger, holding it out at arm's length in front of the open window so that it almost looked as if it floated on the surface of the moon framed there.

"I can't promise you that I'll always believe in the things you believe in. I can't promise that I'll accept that our future is already set in stone by some old women weaving under a big tree. But I agree with what your gods are telling you with this, Christy. We are meant to be one. Both of us are warriors in this life, calling upon the strength of our conviction that we belong together. Both of us have been given the gift of rebirth into a new life."

He lifted her palm to his lips, pressing a kiss to the spot before replacing the rune into her hand.

"You hang on to that, love. I don't know what's to come for us, but I do know that little treasure in your hand is the best symbol I can imagine for our new life. Here. Together. As one."

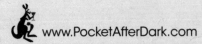

HIGHLANDER'S CURSE

"An enthralling and captivating romance. . . . A page-turner if there ever was one!"

—*RT Book Reviews* (4½ stars)

"Time after time, Mayhue brings her readers tantalizingly close to emotional satisfaction."

—*Publishers Weekly*

HEALING THE HIGHLANDER

"Deeply moving characters, fraught with emotional turmoil, the subtle entwining of Faerie magic and a highly charged, ever-expanding romance. . . ."

—*RT Book Reviews* (4½ stars)

A HIGHLANDER'S HOMECOMING
Finalist for the 2011 RITA Award for Paranormal Romance

"Enthralling. . . . The combination of plot, deeply emotional characters and ever-growing love is breathtaking."

—*RT Book Reviews* (4½ stars)

A HIGHLANDER'S DESTINY

"The characters are well written, the action is non-stop, and there's plenty of sizzling passion."

—*RT Book Reviews* (4 stars)

"This is one of those series that I tell everyone to read."

—*Night Owl Reviews*

"An author with a magical touch for romance."
—*New York Times* bestselling author
Janet Chapman

WARRIOR'S REDEMPTION
Winner of an RT Seal of Excellence Award

"Melissa Mayhue brings the Scottish locale to life with a colorful vividness. . . . An emotional romantic adventure with unforgettable characters and a magically imaginative premise." —*Single Titles*

"Fan favorite Mayhue's time-travel series certainly gives readers everything they want in a medieval and a time travel. Characters of vastly different backgrounds—Nordic and Texan—emotional turmoil, magic, and an ever-expanding love coupled with an unusual plot make this an extraordinary read."
—*RT Book Reviews*

"A wonderful job . . . fun, filled with action and danger."
—*The Reading Café*

"Marvelous, magical mayhem."
—*Genre Go Round Reviews*

"With strong characters, witty dialogue, and an easy to follow plot, what's not to enjoy? A must read."
—*My Book Addiction Reviews*

"You can't go wrong when you pick up one of Ms. Mayhue's books." —*Night Owl Romance*